TERMS OF SERVICE

Subject to Change Without Notice

CRAIG W. STANFILL

To Representative Stefanik,

from us upporter and admiror.

I am <u>awed</u> by what you
have accomplished; you are going
places, and our country desporately
needs you and others like you in these
dark times.
Take back the House,
Take back the Senate,
Take back America!

5/25/2021

Terms of Service: Subject to Change Without Notice

Hardcover ISBN: 978-1-63877-835-6

Published April 2, 2021 by Bad Rooster Press, LLC

A Note On The Translation

The translation of this novel from the original Panglobal into English presented certain difficulties, due to the absence of ungendered personal pronouns in English and the absence of gendered ones in Panglobal. She/her/hers have been used throughout. Similarly, there are no exact analogs to the 'inclusive' and 'exclusive' first-person pronouns found in Panglobal. The inclu-sive form has been translated as 'we,' and the exclusive form is as 'I.' Passages and words which were originally spoken in English have been indicated as follows: *[English] This sentence is in English.* This notation has been omitted for loanwords such as *mother* and *love* which have crept into Panglobal despite the best efforts of the authorities.

Terms of Service

As a condition of doing business, the customer agrees to the following Terms of Service*, summarized below with the full text incorporated by reference.

1. The customer shall not use The Company's goods, services, or property to engage in divisive behavior or to promote any religious sect or cult.
2. The customer shall not use The Company's goods, services, or property to cause harm or distress to any person, corporation, or Artificial Intelligence.
3. The customer shall not demand more than their fair share of The Company's goods, services, or property, or ask for special privileges.
4. The customer shall not use The Company's goods, services, or property for unauthorized purposes, such as conducting commerce or facilitating unauthorized sexual liaisons.
5. The customer shall not use The Company's goods, services, or property to spread lies or disinformation.
6. The customer shall not use The Company's goods, services, or

property to slander or disparage any person, company, or Artificial Intelligence in a position of authority.

7. The customer shall not use The Company's goods, services, or property to invade the privacy of any group or individual.

8. The customer authorizes The Company to collect data pertaining to the use of its goods, services, and property, and to share such data with other Companies.

9. The customer shall not question the fairness and impartiality of The Company, its agents and representatives, or the Artificial Intelligences tasked with enforcing these Terms of Service.

10. The customer acknowledges that The Company may downgrade, suspend, or terminate service at any time, at its sole discretion, should it determine that there has been a violation of these Terms of Service, and agrees to accept all such determinations as final.

*Subject to change without notice.

Part I: Spring

1. An Ordinary Day

Kim awoke at the usual time with the usual pounding headache as the alarm clock blared away. She had once again ended up drinking more than intended, and the night had been difficult, her sleep haunted by unwelcome dreams. Her eyes blinked open then closed again for a few moments as she wished she could sleep a bit longer, but the wakeup alert was insistent and there was no way to turn it off. After a few more seconds she opened her eyes and looked around her tidy but nondescript sleeping chamber, trying to clear her head. Beige carpet, beige comforter, beige pillows, beige walls, and on the nightstand her VR headset, perched perilously close to a tumbler half-full of vodka remaining from last night's binge. The damnable alarm continued its nagging ever more insistently. There was no point in trying to resist. Time to get up.

The lights came on as Kim clambered out of bed, pulled on a pale-beige robe, and sat down at the desk, staring at the terminal's screen for a few moments. There was a soft *feep* as the housebot came into the room. *Ahh!* The coffee pot had sprung into action even before she had awoken and, as always, expertly prepared a hot, steaming mug exactly the way Kim liked it—just strong enough, served black, no sugar—and given it to the housebot, which had dutifully brought it to her desk. It was uncanny the way the appliances knew exactly when Kim would want her coffee, but not at all mysterious—it was just a neural network driven by the health monitors implanted in her body, the sort of basic AI technique she had learned years ago in school. And yet, there were times when it seemed like magic.

"Thank you, Housebot."

Feep?

"Yes, that will be all. Oh, wait, hangover meds please. Breakfast in half an hour."

Kim glanced at the morning Chit-Chat and let the caffeine seep in. No friends were online at the moment (unsurprising this early on a work-day), but there were a few messages to attend to.

First up was a note from Cy, reminding Kim that they had tickets to tonight's ballgame, Tigers vs. Giants. This was accompanied by the usual complaints about doctored replays and crooked AIs. Kim responded with noncommittal sympathy, being careful not to imply that the game was in any way dishonest or rigged, thanking her once again for the invitation. *Sigh.* Yes, of course the game was rigged. Yes, of course the AIs blatantly cheated. Everyone knew that, but only Cy had the poor sense to say so out loud.

A couple more messages and quick responses; nothing important.

Feep!

Kim accepted a handful of hangover pills from the housebot and washed them down with a big gulp of coffee before returning to the screen as she yawned, almost awake.

"Terminal, today's weather report, please."

A moment later, the morning news show came up on the screen.

"Hello Merv!"

"Why hello Mel!"

"So, how's the weather today?"

"The weather?"

As usual, the terminal had brought up that morning-time staple, *The M&M Show,* and they were at it again with their trademarked banter, yacking away pointlessly and sometimes finishing each other's sentences on the dubious theory that the morning news should be 'witty and engaging.' The back-and-forth (repeated almost word-for-word each morning) continued for a few more seconds, until they finally got to the day's forecast, finishing the segment with one of their famous taglines.

"Great weather, if you're a duck. NOT!"

The video then cut to a clip showing two soggy mallards waddling into a coffee shop and ordering a latte, accompanied by the inevitable green flashing box in the middle of the screen:

Order a latte NOW! 10% discount!

Eyeroll.

Why couldn't they just say, "Cold and rainy all day?" Not that it mattered; there was no reason to go outside for even a moment.

After the weather report was over, Merv and Mel moved on to entertainment, raving about the hottest new flick, *Dr. Kro and the Punkmetal Gang.* Kim loved Dr. Kro! Lots of music, lots of dancing, beautiful people and beautiful sets, what's not to like?

"Terminal, please add *Dr. Kro and the Punkmetal Gang t*o our playlist."

"Affirmative," responded the terminal in a smooth, soothing voice. "Is there anything else this unit may assist you with this morning?"

"Negative, terminal, that will be all."

5

Bah! An entire year's worth of Dr. Kro movies were now queued up; evidently there was some sort of promotional deal in effect. That wasn't what Kim had wanted, but it was too much trouble to take the extras off the list, and besides, she was about due for a Dr. Kro binge, so why not? Meanwhile, M&M kept at it without a break. The wonders of superfoods: tofu, spelt, and kale. The latest fashions. And, of course, cue the hottest new band playing the hottest new musical sensation— Afro Punkmetal.

Catchy!

––––––

It was now time for breakfast, so Kim stood up and walked stiffly into the kitchen, where the refrigerator had just disgorged a breakfast packet. She was hoping for sausage and eggs—a favorite—but no such luck. Instead, scrambled tofu and whole grain spelt toast.

Ugh.

"Refrigerator, sausage and eggs, please."

"Negative, Kim. The Food Company recommends that you begin the day with a nutritious breakfast low in fat and high in protein."

Kim was indignant.

"Since when? We've had sausage and eggs every day for the last week. What gives?"

"The latest guidance from The Food Company's nutritional experts confirms that the best breakfast is one high in protein and low in fat, supplemented by healthful whole grains. Tofu is an ideal source of plant-based protein and spelt is widely held to be a superfood that will improve both your health and your outlook on life."

Kim continued to argue, but to no avail. She eventually gave up and asked the housebot to pop the tofu into the microwave and the spelt into the toaster, then sat down at the table to wait, dreading what would doubtless be another tedious week at work. Kim remembered the day she had joined The Artificial Intelligence Company, just five years ago, excited to have a job working with the AIs after majoring in the subject at school. She had even gotten to meet an Order Four AI at orientation on her first day of work. She'd had no idea what an Order Four AI might be at the time, but it seemed quite impressive. It had even given them all a brief demonstration of its ability to multitask, spawning over a hundred independent personae which had individually greeted each new employee and briefed them on their assignments. It had been quite a letdown when she had been assigned to help train the operational automata, simple devices incapable of thinking for themselves. Even that had been interesting for a while, but over the last several years it had settled into an interminable grind and Kim was more than ready for a change.

Ding! Pop!

Breakfast was ready.

The toasted spelt was blandly acceptable if somewhat wanting in texture, but the tofu was beyond redemption. Kim was tempted to dump it into the bin, but waste was a violation of The Food Company's Terms of Service, so she grimaced and washed most of it down with a second cup of steaming hot coffee, once again brewed to perfection by the coffee pot, which catered to every nuance of her preferences even as the refrigerator seemed malevolently indifferent.

After finishing her disappointing breakfast, she returned to Chit-Chat, losing track of time until her watch started buzzing insistently. *Crap!* Time to leave already? Where had the morning gone? She jumped up from the table and ran into the bathroom at full tilt. There was just enough time for a brief, lukewarm shower, after which she waited impatiently while the housebot applied a perfect layer of light-green skin toner. Next, into the closet. Which smock would she wear today? Pale blue, pale green, pale yellow, or pale beige? Kim picked pale blue on the dubious theory that doing so was somehow edgy or daring or whatever. Okay, that was a stretch. It was boringly conventional, but at least it wasn't beige. The watch was now buzzing and beeping ever more angrily. Second warning? *Yikes!* She threw on a dark-blue mane and a pale-beige rain jacket, grabbed her VR headset and ran out the door, which latched behind her as the lights turned themselves off and the apartment powered down.

———

Kim activated the navigational overlay on her headset and was directed down to the main floor via the elevator. She made her way through the lobby, and out onto a broad plaza flanked by identical high-rise apartment buildings that marched nondescriptly off into the distance in two tidy rows. It was gray, rainy, and cold (exactly as forecast). Kim had dawdled a little too long this morning and had therefore been routed via the surface walks instead of the more comfortable but congested underground tunnels. On a warm, sunny day the walk was pleasant; the area was nicely landscaped and afforded a stunning view of the lofty towers of the corporate district off in the distance. But there was nothing nice about the weather today, so Kim pulled her rain jacket tight around her as she scurried along as quickly as possible, partly to get out of the weather, but mostly to avoid missing her bus.

After a few minutes half-walking, half-trotting, she arrived at the station and placed her right wrist in the scanner, which read the embedded ID chip and flashed green to indicate admission. A nervous glance at her watch and a sigh of relief. She had been slow leaving her apartment this morning but had managed to make up most of the lost time along the way, arriving at the turnstile only ten seconds behind schedule. This was fortunate, since the last thing she needed was to annoy the AIs by forcing them to reroute her at the last moment. She had been working in the company's transit support division for the last six months and she knew exactly how much tolerance the AIs had for tardiness—none whatsoever. The entire system was demand-driven, with tens of millions of passengers and countless busses and trains routed and dispatched on a real-time basis. Depending on your boarding priority and which stations the AIs sent you through, your commute could be quick and comfortable or slow and painful. It was important to stay on their good side, and few things were as certain to provoke a week of long and grueling commutes than carelessly missing a bus and forcing them to adjust your routing at the last moment. It was always a bad idea to be late.

Following the directions of her headset, she sprinted through the station and found her assigned place in the twelfth slot of the mid-priority queue, arriving moments before the bus rounded the corner and pulled into the loading zone. *Whew!* The doors opened wide, and she rushed in along with dozens of other bland, interchangeable commuters, quickly finding a nice spot between a stanchion and the side of the bus. Moments later, a latecomer tried to wedge herself in, but Kim stood her ground and glared to warn the interloper off. This was *her* spot, and nobody was going to chase her away.

The driver pushed a button on the console and off they went, first gliding in near-silence along a surface road, then picking up speed and joining a long convoy as a dozen busses locked up head-to-tail merging onto the elevated express lane. Within moments of departure, everyone had their faces stuck in their mobiles, including Kim, who brought up a mindless solitaire game to pass the time. She was halfway through a second hand when she felt someone trying to pry her away from the all-important stanchion. It was the latecomer once again. Kim looked her nemesis in the eye, glaring angrily to warn her off, which seemed to suffice. It would not do either of them any good to be caught jostling one another on the bus. But then, a few minutes later, she was at it again, trying to squeeze into Kim's prime spot. *Damn! What is her problem?* Kim grabbed the stanchion even more firmly, determined not to be displaced. Eventually, whoever-it-was gave up, leaving Kim in peace to finish one more game of solitaire before the convoy plunged underground and arrived at the subway station, where Kim and hundreds of others were disgorged into a vast grotto of concrete and tile. They rushed through tunnels and cascaded down stairways, blindly following their headsets' directions at every junction and branch point until each was deposited on the correct spot to wait for their assigned train.

To her surprise, Kim's headset directed her toward the front of the platform, and she was quite puzzled until she looked down and saw a green message light blinking on her mobile.

NOTIFICATION from The Transportation Company

The Company would like to take this opportunity to thank you, our valued customer, for your patience this morning when a rude and selfist passenger attempted to deprive you of your fair share of space on one of our buses.

In appreciation for your sense of community, The Company is pleased to award you a half-step upgrade to your boarding priority for the remainder of this trip, as well as 0.1 social merit points.

Thank you for your business, and we hope the remainder of your trip will be pleasant.

The upgrade was welcome, as always, and who didn't love a merit award? It was only a tenth of a point, but every little bit helped and she was determined to keep her nose clean, rack up the points, and eventually improve upon her current Baa2 Social Cohesion Rating and move from District 10 to someplace nicer, perhaps the edge of District 8 if she was lucky. The headset then guided her to the medium-high priority queue, where she eagerly waited, anticipating a prized seat toward the front of the train. No more standing, no more jostling for her this morning! When the train arrived, she managed to find a bench in her assigned compartment, the third from the front, just before the mid-priority riders rushed in and wrapped themselves around the stanchions much as Kim had done earlier that morning. She was glad that she had remained calm and let the AIs sort things out, savoring just a bit of schadenfreude at the likely fate of the passenger who had so annoyed her on the first leg of her journey.

After another fifteen minutes of impersonal (but comfortable!) tedium, she arrived at The AI Company's regional headquarters, a windowless tower of concrete and steel situated in the heart of the Corporate District. On a clear day it appeared to soar ever upward into the sky, towering over the lesser structures clustered about its base, but today only the lowest fifty stories were visible, the bulk of the structure disappearing into the clouds and mist on what continued to be a wet and miserable day. She continued to follow the overlay through the security checkpoint, up the elevator to the transportation support division on the twentieth floor, and through the maze of narrow aisles. Straight, left, left, straight, right. At last she arrived and settled into today's assigned cubicle exactly on time, a tribute to the precision of the transit system and the AIs that controlled it.

On to another day of teaching the automatons. They were simple devices, unable to think for themselves, and it was only through constant training by skilled individuals such as Kim that they were able to deal with the ever-changing environment in which they operated. Today, fittingly enough, she was looking for 'malicious jostling.' In the crowded confines of the transit system a certain amount of shoving and jockeying for position was tolerated, particularly at boarding time, but once a vehicle was in motion the passengers were expected to remain in whatever location they had chosen at the start of the journey and avoid unnecessary contact with others. The penalties for jostling were not severe—usually no more than a temporary reduction in boarding priority and tiny demerit—but usually sufficed to deter this sort of unwanted behavior. Selfist outbursts such as Kim had encountered this morning were thankfully rare among the well-heeled residents of the inner districts.

She began plowing through the surveillance data in her queue, with the training manual (frequently updated) and the Terms of Service (likewise frequently updated) close at hand. Today's task was posed as a series of yes/no questions, the first being, *was there significant contact?* In half the cases, the answer was yes, and in half the answer was no. Good. Whoever had collected the data had done a proper job. There was nothing so useless as a training set with excessive numbers of positive or negative instances, which would teach the automaton nothing whatsoever.

Once contact had been confirmed, there was a series of further questions, devised to discern intent. Had the passengers made eye contact? Were there any physiological signs of aggression or fear? Had there been any shoving or jostling between the passengers earlier in the trip? Was the contact repeated, and if so, how often? In borderline cases, she was instructed to consider additional factors, especially the suspect's social cohesion rating. This was yet another reason to keep your nose clean—once your rating began to fall, it was apt to continue doing so as the AIs started citing you for even the most minor, borderline infractions.

Kim's answers to these questions were first compared with those of two other trainers and, if all three agreed, the data was fed into the neural network and eventually deployed across the transit system. Three-way concurrence was essential, as any disagreement would trigger an escalated assessment that would inevitably result in at least one trainer receiving a job performance penalty. Nobody cared whether the answer was correct or not, as long as all three trainers agreed, and Kim had long ago learned the value of dull conventionality. Being the oddball was never wise, even if you were right.

After a morning reviewing hour after hour of surveillance data and resolving over a dozen cases, Kim rode the elevator down to the second sub-basement for lunch and entered the bland, cheerful cafeteria to wait in line for the chef's salad. Today's offering was lentils and quinoa on a bed of wilted kale. *Yuck.* Kim had never been fond of quinoa, and she positively despised kale, but at least there wasn't any tofu. She caught herself starting to smile with amusement at this thought, then quickly stifled it, fearing that the AIs would incorrectly infer that she was somehow pleased with today's offering and add it to this week's grocery order. Sure enough, moments later an urgent message began to flash bright green on her mobile:

Special Discount, Today Only!
25% off on Kale, Lentils, and Quinoa!

Kim replied with an emphatic *no* but wasn't sure it would make any difference. If they wanted you to eat kale, you were going to eat kale, and that was it. Her headset then directed her to a seat in a private dining nook, where she sat down to eat and catch up on Chit-Chat. There was nothing terribly important, but it did help to pass the time and distract her from the sodden green mass that remained upon her tray after she'd picked out most of the lentils and some of the quinoa.

All too soon, it was back into the elevator for the return trip to the twentieth floor.

The afternoon was just like the morning, except for one case which proved both challenging and interesting. At first it seemed to be a routine encounter in which two passengers (subjects A and B) pressed up against one another in a crowded train near the outer districts. There was clearly no jostling involved and Kim was about to mark it as a negative instance, when she noticed that Subject A was wearing gaudy, gender-revealing clothing (prominent mams) and an unstylish mane.

Hmmm. This looks suspicious.

Even though no rules had been broken, Kim decided to replay the surveillance, looking to see if anything else might come to light. Sure enough, she caught Subject B staring at A's mams, which were almost in her face. This was accompanied by a positive physiological reaction from both, indicating excitement rather than the embarrassed revulsion that one would normally expect.

Both leering and encouragement of leering were prohibited by the Terms of Service, so Kim cited them for Level 1 violations but kept probing, certain that a more serious infraction would soon become evident. She replayed the video from several other angles, and eventually caught them whispering to one another. Then she checked the exit logs and, as suspected, the two had left the system together. Holding hands. And smiling. *Damn. This is getting serious.* Kim had seen this pattern before and knew exactly what was going on—they were misusing the transit system to bypass Matchmaker and arrange for an illicit sexual liaison. She boosted the penalty to Level 2, but was certain she could find at least a Level 3 violation if she kept on probing.

Time to check around.

Kim contacted one of the AIs at Matchmaker and was told that both subjects had been banned for gender-selective intimacy violations. Furthermore, The Elevator Company's AIs indicated they had ridden to Subject B's apartment together, and that Subject A had not left the building until several hours later. No further surveillance was available, as all devices within the apartment had been powered down as soon as the two had entered. Nevertheless, there was enough data to form a definitive conclusion—the two subjects had mis-used the transportation system to arrange for an illicit gender-selective liaison, a Level 4 violation. After consulting the training manual, she assessed a two-point penalty to their boarding priorities for a duration of six months and imposed a significant social cohesion demerit. Finally, she notified The Housing Company so they could assess whatever penalties were appropriate under their own Terms of Service. Sadly, the two would doubtless find themselves living far out in the middle districts, if not the outers.

Sitting alone in her cubicle, Kim found herself unsettled by what she had just seen. The notion that these two had cared so much about the difference between a vag and a phal seemed bizarre to her, impossible to explain. Why would anyone risk the severe penalties associated with genderism just to gratify such an odd, irrational fetish? But then, some people seemed to think that they were special and didn't have to play by the rules. Whatever misfortune befell them, they had brought it on themselves through their selfist disregard for the greater good of the community.

About five minutes later an evaluation of her results came in. "Four-point correlation, new pattern established and uploaded for further processing! Well Done!" Kim beamed, both from the praise and in anticipation of what would doubtless be another stellar performance review. *Wow! Just wow!* The company was obviously pleased with Kim's performance. Could a promotion be in the works?

———

After a few more tedious hours, Kim repeated the morning's commute in reverse and, at exactly 1800, arrived at her apartment, ready for a quick dinner before the promised ballgame with Cy.

"Refrigerator, steak, potatoes, salad, and Cabernet, please," she said, with more hope than expectation. Ignoring her request, the refrigerator disgorged packets of boiled synchicken, quinoa, and kale instead, throwing in a glass of cheap Zinfandel as either a taunt or a concession, it was hard to tell which. Kim glared at the uncooperative appliance and could have sworn it glared back at her. Nonsense, of course, but the AIs would certainly pick up on Kim's growing dissatisfaction with the refrigerator's behavior and perhaps relent.

"Refrigerator, steak, potatoes, avocado salad and Cabernet please."

"Negative, Kim. The Food Company recommends a healthy diet low in fat and high in protein."

Kim cursed at the uncooperative appliance, opened its door, and slammed the unwanted packets back into the sorter, which dutifully returned them to their assigned places. She dug through the contents of the bins, but not a shred of red meat was anywhere to be found. *Crap,*

crap, and more crap. Kim eventually settled for baked synfish with poached cauliflower and rice and exchanged the Zinfandel for a small glass of cheap Chardonnay. This was scarcely more appealing than the initial offering, but at least Kim had some small amount of choice in the matter. The refrigerator handed the packets over to the housebot, which popped them into the microwave as Kim sat at the table fuming away.

Ding!

After bolting down the blandness that passed for dinner, she was soon back at the terminal for some Chit-Chat while waiting for the ballpark to open. Mostly it was the usual mindless drivel, catbot videos and the like, and several of Kim's classmates—Quinn, Devon, and Em— arguing about music, as usual. There was, however, a nice note from Keli about a recent visit with Kee, her first child, who was doing well under her mentor, progressing satisfactorily and considered completely unexceptional. It was good to see that Keli had finally gotten over the sorrow of parting, but it was a painful reminder that Kim had never received a visit or even a text message from her own birth-giver, whose name she had never been told.

Finally, a quick note from Shan, her best friend from school. "Bike ride tonight?"

"Sorry, ballgame with Cy, some other time, see you soon."

————

Kim was now ready to enter Virtual Reality for the ballgame. Attendance was expected to exceed five million, spread across the one hundred fifty duplicate instances that had been spun up for tonight. The Tigers and the Giants were bitter divisional rivals, and head-to-head matchups between the two always drew a big crowd. This was going to be fun!

She leaned back in the recliner and immediately felt a familiar sense of detachment as the headset shunted nerve impulses from her motor cortex to the household entertainment system, allowing both movement and speech to be controlled directly via the interface implanted in her brain. The headset turned opaque then brightened, going into full VR mode, and a moment later Kim was sitting next to Cy on the upper deck of the ballpark about halfway down the third base foul line. They spent the pregame warmup busily chatting about the weekly player rotation, the opposing lineup, and of course about the standings and whether the Tigers might make a run for it this season. As they chatted, Kim leaned back and enjoyed the perfect simulation of a perfect day, with its cloudless blue sky and bright sun shining above. True, it was lacking all sense of warmth (one of the limitations of consumer-grade VR), but it was nevertheless a welcome change from the day's chilly and wet weather and an emblem of happy times in the mythical land of baseball where it was always summer regardless of what the calendar might say.

"Play Ball!"

The crowd cheered as the home team took the field and booed as the first hitter for the Giants stepped up to the plate. The pitcher checked the sign, shook one off, then smoked one fastball after another down the center of the plate. Strike one! Strike two! Foul ball out of play, strike three looking! An excellent start, but despite the auspicious beginning, the top of the first inning ended up being a tense affair as the visitors managed to put runners at the corners with one out and score the first run of the game on a sacrifice fly. A timely strikeout completed the visitors' half of the inning and everyone breathed a sigh of relief as the Tigers jogged into the dugout.

"Hey! Couple of beers over here!" shouted Kim, prompting a waitbot with a small keg strapped to its back to pogo over and serve up a couple of cold brews in the obligatory plastic cups, dispensed by their respective housebots. The shunts momentarily disengaged to let Kim take that first, deeply satisfying draft, when a hard-hit foul came rocketing straight at her. She reflexively hit the deck, while Cy went for the catch but only managed to deflect the ball downward, where it bounced and rattled around between the seats. Kim, still unshunted, lunged and came up with it just ahead of another grasping hand.

"Woohoo!"

Phantom fist bumps, virtual high-fives.

"That one had your name on it!" laughed Cy. "A real one should be on the way by the end of the game, you'll have it tomorrow morning."

"It'd better be," said Kim, laughing and getting up off the floor in both the physical and virtual worlds. "The shunts were down and now there's beer all over the place. Be right back."

Kim dropped out of VR to survey the scene, and sure enough everything was now a beer-covered mess. The recliner, the carpet, even the poor housebot, which had been knocked over as Kim had scrambled for the ball. She left it to clean up and went into the bathroom for a quick rinse and a change of clothes, all the while thinking about Cy's wild obsession with baseball. Kim loved the game and was a devoted fan, but Cy had developed an unhealthy fixation on the AIs and how they cheated and fixed games. The Baseball Company didn't care for this sort of second guessing, and she was almost certain to be banned at some point for questioning the integrity of the game.

When Kim dropped back in, it was the bottom of the third inning and the game was completely out of hand, with the Tigers now leading 14-12.

"So, what do you think about tonight's lineup? Pretty sweet, eh?" said Cy, enthusiastic about the results of the weekly player rotation and the nonstop barrage of hard-hit doubles and base-clearing homers they were witnessing.

"You kidding? This isn't a ballgame, it's batting practice!"

"Cut it out!" laughed Cy, mercilessly pummeling Kim's shoulder. "You'll jinx us for sure!"

And then, as if on cue, the bats on both sides went abruptly silent; the umpires, perhaps realizing that the game was becoming a travesty, had dramatically expanded the strike zone. Balls in the dirt, balls at chin level, inside, outside, swing and miss or watch it go by—the call was always the same, and the scoring ground to a halt while hits became few and far between and the pitchers threw junk, not even trying to hit the plate. This was a situation that pleased no one, but after a few innings the umps eased up a bit and fiddled with the strike zone again until it was just the right size to generate some offense without turning the game into a farce.

Soon it was the bottom of the ninth with the Tigers trailing by a run. Banners waved, horns blared, and everyone chanted in unison to cheer their team on to victory. The Tigers were down to their final strike with runners at first and second when the cleanup hitter made solid contact with the tenth pitch of a classic duel. The ball shot past the diving outfielder and rolled to the center field wall. The tying run scored, and the winning run rounded third going hard for home. The relay was good, the ball was in time, the catcher applied the tag, and the game seemed destined for extra innings until the ump's arms extended wide. Safe! The Tigers had won it in dramatic fashion, and the crowd went wild as fireworks lit up the sky. Kim was sure that the runner had been cut down at the plate and that the AIs had cheated, but that was part of the game and a win is a win is a win is a WIN!

Even Cy was happy.

———

It was late now, so Kim undressed, poured a glass of vodka, and settled into bed to watch the videos that the terminal had queued up that morning, starting with *Dr. Kro and the Punkmetal Gang*. As expected, it ended up being a typical Dr. Kro flick. The ne'er-do-well youngster was whisked off to the 'mysterious secret lair' where she had numerous adventures, all leading to a massive, choreographed dance number set to—surprise!—Afro Punkmetal, and a final celebratory feast featuring kale, spelt, and tofu. It was incredibly lame, but Kim was bemused by the sheer crassness of the tie-ins and cross-promotion.

The binge continued, with one Dr. Kro flick after another, but Kim paid no attention as the cheap vodka proceeded to do its work. All in all, it hadn't been a bad day. Nothing awful had happened, she had gotten an opportunity to rise above the pack at work, and the ballgame had been a blast. And yet she was sad, without really understanding why, and she sank into that melancholy mood which often struck her in the wee hours of the morning. The bottle gradually emptied, and she eventually drifted off into a shallow and troubled sleep interspersed with dreams of soft warm arms and a dimly remembered song that was somehow comforting despite the sadness it provoked. The vodka finally won, and an ordinary day in the ordinary life of Kim ended as it had begun, in oblivion.

2. Crackdown

It was 1000 on a Oneday morning when an urgent message arrived at Kim's desktop terminal:

MEETING NOTICE from The Artificial Intelligence Company

Report to Conference Room 27.01 immediately.

Kim sighed, put her current assignment on hold, and hurried to the elevator, all the while wondering what this was all about. Unscheduled meetings, while rare, were usually uneventful and this was probably just a dull administrative matter. It might, however, be the start of a special investigation or some other high-profile project. That would be exciting!

One elevator after another arrived on the twenty-seventh floor and Kim was swept along with a steady stream of trainers on their way to the briefing. What was up? Something good or something bad? *Hurry! Hurry!* But not too fast. Mustn't be late, mustn't be early. Into the room they poured, dispersing and quickly taking their assigned seats with hands folded neatly in their laps and eyes focused straight ahead, anxious not to be noticed. The minutes ticked by, nobody making a sound or moving a muscle, the room a sea of pale beige, except for one oddball—Kim had worn pale blue today, as she often did on Onedays. While there weren't any rules against wearing blue, neither was it wise to draw attention to yourself by being different. Beige from here on. That was a pity; Kim liked blue.

After ten minutes of needless suspense and gratuitously wasted time, Supervisor Cam strode into the room and mounted the podium to address the assembled trainers.

"A few hours ago, The Housing Company detected an Anti-Mentorist cult holding children captive in one of the middle districts. This has been kept quiet so far, but sooner or later word is bound to get out, so it is vitally important that we crack this case before the Hierarchy gets wind of it. We trust you all understand the gravity of the situation."

A murmur went through the room as the trainers expressed the required degree of shock and anger. Everyone knew the rules—children must be handed over to a mentor no later than their fourth birthday, no exceptions. Despite this, there were those who refused to honor the terms of the birthing contract and tried to keep 'their' children for themselves. This was illegal and could cause irreparable damage to both birth-giver and child, so such matters were always taken seriously. Kim murmured along with the rest, feigning outrage despite decidedly mixed emotions. There was broad agreement that parting was in the best interest of both the child and society, but Kim's experience in the mentoring system had been quite unhappy, and the topic caused her considerable distress.

The room quieted, and the briefing continued.

"We have assembled a cross-division task force to assist in unraveling the network of safe houses. Transit, Food, Housing, even Clothing and Elevators will be involved. We have half a dozen companies working on this project, and sooner or later we'll find the culprits. This is a difficult undertaking because the Anti-Mentorists are particularly adept at hiding in the shadows, never staying in one place for more than a couple of nights. There are occasional raids, but by the time the authorities arrive they have already moved to another location, taking the children with them. Due to the need to act swiftly once the targets have been identified, you will be using live surveillance data, and any information you uncover will be acted on immediately. You will also be working directly with some of our AIs in order to close the loop as quickly as possible. This is, of course, an extremely sensitive operation, and any breach of confidentiality will result in immediate dismissal... Is that clear?"

All agreed, in chorus as required. "Yes, Supervisor!"

"Very well. Return to your desks."

Kim sighed. *Here we go again. Cult-suppression duty. Prepare for the grind.*

———

When Kim returned to her cubicle a message was waiting:

MEETING NOTICE from The Artificial Intelligence Company

Stand by for further instructions from Raphael.

Raphael was an Order Three Artificial Intelligence with which Kim had worked on occasion, the sort of mid-level AI that formed the core of the company's operations. Kim sat down, anxious and excited at the chance to work with a real AI, as the headset overlaid a portal above her desk. This appeared as a stark, black-bordered rectangle superimposed upon reality, through which you could peer into the virtual world where the AIs lived without entering it yourself.

Beyond the portal was a humanoid avatar with a short, cropped mane, looking back at Kim from the middle of a circular desk heaped high with terminals and communication devices. In the background, Kim could make out the interior of a large white room, bustling with activity as hundreds of identical avatars went about their work.

"Greetings. I am Raphael. You are speaking with a sub-deputy."

Kim was always a little startled by the way AIs casually dropped the 'I-bomb.' While most considered the much-despised pronoun acceptable in private among friends, in public it was always considered both selfist and rude, an attempt to draw undue attention to the speaker. AIs used it all the time, a practice which had taken Kim quite a while to get used to. Her mentor, Zani, had been particularly strict about selfist language, to the point where she was afraid to even *think* that particular word, lest it slip out and draw a severe reprimand. Her friends mercilessly teased her about her stodginess, and she had to admit they were right.

"Greetings. We are Kim. You are speaking with an assistant trainer."

Conversely, the AIs sometimes expressed puzzlement as to why humans, with their unary minds, constantly used the word 'we.' Kim had to admit that this was oddly irrational. If anything, it was the AIs that should use 'we' and the humans that should use 'I.' There was clearly something backward here, but social conventions were not required to make sense.

"I will begin with an explanation of your part in this effort," said Raphael. "One of the major challenges faced by the Anti-Mentorists is obtaining food for the children. They obviously can't eat in the dining halls, where their captives would be immediately identified and taken away by the authorities, and they can't order extra portions from The Food Company or their AIs will infer that extra mouths are being fed. We believe that they resort to buying food on the gray market and smuggling it home via the transit system, a clear violation of the Terms of Service. You are to assist in the investigation by looking for instances of passengers transporting food in shoulder bags, backpacks, and similar containers. Is that clear?"

"No, not really," said Kim. "Millions of passengers carry bags through the system every day, and there's no way to tell what's inside them. How are we supposed to find food we can't see?"

"No additional guidance is available at this point."

The AI continued with the briefing. "Once you've identified a violation, you should look for additional information to determine whether it pertains to Anti-Mentorism or some other cult. Don't bother with Foodies unless you find something flagrant. Are there any further questions?"

"No," said Kim. "It's all as clear as mud, but we'll do what we can."

"Very well," responded the AI. "You have one hundred cases in your input queue. Work through them as quickly as possible. I'll give you more once you have finished."

The portal closed, and Kim got going on the hopeless assignment.

———

The rest of the day turned into an interminable slog as Kim pored over hour upon hour of surveillance, peering at shoulder bags and backpacks, trying to guess what might be inside. Was the big, lumpy bag full of food? Don't know. What was in the small but hefty one? No idea. Kim would, however, occasionally spot a zipper left unzipped or a clasp that had popped open, exposing the bag's contents to observation. At that point she would step through the video one frame at a time, looking for an unobstructed shot of whatever was inside. For the most part the contents were of no interest, and Kim only identified food items on one occasion. Unfortunately, further investigation indicated that the passenger was a known courier for the Foodies, so Kim ignored the violation and moved on to the next case. That was it for excitement that afternoon.

When work was finished, Kim began the long ride home, sullen and withdrawn as some of the emotions dredged up by today's assignment began to surface. Standing there on the train, grasping a stanchion for support and staring off into space, Kim was overwhelmed by lingering feelings of loss that refused to go away. Loneliness. Sadness. Despair. Feelings of betrayal and abandonment. Almost everyone had a certain degree of parting trauma, as it was called, but Kim's case was more severe than most, or so she had been told. According to the doctors, this was a result of incorrect childrearing techniques during the early stages of Kim's life, mistakes that had led to excessive attachment to her birth-giver. This was why Anti-Mentorism was considered such a serious offense, as any delays in the parting greatly increased the likelihood of emotional damage. Kim had mostly recovered, but still suffered from persistent dreams that, while not frightening in the manner of a nightmare, were still troubling. Fortunately, she had little recollection of the time before the parting—just fragments that emerged from time to time in unguarded moments or while asleep. Memories of happiness, of lying in soft, warm arms, and of a silly little song whose words Kim could not recall. That was all, really.

By contrast, Kim could scarcely forget what had come afterward in the household of Zani, the stern disciplinarian into whose care she had been consigned. Mentors were required to raise their charges according to the great principles of Unity, Community, and Equality, but Zani had been particularly strict, a puritanical zealot with no patience for even the tiniest sign of deviancy. Was Kim sad? "Stop that selfist whining." Was Kim happy? "Lose that selfist smirk." Was Kim angry? "Control yourself, cold showers for a week." Kim had quickly learned to pay lip service to UCE orthodoxy—to do the expected things, mouth the expected words, feign the expected beliefs—without buying a word of it. Year after year she had lived that lie and eventually it became the truth, except on days like today when reality could not be ignored. Kim had never forgiven whoever had delivered her into that sad and lonely existence, and even the knowledge that there had been no choice did little to chase away the lingering sense of betrayal.

That night, Kim queued up a long series of mindless videos to avoid dwelling on the topic and poured out a bit more than the usual quantity of vodka before dropping off into yet another night of troubled sleep.

———

The pace picked up on Twoday morning. Raphael had noticed the extra attention Kim paid to open bags and was now focusing on those in today's surveillance data, which allowed her to identify a good bit of contraband and several more Foodies but, alas, no Anti-Mentorists or anything even remotely on target. She continued to grind away, knowing that the project was doomed from the outset, but unwilling to risk demotion or dismissal due to any lack of diligence. The day was not, however, entirely wasted, as Kim managed to ferret out a number of serious offences unrelated to the investigation, including a Tobacconist who was reported to the authorities and swiftly arrested.

At the end of the day, the trainers were summoned back to the conference room to review the team's progress, or rather its lack thereof. They sat as usual in the auditorium, while the AIs, including Raphael, sent their homunculi, which Kim's headset projected onto the front of the meeting room facing Cam.

"What's the holdup?" demanded Cam, clearly unhappy about the failure to make any significant headway. "Can anyone explain why we have yet to identify a single lead that might help us unravel this case?"

None of the trainers ventured so much as a word, but Raphael did speak up.

"Efforts to trace the cultists' food supply through the transit system have so far failed. Several cases of smuggling have been detected, but none has yet been tied to anything other than the usual Foodies."

"And why is that?" snapped the angry supervisor. "Is there perhaps a lack of diligence on the part of team members? We are beginning to suspect that not everyone is fully on board with this investigation and that someone may be secretly hampering its progress."

This set off a wave of panic in Kim, whose parting trauma was well known to management, and there was no way to hide her anxiety from the health monitor. If they even *suspected* that Kim was somehow letting her personal feelings interfere with the mission, the consequences would be dire.

Fortunately, Raphael spoke up to defend the integrity of the trainers.

"All team members are diligently performing their duties, despite signs of stress and anxiety which have been detected in certain individuals. The normal three-way quality control checks indicate no more than the usual level of disagreement, so sabotage seems unlikely. The underlying problem is a lack of data, specifically the impossibility of determining the contents of shoulder bags and similar containers unless they happen to fall open by chance. Food is sometimes found, but the rate of primary detection is too low to make any progress."

Kim suppressed a sigh of relief.

"Very well," said the supervisor. "Fortunately, we have an easy remedy available. That will be all."

———

Kim's puzzlement as to what this 'easy remedy' might be was resolved when an urgent message arrived immediately after dinner that night:

NOTIFICATION from The Transportation Company

In order to ensure the safety of the traveling public, it is no longer permitted to bring any shoulder bag, backpack, or other container onto the transit system unless its contents are plainly visible. Noncompliant bags will be confiscated and replacements issued.

The company advises all passengers to arrive at their assigned transit station at least thirty minutes earlier than normal to allow for any disruptions caused by this necessary security measure.

These terms are effective immediately upon receipt.

Predictably, not everyone saw the updated Terms of Service in time to obtain a compliant bag, so when Kim arrived at the bus station on Threeday morning there was a long line of passengers waiting for replacements. Making matters even worse, many only became aware of the new policy after passing through the turnstiles, whereupon they attempted to double back and leave, disrupting the normally smooth flow of passengers. Many others had neglected to heed the earlier wakeup alerts, convinced that their alarm clocks had somehow made a mistake. As delays mounted and frustration grew, people began pushing and shoving, even jumping to the fronts of queues or packing the trains past the point of maximum capacity, trying to avoid being late for work. Kim managed to arrive at her desk exactly on time, but only after a chaotic and uncomfortable hour and a half in transit, knowing that the updated security procedures would prove a colossal waste of time.

Sure enough, not a single item of food was detected that entire morning. Neither was any other form of contraband found. Instead, they observed an abundance of extra clothing, towels, and even plastifoam packing material—things that could easily be used to conceal the contents of a bag from prying eyes. Smugglers were not idiots and had instantly realized that a crackdown was in progress. They took some simple precautions and turned the entire operation into a farce, inconveniencing every single traveler in the system while rendering the already difficult task of interdicting the cultists' food supply impossible. Nevertheless, Kim soldiered on, focusing on the task at hand and trying not to think too much about the stupidity of her assignment.

The predictable summons came in mid-afternoon, and once again Kim trudged into the conference room along with the others to take a seat and stare into space, the minutes ticking by as everyone waited for the meeting to begin. After a good bit more than the usual delay, Supervisor Cam arrived and once again mounted the podium.

"Show the clip."

The bank of video screens behind Cam lit up, showing the soft, glowing face of the Deputy First Minister Lo, a senior potentate of the UCE hierarchy, making an unexpected statement on an urgent matter.

"We are alarmed to hear of a great evil that has surfaced once again in this good and gracious city, a terrorist gang of Anti-Mentorists who are kidnapping and holding innocent children under deplorable conditions and, even worse, treating them as the personal property of their birth-givers. This heinous cult is not merely a danger to the children they abuse in this fashion, it is a dagger aimed at the heart of civilization itself. We condemn this wanton criminality and ask that any citizens with information on this cult to immediately contact the police so they can rescue the children and bring the cultists to justice."

Deputy First Minister Lo continued talking, but the video screens went silent as a murmur went through the room, this time entirely genuine. Once the Hierarchy got involved, things were certain to heat up in a hurry.

"This *is your* fault!" The ritual beratement had begun.

The supervisor spat out the words while glaring venomously at everyone in the room, accusing the entire team of every crime and shortcoming imaginable. "Which of you tipped off the Hierarchy? Who sabotaged the investigation? Which of you is helping the smugglers evade the dragnet? You will all pay for this!" On and on it went without letup for nearly twenty minutes, after which the team was sent back to their desks without any further instruction as to how to proceed.

––––––

That evening, Kim picked disconsolately at the unpalatable mass provided for dinner, the composition of which was uncertain except for an abundance of kale and tofu. Was tonight's disappointing fare due to the supervisor's promise of retribution, or merely The Food Company's general indifference to Kim's likes and dislikes? Whichever it was, the result had been another fight with the damnable refrigerator, putting Kim in a thoroughly foul mood. On top of that, now that the Hierarchy had gotten involved, nothing was certain except that tomorrow would be even worse than today. Sure enough, a few minutes later another urgent message arrived:

NOTIFICATION from The Transportation Company

In order to ensure the safety of the traveling public, all shoulder bags, backpacks, and other containers will be subject to manual search immediately upon entry to the system. Failure to comply will be severely penalized.

The company advises all commuters to arrive at their assigned transit station at least one hour earlier than normal to allow for any disruptions caused by this necessary security measure.

These terms are effective immediately upon receipt.

Kim's mood further deteriorated after the lead story on the evening news show, in which a mob of drably clad UCE Zealots had appeared in front of The Housing Company's headquarters to protest the company's failure to immediately bring the Anti-Mentorist cult to justice.

They shouted the usual slogans: "Unity! Community! Equality! All are One when One is All!" Meanwhile, Deputy First Minister Venn, a notorious firebrand, was giving an impassioned speech, only fragments of which were audible over the chanting mob.

"How could they let this happen?"

"They are treating our children as property!"

"They must be found and rescued at once!"

"This is an outrage!"

Fortunately, the demonstration had been scheduled for the evening hours and the riot shutters had been closed well in advance, so there was no disruption to business or damage to property. Lacking any targets on which to vent their anger, the crowd soon dispersed without the necessity of bringing in the copbots.

———

On Fourday morning, Kim was waiting in a line that stretched halfway across the plaza when everyone began to rush forward into the station. Had the company brought in additional bots to speed the inspection? Doubtful. Had they relented? Fat chance. And then the screaming began. Far ahead in the line, Kim beheld an ugly scene as desperate commuters surged past the checkpoint and into the station while the copbots tried to restore order, liberally applying the feared stun-batons to all within reach. Despite their best efforts, the copbots were quickly overwhelmed and Kim was swept along with the press of humanity through the station in no particular direction, the navigational overlay saying only "Emergency Service Suspension. Shelter in Place."

The situation deteriorated rapidly as even more commuters, desperate to get to work, crowded into the station with no place to go. Suddenly, the riot shutters slammed shut with a loud, metallic *clang* as the transit system ground to a halt and, with it, the city itself. Kim knew this could not last much longer, and indeed it did not; a few minutes later a new message arrived, a thousand mobiles beeping and booping in synchrony to the cheers of the crowd:

NOTIFICATION from The Transportation Company

Due to the resolution of the security threat, restrictions on carrying shoulder bags, backpacks, and other containers on the transit system are hereby lifted. Thank you for your selfless cooperation and sense of community.

These terms are effective immediately upon receipt.

Despite everything, Kim still arrived at work on time, and was immediately directed to room 27.01 for yet another briefing. After the obligatory period of obsequious silence, someone new mounted the podium at the front of the room. Supervisor Rin. This time the meeting was short and sweet.

"We have determined that the cultists are not, at this time, using public transportation to smuggle food to their safe houses. Entities assigned to transit system monitoring are released. Everyone else, stand by for further instructions."

Kim could not help feeling sorry for Supervisor Cam, who was never heard from again.

———

The rest of the week went by in the usual fashion as the crackdown continued, thankfully without Kim's participation. There were more demonstrations, further posturing from the Hierarchy, and reports of flash mobs in the outer districts. Finally, the expected news bulletin arrived while Kim was sitting in the cafeteria at lunch on Fiveday, right on schedule.

"We interrupt the regularly scheduled programming to bring you this special update."

The video shifted to show a live drone shot of events unfolding "somewhere in the middle districts," as a pair of manacled adults were led away by the police to the cheers of the zealots who had gathered to watch the spectacle.

"Breaking News! Authorities have just concluded a successful raid on the notorious Anti-Mentorist cult known as 'Our Children, Ourselves.' Members of this outlaw terrorist organization have been caught holding three children captive under deplorable conditions in a safe house somewhere in the middle districts. Representatives of The Housing Company deny accusations of lax enforcement, complaining that archaic laws against surveillance within a housing unit had hampered the investigation. The new management team for that district has apologized on behalf of the company and promised to redouble efforts in the future.

"The break in this case reportedly came when an AI assigned to The Elevator Company noticed unusual activity in the building, leading to a unit-by-unit search after the housing project had been sealed off. The children have been rescued, and the ringleaders are now being taken away to await trial. More details at 1800. We now return to our regularly scheduled program."

The raid was all over the news and Chit-Chat for the rest of the day and long into the night, as the Hierarchy and the talking heads proclaimed victory and thanked the public for their diligence and sense of community. On Sixday afternoon, they were treated to the usual show trial as the ringleaders were brought to the dreaded Halls of Justice to confess their crimes, after which they were sentenced to five years in a work camp and relegated to the outer districts. No further raids or trials were announced and the crackdown was officially over, problem solved.

Had the entire city been turned upside down to locate just one pair of violators? Evidently so.

———

It was Sixday evening and time for the UCE Dance Spectacular, a fixture in Kim's life for as long as she could remember. Attendance had been mandatory in Zani's household, and Kim had enthusiastically complied, racing through dinner to be ready in time, though for reasons unrelated to any enthusiasm for the UCE movement. Even back then, Kim had loved nothing so much as dance, and the spectaculars were unrivaled in that regard, with their epic settings and massive crowds writhing in unity. Above all she had loved them for the head-pounding, chest-thumping power of the music. Kim wasn't nearly so gung-ho these days and usually watched while eating dinner, passively enjoying the spectacle with the shunts disengaged rather than actively participating, but she still attended nearly every week. The social cohesion bonus you got for attending had nothing to do with it, of course. Okay, that was a lie, but the spectacle was still a hoot if you could get past the preening and posturing of the Hierarchy.

Kim dropped into VR and was transported to a lofty chamber of indeterminate size, immersed in an ocean of avatars swaying in unison to the vibrant pounding rhythms of Afro Punkmetal, loud and energetic. The illusion was nearly perfect. She was moving without moving, dancing without dancing, the avatar doing the work while Kim was eating her dinner. Soon she was whirring in synchrony with countless thousands of others, mind in one place and body in another. The first number led into the second, the music slowing a tad as the assembled multitude fell into formation for a solemn processional, marching in unison around the bright, shining dais in their midst. There was a brief, expectant pause as the procession ended and the Cadre, fulfilling its role as the leaders of the community, took its place atop the rising platform, arms uplifted, tension building as the people clapped and stamped their feet in time to the power of the music.

Fireworks! Explosions! Shooting stars and geysers of fire! The Cadre broke into frenetic gyrations and the crowd went wild, the energy of each feeding off of the other. On and on it went, wave after wave, until the storm subsided, the music calmed, and all became serene as the assembly swayed and chanted the mantras, "Unity, Community, Equality! All are One when One is All," over and over, passion spent.

And then a cheer rose up, "UCE! UCE! UCE!" proclaiming the arrival of a flock of dazzling white doves descending from on high and alighting atop the pinnacle of the dais. As they landed, the doves transformed into the familiar forms of the Upper Hierarchy, along with numerous lesser ministers, acolytes, and potentates. This week's inspirational talk was to be delivered by Deputy First Minister Lo, and after the usual platitudes and exhortations the Esteemed One began her oration.

"This week has seen a great victory against one of the great scourges of our time, the hideous cult known as Anti-Mentorism. Like all cults, it is founded on selfism, the desire to place oneself at the center of the universe and claim special privileges to the detriment of others. But what form of selfism could possibly drive a birth-giver to dehumanize her own offspring and treat it as her personal property, to do with as she pleases? The answer is deceptively simple. It is a form of *bipolar* selfism, similar to that which leads to pair-bonding, another practice which we have long spoken against. In this case, the person who bore a child teaches it to love her and her alone, above all others, thereby validating and reinforcing her own delusion that she is somehow entitled to a special place in the cosmos. Society tolerates a certain amount of this as being necessary to the essential function of reproduction but prolonging it beyond the four years allowed by law can make this unnatural attachment permanent, creating a lifelong bond in which the child-bearer attains a lasting, special importance to the child, and vice versa. We will continue to press, as always, for abolition of certain archaic child-rearing practices that allow this unhealthy bipolar selfism to flourish, guided by clear scientific ..."

This was becoming too intense for Kim, dredging up deeply buried memories faster than they could be suppressed. She managed to tune out for the next several minutes, distracting herself by focusing on the shortcomings of dinner while doing her best to ignore the rest of the sermon. Mercifully, the rally didn't last much longer, and soon the Hierarchy took wing, the Cadre waved goodbye, and the show ended with a final volley of fireworks.

She drifted back to the real world, scraped the last of 'dinner' into the bin, and commenced her nightly ritual of videos and vodka, thankful that she would have the entirety of Sevenday to recover before the week began anew.

3. Kim's Big Night

It was late on Fivenight and Kim was on a date with someone named Jael at a nondescript nightclub called VOO in the heart of the Entertainment District. Her finger hovered nervously above the *Offer* button on the Matchmaker app, trying to summon the courage to invite her partner for the night to one of the intimacy booths lining the back wall of the nightclub. She had been on many dates but had always chickened out at this point, terrified by the final rite of passage into adulthood, something she had long desired but never quite gone through with.

The person looking at her from across the table, although strong and muscular, was a mediocre dancer, and the date had gone only moderately well. Despite this, they had drunk, danced, and drugged into the wee hours of the morning in anticipation of this moment. Offer or not, yes or no? Jael smiled encouragingly (though no more so than was proper), and there was no doubt in Kim's mind that an offer was already pending, needing only reciprocation.

And then she froze, as she had on previous occasions, unable to proceed. After agonizing for what seemed like hours, Kim finally put her mobile away, at which point the date was essentially over, though they did dance to another couple of songs before parting with a polite kiss on the cheek. Kim paid her half of the bar tab and exited the club onto the street, while Jael remained behind, most likely hoping for better luck with whatever backup option the AIs might come up with. She stopped for a moment just outside the club and briefly considered going back in to give it another try, but instead continued to the train station for the lonely ride home.

––––––

Three days later, another week began with the usual hangover pills and hot coffee as Merv and Mel went on and on about this and that. The latest in videos, music, food, blah blah blah, but eventually they cut to a representative of The Clothing Company making an important announcement. Kim's ears perked up.

"The Clothing Company is pleased to unveil this week's exciting new fashion sensation! Boring is out, and dazzling is in with our stunning new collection of double-pocketed tunics in a bold new palette of spring colors. Vibrant pale blue! Vibrant pale green! And no wardrobe could possibly be complete without this week's amazing new fashion sensation, vibrant pale beige!"

Amazing offer! 25% off if you order NOW!!!

Vibrant pale beige? What the heck was vibrant pale beige? How can you make beige pale and have anything left to make vibrant? But Kim liked pockets and wearing last week's fashions would certainly get her noticed (not in a good way), so she ordered two in beige and one in blue with triple pockets that seemed quite daring. The constant expense of keeping up with the ever-changing fashions was a major drain on her finances, and most weeks she would rather have spent less on clothes or, at least to have spent it on clothes that weren't quite so dull, but today's offerings struck her as rather nice so she happily made the purchase. And, hey, at 25% off, who could resist?

She had almost finished eating when a personal message arrived from Quinn, Kim's musician friend from school. She was invited to come over for dinner at 1900 on Fournight and listen to some of that ancient music she was always going on about. Kim needed to be careful. While there was no prohibition against pre-unification culture, the last thing she needed was for the AIs to label her as an Aficionado, with the implication that she was some sort of cultist. This would not make her popular with either the Hierarchy, who despised any hint of decadent culture or art, nor with The Music Company, which saw irregularly provisioned songs as a threat to their commercial interests. However, there was no indication that a crackdown was in the works any time soon, and Kim was curious about why Quinn seemed to love those dusty old tunes so much, so she decided to take a chance.

Just as she finished sending her response and scraping the remnants of breakfast into the bin, the delivery chute buzzed and the housebot brought her a box containing her new tunics, express shipped just in time for work. After a brief spray of lukewarm water and an application of this week's skin toner (coppery brown), Kim got dressed and was out the door in plenty of time. *Hmm.* The beige did look nice with the toner, and the double pockets were definitely sharp.

Nothing of any interest happened that week at work, which was fine with Kim.

—————

"Headset and mobile go in the bin. You know the drill."

Kim smiled sardonically. She dropped the items into a soundproof isolation box and shut the lid, which snapped firmly shut with an audible *click*. Quinn had a strange obsession with privacy, as if such a thing were possible. Kim knew far too much about how the AIs operated to indulge in such wishful thinking. Any attempts to hide from them would only draw increased scrutiny, and any belief that they weren't listening would at best lead to a dangerous sense of complacency. But Quinn's home, Quinn's rules, so she complied.

Located in District 2, one of the most prestigious of the inners, Quinn's residence was no larger than any other but distinctly more luxurious, with an awe-inspiring view of The AI Company's regional headquarters. Kim had often seen this prestigious building from the entrance plaza or off in the distance as she walked to the bus station, but from the unobstructed vantage of Quinn's apartment on the seventy-eighth floor the view was stunning. Up and up it soared, a vast expanse of concrete, steel, and ventilation fans towering far above the lesser structures clustered around its base. They said it reached more than a thousand meters into the sky, though Kim had never been above the thirtieth floor, the highest level to which trainers had access. Above that lay the realm of the AIs, forbidden to humans and tended to by an army of robotic maintenance workers which kept everything humming smoothly along. And then, at the very top, she could just make out a light shining through the one window in the entire building, rumored to be the abode of a mysterious and much-feared potentate known only as 'the Director'—the shadowy master of the AIs.

"Kim, are you okay?" asked Quinn, who had noticed her staring out the window.

"Oh, sorry. Just looking at the company's headquarters, wondering what goes on up there where the real AIs live."

After exchanging further pleasantries, they sat down to a sumptuous dinner. Everything looked amazing, from the perfectly roasted chicken to the mouth-watering tart prepared for dessert. Kim had only been served such a meal a handful of times in her entire life, and said little, wanting to savor every bite as Quinn yacked on and on as if this were just a normal dinner, which undoubtably it was for the A3-rated musician.

"It's so frustrating!" Quinn said. "There is so much amazing material out there, century upon century of amazing music, hundreds of cultures, thousands of genres, all valuable, all distinct, and all with something to say, but it's locked away in the Music Company's vaults, probably forever. And what do we have today? Complete and utter garbage, bits of this and pieces of that, spliced together by the AIs."

Kim sliced off a bite of chicken. It was delicious, as expected.

"So why did you go into music, if it's such a wasteland?"

"You'll laugh when you hear this, but I dreamed of being a rock star!"

"A rock star? What's that?"

"Once upon a time there was a golden age of music, an era of unparalleled creativity and energy. The musicians of that day were infinitely inventive, writing thousands upon thousands of songs the likes of which haven't been seen before or since. It was primal stuff, pulsing with passion and creativity, unlike the junk they make us play these days. Devon played a little snippet for me one day after class, and I was hooked."

"Devon? You're kidding. She hates all that old stuff."

Quinn's voice lowered to a whisper, instinctively trying to avoid being overheard, though it didn't really matter—if the AIs were listening, they had already heard more than enough to make any number of unwelcome inferences.

"She's a closet Afficionado, believe it or not. All the noise she puts out about how wonderful the new stuff is? It's all a smoke screen. The only reason she argues with me is so we can talk about music without her getting into trouble."

"So, anyway, what happened to the rock stars?" asked Kim before taking a bite out of a thick slice of freshly baked whole wheat bread.

"The Music Company realized that if they let the AIs write the songs, they didn't have to pay royalties to the artists. And today, if you even *try* to perform something of your own, they compare it with every song that's ever been written, find something that's similar, claim you stole it, and ban you. Real music has been dead for hundreds of years."

After they finished consuming the delicious tart, Quinn lit a couple of candles and powered down the apartment. Lights, housebot, refrigerator—everything went dark at the flip of a switch, leaving the room lit only by a flickering yellow glow accompanied by a pleasant aroma that she referred to as 'sandalwood,' whatever that was. She then opened up a cabinet to reveal some odd equipment, made of brushed aluminum and covered with knobs, dials, meters, and other similar gadgets. Quinn flipped a switch, and it powered up as a warm, reddish glow began emanating from inside.

"What's this? It looks like some sort of contraption out of a mad scientist video. Where'd you get that antique?"

"It's not an antique. It uses some old and very primitive technology, but it's simple enough that people can recreate it without a full-fledged fabrication line, and the sound is incredible."

Damn! On top of everything else, Quinn is an Audiophile. How does she get away with this?

Quinn opened another drawer and pulled out a flat, square envelope with colorful designs on the front and back. She carefully removed a black disk about thirty centimeters in diameter, set it down on the contraptions' circular piece of metal with a rubbery surface on top, and flipped a switch to set it spinning. She lowered a long, thin arm onto its surface and the moment it made contact a crackly sort of sound could be heard through the device's speakers, followed by some soft, vaguely musical sounds.

A voice filled the room, full of passion and raw energy.

[English]Hey hey momma said the way you move,
gonna make you sweat, gonna make you groove.

After a moment of silence, an explosion of drums and guitar filled the room, loud and primal yet simple and sparse, while the singer continued to belt out lyrics laced with raw sexuality. Kim listened in awe, following as best she could with her spotty recollection of classical English, and instantly understood why it invoked such enthusiasm in Quinn and such loathing in The Music Company.

"That's where it all began for me," said Quinn when the arm retracted and the disk stopped spinning. "But here, let me show you what I really love. This one is even older, even better."

She carefully put away the rock star's music and extracted another disk from the cabinet, placing it carefully on the strange music machine. The sound was distorted, tinny and scratchy, but sublime in the subtlety of nuances, and Kim could well understand why people would risk being labeled as Afficionados and treated like outcasts to listen to it.

"*[English] Piano, string bass, drums, reeds, a few horns, Mood Indigo,*" Quinn said, mixing languages in the way she did whenever she thought Panglobal lacked the proper words. "Music pared down to the basics, sparse and uncomplicated. *[English] Jazz like it was meant to be played, from the heart.*" After a while, she grabbed a battered old acoustic guitar from its perch on the wall and began to subtly embellish, never more than four or five notes at a time, "*[English] just to give it a little personality, keep it fresh and alive, add my voice to the masters of the past.*"

Kim sat enraptured as Quinn jammed with kindred souls long dead. There were those who would have given a month's pay to be in that room and listen to her play, had it been permitted. But even Quinn could not step that far out of bounds without risking severe penalties for conducting commerce in her living quarters.

"So, any luck last week?" asked Quinn after the recording finished playing. "In the booths, I mean. I'm assuming not, otherwise it'd be all over Chit-Chat by now. High time you 'got some,' in my opinion."

"No," said Kim. "We didn't exactly hit it off, it just wasn't happening. Our love rating must be in the toilet by now."

Quinn started to chuckle. "You're probably right about that, but I have some pull and can fix you up with an off-the-charts hot date at a top-notch club where they don't cut the drugs. Full potency. Trust me, one hit of Firefly and you'll do fine, just promise you'll push the damn button this time. Go out and get laid! Sheesh, you're more than due."

Kim protested that she didn't need anyone to fix her up with a date, hot or otherwise, despite the obvious falseness of that statement. But Quinn insisted and made sure that she put in the request before leaving to go home.

———

Kim was eating breakfast the next morning when she received a message from Matchmaker—the AIs had had found her a date and, just as Quinn had promised, she looked amazing, the sort of hookup Kim could never have scored on her own. She had a five-star love rating, was a great dancer as well as a snappy dresser, tops in every category. Even more impressive, the date was to be at the legendary Tropicana, one of the hottest, most exclusive nightclubs in Sector 5. It was also one of the most expensive, alas. Kim accepted the date before there was time for second thoughts, then fired off a quick *Thank You* to Quinn. It was too late to back out now.

She spent much of that day at work staring off into space, distracted by the prospects of what the night might hold. Dancing, drinking, drugging, flirting … more and more, around and around, building up until finally, in the wee hours of the morning, the moment of truth. Offer or not? This time the answer would be yes! And after that? This was the point where things started to seem a little scary, as Kim tried to imagine being naked with a complete stranger. *Dammit, Kim, don't think, just do.*

The ride home after work was quick and comfortable. Express queue, front of the train, first bus. Kim knew every detail of the priority scheme and realized that her trip reflected a two-step priority boost. Temporary upgrades of this sort were routinely granted on request from other companies; it would appear that Matchmaker's AIs were pulling out all the stops. The outrageous pampering continued at home as the housebot set up a self-contained grill and the refrigerator disgorged one hundred grams of genuine rib eye steak; an indulgence as surprising as it was welcome. Kim suspected this was once again Matchmaker's doing but didn't really care and gave the fridge a great big hug.

The meat was perfectly cooked—medium rare—and accompanied by a generous scoop of creamy mashed potatoes, a huge garden salad, and a glass of decent Cabernet. Not quite Quinn-worthy, but still an amazing improvement over the usual fare. Kim lingered over every savory bite, slicing off the thinnest possible slivers, popping each into her mouth, slowly chewing while relishing the warm, moist … *Lol! try not to think about sex for just thirty seconds. Can't do it? Then go for it!* The rest of the steak disappeared in a single huge and satisfying mouthful. *Screw moderation!*

After dinner, Kim gave only the most cursory attention to the news feed and Chit-Chat. Weather report blah blah blah. Cults and crackdowns, yeah whatever. Merv and Mel blither blather blither. Em, Devon and Quinn going on and on about music and culture. Shan wanting to go bicycling. Dammit, why'd she always have to pick a night when Kim was busy? Her mind wandered. What would tonight's date be like? Innie or Outie? Soft and curvy, strong and muscular, or something tastefully in between? Not that it mattered; one was as good as the other, as everyone agreed. "Sorry, some other time," she wrote back at the last minute, almost forgetting to send a response.

Crap!

Quinn had just blabbed about tonight's hot date, and Chit-Chat was suddenly abuzz with words of encouragement and threats of never-ending torment should Kim chicken out again. They meant well but it wasn't helping, so she blocked all further messages for the evening, setting her status to "Do Not Disturb—hot date! Details tomorrow!"

Meanwhile, the latest rage on the music scene was blaring away in the background—Sino-Indian Thrash. Quinn would doubtless condemn it as lacking even the smallest spark of creativity, but so what? Kim jumped up and pranced around the room. *Dance baby, dance! Shake it baby, shake it!* Then she fell down laughing at the absurdity of it all. Tonight, tonight, yes tonight. Hot and flushed, heart racing, and again the sweaty palms and trembling hands. What if it didn't happen? But even more unnerving, what if it did?

Calm down Kim. You'll blow it again.

Her watch vibrated once again, very insistently. Only sixty minutes until time to go. Kim muted and blanked the terminal, went into the bathroom, and hopped in and out of the *steaming hot shower.* (Wow!) After that, she grabbed a razor and meticulously removed every last vestige of hair before the housebot applied a fresh coat of toner, achieving a uniform coat of light coppery brown with just the faintest hint of orange tiger stripes to add an air of mystery. Perfect!

Kim wondered if perhaps the tiger stripes were a bit too daring, and if the huge investment of effort and the perfection of the results wasn't itself verging on distinctivism. *Hell yeah!* This was going to be a very distinctive night. To complete the look, she went into the bedroom, where the housebot had laid out the blue smock with the triple pockets. The whole household was in on it! There was magic in the air, and the stars (or at least the AIs) were in perfect alignment. A bright-orange mane completed the look, and she stepped back to admire the effect before walking out the door, which obediently latched behind her.

———

Kim emerged from the station and into the riot of sight and sound that was the Entertainment District. Green and purple. Blue and orange.

Gold, hot pink, flaming orange, and more hot pink. Spectacular signs in garish hues vied to draw the revelers inside, insistently different yet somehow all the same. The head-splitting sound of Sino-Indian Thrash poured out of every door, a cacophony of conflicting tunes and rhythms, confused and intoxicating. Neatly groomed revelers pushed and shoved toward whatever venue suited their fancy, each trying to be more spectacularly nondescript than the next, except for the occasional oddball who shrugged off the scowls and opprobrium heaped with abundance upon anyone who dared to be truly different.

There was time to kill, so Kim decided to sample the sinful delights of the zone, inching through the writhing mob of partiers. Bars and drug dens aplenty—no thank you, save it for the club. Dance hall? Nope. What about the gambling house, full of flashing lights and jingling machines? Kim paused at its entrance for just a little too long and was dragged in by one of the touts and given a "free pull on the loosest slots on the strip." Naturally, it paid off—the oldest trick in the book. Kim grabbed the gambling tokens pouring into the hopper and tossed them to some poor sucker sitting zombie-like at one of the machines, which resulted in her immediately being hustled out the door. Kim had long ago learned that this was the quickest and easiest way to escape from such establishments without being immediately pulled back in. The next block was dominated by theatres with live stage shows, some savory, some not, but tickets were expensive and there was not enough time even if Kim had the inclination, which she did not.

Maybe a VR parlor? *Sure! That would do the trick.* Kim paid the modest entry fee and was treated to the always-amazing experience of a commercial-grade rig, far more capable than a typical home unit. How about a dungeon crawl? *Yeah!* Kim punched in and entered a spooky subterranean world inhabited by ghouls and goblins, shoulder to shoulder with two other brave heroes who had entered at the same time. Kick down the door, kill the monster, take its stuff—an ancient format that never grew old, enhanced by the full-touch sensory experience. Awesome! The heft of the sword, the weight of the armor, and the searing heat of a near-miss by a hostile fireball were all totally real-

CRAIG W. STANFILL

istic except for the absence of smell, a feature that never quite made it out of beta, or so they said. Kim did pretty well, collecting a heavy sack full of gold and gems before dying. *Ouch!* That hurt! Okay, it only stung a little, just enough to make you sweat and remember to watch out for thieves hiding in the shadows. Kim respawned and went in again, but the brave adventurers kicked down the wrong door and got chased down the corridor by an angry wizard before falling into a pit where they were all eaten alive by a giant carnivorous bug.

Game over.

Oops, almost time, mustn't be late.

Kim quickly found the public toilet and entered one of the stalls, which provided a bit of quiet time to regain a degree of composure. The VR parlor had been fun, but perhaps the adrenalin-charged dungeon crawl hadn't been the best choice, and Kim was now more than a bit flustered due to the residual stress of being eaten alive and the anxiety over what the evening might hold. Might hold? Would hold. What the evening totally and definitely would hold, no question about it. It was absolutely going to happen.

That didn't help.

Kim sat there for a couple of minutes, feeling lost and alone, until her watch buzzed with the fifteen-minute warning.

Don't think, just do, like Quinn said. Good advice. One step at a time.

Kim finished up, went to the washstand, and crowded around the mirror for a final check. The perfect layer of toner so carefully applied that evening was starting to smear, but not too badly and it only took a moment for her to touch it up. A final check of the tunic (perfect!) and her mane (a little askew, nudge it back into place). Everything was good.

Okay, here we go.

And there it was, the legendary Tropicana. Lights blinking white and crimson, with jade-green palm trees and a blue and gold parrot flapping its wings in time to the music. Kim's date stood at the entrance, clearly identified in the overlay. As they drew near, their headsets automatically switched into vocal-shunt mode, intercepting the nerve impulses in their speech cortexes and transmitting them directly to one another's auditory nerves.

"Kim."

"Rey."

Introduction completed, they tapped their mobiles, indicating the start of the date, and stepped into the club. Live music! Classy!

Rey was impeccably groomed, eye-catching in a pale green smock trimmed in bright blue. It was a little last-weekish but snazzy, and Kim immediately noticed the precise tailoring of its pockets and the silky smoothness of the fabric. Rey also sized up Kim's more modest pale-blue tunic, smiled, and offered her a hand as they walked into the club together. IDs were scanned and the light blinked green twice, indicating the entrance fee had already been paid through Matchmaker. They were then shown to a private table on the second terrace of the seating area, not far from the dance floor. Time to order—vodka for Kim, tequila for Rey, and one Elation for each.

The two made forgettable small talk while waiting for the drinks and drugs to take effect. Baseball, the weather, music, the usual sort of unimportant chatter, with a lot of fashion thrown in. Rey feigned embarrassment about her smock, claiming that pale green was somehow retro and cool, while raving about Kim's daring triple pockets. They dished unrelentingly on the dancers out on the floor, making snarky comments about who was wearing what, and even snarkier jabs at the awkwardness of one couple's dance moves. "*Where* did they learn to dance and *why* does their teacher still have a job?"

Despite the booze and drugs, Kim was wound up and nervous. Was the date going well? Was Rey sufficiently entertained by the conversation?

Kim also considered the expensive cut and fabric of Rey's clothing, way out of reach for her own modest means. Perhaps the day's indulgences had not come from Matchmaker, but from Rey, who obviously possessed both a stellar social cohesion rating and a lot of money. Kim was uncertain whether to be happy about this or not, but with the Elation starting to take effect there really was no other option so happy it was. Not merely happy, but insanely, ridiculously happy. *Wow!* Quinn hadn't been kidding, the drugs in Tropicana were *potent*, full strength and uncut, unlike those in lesser clubs.

Now that they were fully prepped for an evening of hard-core partying, Rey took Kim's hand and led her to the dance floor. Mesmerized by the dazzling lights, they soon lost all sense of one another and even themselves, merging with the crowd as they danced to the loud incessant beat. Step left and sway right, spin forward and swirl back, over and over in seemingly endless permutations, guided by subtle cues and nudges provided via their headsets as the club's dance synchronization system kicked in. Dance after dance after dance, song after song after song, hour after hour after hour. And yet they always remained within reach, an island of two within a sea of many, touching hands, bringing hips together, looking into one other's eyes perceiving neither self nor other and yet somehow together. Occasionally they would take a break and return to the table to rest and order another round of drinks or top off on chemical enhancements, but only for a moment before returning to the dance floor to merge once again with the crowd.

"Two Firefly," said Rey, ready to amp things up, and Kim was all in. "A couple here, too!" said Kim, doubling down. Rey was momentarily taken aback but smiled wickedly, not saying a word. They washed down the bright purple pills with a glass of champagne (yet another extravagant luxury), looking at one another with anticipation. Ten seconds, twenty seconds, thirty seconds. *Bam!* The potent drug hit both of them like a transit system bus, bringing lust and desire to an irresistible crescendo and erasing all vestiges of caution or hesitation. Heart pounding, skin tingling, head spinning, Kim reached for her mobile with a sense of unreality, as if watching from afar. And there it was, the *Offer* button, that final barrier that she had so often failed to surmount. Panic and hesitation welled up once again from somewhere deep within Kim's psyche, but was swiftly overruled as a finger reached out and swiped right to *Yes* as if it belonged to another person or was operated by remote control.

There. It was done, and the answer came back almost instantly. *Accepted.*

———

Kim felt Rey's warm embrace as their smocks dropped silently to the floor in the darkness of the privacy booth. Body on body, lips on lips, skin on skin. Kim felt ever so many emotions at once—excitement, apprehension, anticipation, dread, hope, fear, but above all a full measure of raw animal passion such as she had never experienced before. There was no longer any slowing down or holding back, only rushing forward and the realization that nothing would ever be the same again.

Sensing Kim's inexperience, Rey took the lead. Stroking, exploring, caressing, kissing; not rough but not exactly gentle, with ever-growing intensity as Kim began to respond. For a while she lay back, enjoying the sensations and the building passion, simultaneously excited and terrified, anxious and uncertain. It felt *so good.* Scarcely realizing what she was doing, she began to eagerly explore Rey's body, feeling the delicious softness of her mams, the musty wetness of her vag, the curve of her hips; these aroused in her ever-greater heights of excitement and unbridled lust.

And then the consummation. Wave upon wave, building and crashing. *Is this really happening? OMG, this is for real.* Panting, sweating, moaning bodies thrust together, building to a moment outside of time and consciousness, an instant lost in eternity, followed by sweet release shared equally between the two.

Eventually Kim returned to the world. *YES! YES! YES!* It had been as good as—no, infinitely better than—she had ever imagined. The two lay silently beside one another as she continued to slowly, gently stroke Rey in all the secret places, reveling in the warmth and softness of her body. More caressing, soft lips together once more, eyes gazing into eyes as passion arose for a second time. Another wave of pleasure and release; then yet again. The two drifted off into blissful sleep, entwined in one another's arms.

When Kim awoke it was nearly dawn and Rey was gone. Had it really happened? Evidently so. Lying there naked in the darkness, she smiled, happy to have finally done the deed while wondering how something so pleasurable yet meaningless had come to provoke such anxiety and fear. It was good, great even, but in retrospect a bit of a letdown.

Kim found her mobile, pressed the *Add Contact* button, and eagerly awaited a response that never came.

———

Kim woke up around noon to a pounding, well-deserved headache. Half dozing, half dreaming, she had spent the morning recapturing the sweetness of Rey's caress, the softness of her body, the waves of pleasure and release, replayed endlessly in an attempt to savor the memory of each and every sensation before it faded into obscurity. *Is this love? Is this what love feels like?* Kim kept checking her mobile, hoping in vain for the contact request to be accepted, sighing with the bittersweet knowledge of what had been and what was not to be.

Hunger eventually overcame her torpor and the lingering effects of the vodka and other drugs. Out of bed. A quick shower (back to lukewarm). Coffee, coffee, coffee, and a double handful of hangover pills. Kim paid no attention to whatever it was that came out of the refrigerator, whether it was breakfast or lunch or something else entirely, as long as it quieted her growling stomach and brought back a measure of strength.

Kim's big date was the talk of the town on Chit-Chat, and everyone wanted to know, Yes or No? Rather than answering each inquiry individually, Kim set her status to display a big thumbs-up emoji with animated party balloons, skyrockets, pinatas, more balloons, and exploding firecrackers practically leaping off the screen. The congratulations and the high fives began pouring in almost immediately.

"Details! We want Details!"

"How many times? Three?"

"OMG!!! WAY TO GO!"

Kim was more than happy to share it all, except for details of body form. Never ask, never tell; some things simply weren't spoken of, at least in public. Kim was quite the celebrity all afternoon, reveling in the attention and the opportunity to relive the night over and over.

That evening, Kim accepted a VR request from Keli, who remained one of her best friends from school. They spoke heart-to-heart for nearly an hour as she opened up about details of the encounter not shared with others; about the warm, wet, softness of Rey and the depths of passion it had aroused. Keli listened sympathetically but cautioned Kim not to get too wrapped up in this one encounter as there were doubtless many more to come. "Go slowly, learn what you like, and don't give over your heart too soon or too easily." Kim was touched by the easy intimacy she enjoyed with Keli and the confidences shared between them. It was all good advice. Kim would never see Rey again. Move on, but never forget.

Afterward, she surveyed the bill from her date and gasped. Matchmaker had paid the entrance fee, but all other expenses had been split 50/50, as per the Terms of Service. The drinks were pricey, the drugs were pricey, and on top of all that, four hours in the privacy booth. At least Kim now knew how long they had been at it. There was not the least feeling of regret, but still, *ouch*. Adjustments would have to be made. A voluntary reduction in transit priority (leave half an hour earlier); no new clothes for a while (suck it up); an economy-grade menu (smirks from the refrigerator). There was not the least chance of another date for at least a month or two.

As the evening wore on, Kim became increasingly restless, still trying to process the big night, so she put the terminal on *Do Not Disturb* and queued up a long sequence of mushy romance videos. As they droned on, she poured a bit more than the normal quantity of vodka and lay upon the recliner while her mind kept wandering back to the momentous events of the previous night, replaying the evening over and over. She reveled in the preparation, the building excitement, the trance-like frenzy of the dance, the dark confines of the privacy booth, the gentle caresses of Rey's hands, the sweet softness of Rey's body, the climax, the release, the soft afterglow, the second and third reprises, and the brief contented slumber afterward.

But for all the pleasant memories forged that night, she could not forget the emptiness that followed.

Waking up. Alone.

Walking to the train station. Alone.

Returning home. Alone.

All was as it should be, pretty much like in the videos Kim was barely watching, and yet ... *Stop it Kim. The evening was perfect, exactly as it was supposed to be.* Another video, another slug of vodka, around and around, somehow always ending with the same vague feeling of emptiness as if something were missing. The hours ticked slowly by.

Eventually sleep came and with it once more dreams of a soft warm voice singing quietly in the dark, again bringing both sadness and comfort to her troubled soul.

4. That Empty Feeling

The weeks drifted by, the days grew longer, and life went on with little to mark the passage of time, an empty void casting an empty shadow on an empty space, with only the big night at Club Tropicana to look back on with anything approaching fondness. As pleasant as that night had been, in its aftermath her ordinary life had become even more ordinary. Nothing new in the closet, everything now weeks out of style. When tunics went out and pantavests came in, Kim was left hopelessly behind. Okay, one new outfit, but that was it. No dating—even the most basic level of Matchmaking was out of the question, and what was the point if you were too broke to afford a privacy booth?

Every day was much the same as the one before. For breakfast, Kim had now discovered the joys of oatmeal. Cheap, lots of energy, filling, and *it didn't need refrigeration*. Just stir in a little butter and cream (if the refrigerator was feeling cooperative), and she was set.

Work likewise continued drearily. The neural nets had an innate tendency to drift if not constantly updated, and even the most basic rules had to be reinforced and retrained, day in and day out. Jumping the turnstile was forbidden yesterday, today, and tomorrow, but the necessary adaptability and fluidity of the learning algorithms meant that anything not constantly retaught was soon forgotten.

And what was there to bring excitement and mystery into Kim's bland and boring existence? Dinnertime! A new adventure nightly, as the refrigerator took advantage of every discount and promotional deal available, no matter how bizarre. One night it was stir-fried broccoli with synchicken liver and mango salsa. What a horrible fate! What did that poor broccoli ever do to anyone? The next evening Kim was presented with a taro tofu omelet—criminal egg abuse ... *Oh, wait, that's not egg. Eww.* Horror after horror, convincing Kim that the damned machine was intentionally taking revenge for the verbal abuse it had absorbed over the last few months.

The only break from this monotony, if one could call it a break, came when Kim was assigned to special investigative teams at work, something that was now happening with increasing frequency. Apparently, the outer districts were crawling with cults and subcults of every sort, and their activity spilled onto the transit system, where they would use the poorly regulated contact between passengers to advertise their presence and recruit new followers. The Fashionistas, for example, were constantly prancing around the system wearing gaudy, eye-catching garments which they made in clandestine workshops in the outer districts. This illicit commercial activity cut into the profits of The Clothing Company, and the cultists' flamboyant distinctivism offended the sensibilities of the UCE zealots, leading to loud confrontations for which The Transportation Company was compelled to provide compensation.

For a typical crackdown, Kim would be called into room 27.01 on Oneday and paired up with an AI, after which they would spend several days tediously collecting and analyzing data in order to identify just enough offenders to satisfy the companies and the Hierarchy without causing the kind of disruption that had led to the disappearance of the hapless Supervisor Cam. One could not crack down on the Fashionistas by simply banning anyone dressed 'oddly'—not without causing a riot. On Threeday there would be a leak, heads would roll, protests and flash mobs would erupt, and the Hierarchy would proclaim its outrage, at which point the newly retrained neural networks would be uploaded into the surveillance system and the updated Terms of Service published. Arrests and show trials would follow, and the senior ministers would wag their fingers and warn the faithful about the evils of the cult-of-the-week on Sixnight. In most cases these crackdowns were entirely ineffective because their targets quickly adapted to the enforcement strategy, making it seem as if the problem had been solved when nothing of the sort was true. The companies understood this but indulged the Hierarchy anyway, expending considerable resources in doing so and writing it off as the cost of doing business.

These special assignments did provide a welcome opportunity to work with some high-order AIs, such as Raphael, but they quickly became demoralizing as Kim was called on to help catch and punish members of even the most harmless cults—Foodies, Afficionados, and the like—or to persecute adherents to various archaic religions whose teachings contradicted the tenets of the UCE movement. In theory, everyone had 'Freedom of Belief,' whatever that was, but the Hierarchy nevertheless manufactured one excuse after another to go after these forces of disunity. Abrahamics, Wiccans, The Followers of the Way, even 'The Baldies,' as one orange-robed sect was called with considerable disdain. Each was singled out for persecution on a rotating basis, along with genuinely menacing cults such as Tobacconists and Anti-Mentorists. It all seemed like a pointless waste of time at best, and more often than not like needless oppression. But what was one to do? Resign? Rumor had it that people did quit on occasion; supposedly they were then consigned to the middle districts and given over to a life of tedium under barely adequate conditions. But what was the point? There was always someone new to take their place and they were only hurting themselves.

After a month of austerity, Kim's finances recovered sufficiently to allow a return to normalcy. The refrigerator came off economy mode, and the two reached an uneasy truce—Kim agreed to not complain about synchicken, and the fridge agreed not to serve tofu, at least for the moment. Oatmeal, now a comfort food, remained on the menu, though the refrigerator continued to be stingy with the cream and butter, demands for which always elicited the standard recommendation of "a breakfast low in fat and high in protein," but usually it let Kim win. She also went on the occasional date, though only once agreeing to intimacy. In the aftermath of her night at the Tropicana, the matter no longer provoked the same level of either urgency or anxiety, so Kim generally signed up for group dates, more interested in finding dance partners than bedmates.

———

On a Oneday evening later that spring, Kim dropped into VR and found her way to a beach where Keli and her life-mate, Jo, were throwing a party and promising some sort of big announcement. Kim had accepted the invitation, though not without misgivings; she had a good guess as to what the 'big announcement' might be, and had thought about skipping the whole thing, but Keli would be disappointed if she begged off so she had reluctantly agreed. This being a toon night, Kim was in the form of a cheerful yellow bird with black and white wing bars, a black cap, and a pointy orange beak, rendered in such minute detail that it could have been mistaken for the real thing even if one knew a lot about birds. The beach was likewise rendered in vivid fashion, and just as with baseball it was always summer, with the sun high in a cloudless blue sky and waves gently breaking and rolling ashore, although they could order up a storm if people were in the mood for some excitement. Inland, there were dunes and marshes, with paths winding through thickets and along the margins of the backwaters, provided in case one wished for solitude or a quiet moment with a friend.

She immediately spotted tonight's guests-of-honor: a tiny waif wearing a plum-colored tunic that came down to just below the knees, and a sky-blue mustang with cobalt mane and tail. Keli and Jo, of course, preparing for their much-anticipated announcement. Both looked splendid as the VR matched their appearance to their mood, with Keli's big, soulful eyes looking particularly deep and full of compassion, and Jo prancing around as proud as any monarch from a bygone age, tail and mane elegantly braided and adorned with bright crimson ribbons.

When their guests had arrived and mostly quieted down, Jo reared up and let out a loud whinny to get their attention.

"You may remember that we had a very rough time after our first child, Kee, was sent off for mentoring, and Keli swore that she was never going through *that* again."

Everyone laughed uncomfortably.

"Well, we all know that none of you really believed her, and you were right. The permit just came through, we're going to have another baby! We just got back from the doctor, so it's official. And now … it's time for the name lottery."

A huge rotating drum filled with brightly colored pieces of paper appeared in front of them, spinning to mix up the names, adding an air of mystery and expectation to the process. It was all for show, of course; the AIs just picked something according to the whims of a random number generator. But everyone enjoyed the drawing, the one aspect of the birth-giving process that even the stodgiest of zealots could enjoy.

The drum stopped spinning, Keli reached in, extracted a bright-purple slip, and announced the results:

"Hollis. We got Hollis! We've always loved that name."

After the cheering had died down, Kim flew up to congratulate the couple then perched on a twig, thinking about their decision to forego moderation and enroll in the birth-giving program. It was unusual enough for them to have defied convention and paired off right after graduation, but their decision to have children was downright odd, almost unheard of among the well-heeled residents of the inner districts. And *everyone* remembered that first parting—weeks of crying and moodiness, followed by bursts of excitement whenever a visit was allowed. Kim had always wondered why anyone would endure nine months of pregnancy followed by years of diaper changes and all the work that went with caring for an infant, only to go through the inevitable trauma of parting and having to start all over again.

There followed a round of congratulations, more polite than heartfelt. Everyone liked the young couple, but it was difficult to get excited about something you did not understand, and there was always an undercurrent of snobbishness toward anything or anyone associated with the middle districts, such as child-rearing. In some circles, birth-givers were considered little more than livestock, renting out their bodies for a supplemental stipend and a larger apartment. Not that anyone would ever accuse Keli and Jo of doing such a thing—indeed, everyone considered them to be both genuine and caring, the best of friends—but their choice had cost them a bit of respectability, at least with some.

As the group dispersed, they broke up into twos and threes, chatting about this and talking about that, except for one trio who were creating quite a ruckus. Guess what? Quinn, Devon, and Em were going at it again.

"Derivative crap!" said Quinn dismissively, before transforming into the form of a kitchen blender as everyone joined in her ritual denouncement of all contemporary music. "Toss it in, push the button. Whir! Mush!"

"You say that about everything!" laughed Devon's purple panda. "Everything but that ancient crap you love so much!"

Quinn was indignant. "Ancient crap? That's real music you're talking about, not the garbage they make us play in the clubs."

"Hey, there's Kim!" said Em's big orange cat. "Let's ask Kim!"

Everyone agreed, and they put forth their question. Was Sino-Indian Thrash great music or derivative crap?

"An interesting question," said Kim, stalling for time, looking for a way out. She knew Quinn was absolutely right, but the AIs were always listening. A moment's thought, and then the answer. "It's both! Great to dance to, but why would anyone actually listen to it?"

Everyone laughed at the clever escape and went on to the next discussion, this time on the topic of videos, which was Kim's cue to beat a hasty retreat. The announcement was over, Kim had said hi to everyone that mattered, and it was already getting late. She was about to punch out, when a big blue squirrel wearing red running shorts and a bright green jersey came riding up on a bicycle.

"Beastie! You made it!"

It was Shan, Kim's best friend from school. The two were die-hard bicyclists, nicknamed "The Beasts" by one and all. They had been inseparable until the week before graduation, when they had been caught breaking into the chemistry lab late one night to filch the final exam. Afterward, Shan had been expelled and sent off to a menial job on the west coast, over 4500 kilometers away. Kim, however, been allowed to graduate; she had been a stellar student, and the head of the school had put in a good word for her at the disciplinary board. The disparity in their fates had made things awkward at times, but in the end nothing could come between the Beasts and they were as close as ever. Maybe even more so—absence making the heart fonder, as they say.

"You missed the big reveal," said Kim, briefly dropping into proper form and giving the giant squirrel an extravagant air-hug.

"Yeah, sorry," said Shan. "I drew a double shift. Somehow that always seems to happen when there's something fun going on."

Shan grinned with a mischievous sparkle in her eye, looking up and down the beach at the assembled crowd.

"Let's ditch this party and go for a quick ride," she suggested. "Up for it?"

"Super! Sounds like fun!"

––––––

A series of whirs and clicks, and Kim's recliner (a sports model, naturally) deployed a pair of pedals and she began to crank away like mad, helping to propel them through a racecourse at breakneck speed while Shan controlled the bike. Their avatars rambled on, with Kim's cheerful little bird perched on the handlebars of the big blue squirrel's bike, the two of them chatting away amiably as they hurtled through a virtual landscape strewn with hazards and death at every turn.

"So, what's new?" inquired Shan as they rounded the corner, narrowly avoiding a deadly tumble over a sheer precipice onto the jagged rocks below.

"Same old, same old. Training the automatons." Kim paused to duck under a tree limb. "It was fun at first, but now it's just a grind. How about you? How's life at The Delivery Company?"

"Not bad," responded Shan as they jumped over an impossibly wide chasm, flying fifteen meters through the air then landing with a spray of gravel as they skidded down the trail.

"Mostly I just sit in the cab in case something goes wrong. The truck drives itself, but once in a while some idiot in a pedicab darts out in front of me or a pedestrian wanders into traffic and I have to push the emergency stop button. 'The AIs aren't perfect,' as my boss is always saying. I guess that's why I have my nice, cushy job."

They both laughed at the joke that wasn't a joke.

Kim flitted around to the maniacal squirrel's left shoulder as she dodged and wove through a grove of trees that had suddenly sprung up in their path, cool and calm as always. They rounded another bend, and suddenly—Cliff! Shan had missed a turn! Tires skidded, spraying dirt everywhere as she slammed on the brakes, but it was too late and the bike sailed over the edge, carrying the crazed squirrel with it to crash upon the boulder-strewn creek bed below.

"Sheesh! Good thing the AIs don't let you drive. There'd be no survivors!" said Kim, laughing as she glided gracefully down to perch on the twisted remains of Shan's bike.

The two had a good chuckle, then settled down in a quiet spot next to the stream, Shan sitting on a rock and Kim perched on a nearby bush. They chatted amiably for a while about this and that. Music, clothes, dancing. And, not surprisingly, about dating. The latter topic made Kim feel rather awkward due to an incident that had occurred during intimacy training back in school, when the two of them had gotten a little too enthusiastic a little too quickly. Ever since that day Shan had been acting strangely, for reasons Kim didn't want to guess at.

After a while, Shan got that mischievous look that was hers alone, and smiled a wicked smile.

"Now it's time for *my* big reveal! The company has finally approved my application to transfer back east. Come summer, we can celebrate in style, with real bikes, just like old times. Maybe even visit our old stomping grounds near the school. Beasts forever?"

"Beasts forever!" replied Kim, hopping about excitedly from twig to twig and bush to bush while chirping away nonstop like some sort of demented canary. The two took on their proper forms for a parting air-hug, after which Shan punched out to get ready for her evening delivery runs.

———

Kim was ecstatic at the news, but also worried. On her own, she was careful and disciplined, always mindful of the rules, never stepping out of bounds. The moment she was with Shan, however, all that changed, and the two had gotten into trouble more times than she cared to recall. For the most part it was minor stuff, and they had never drawn more than a week's detention, until that fateful incident in the chemistry lab. She still didn't understand what had come over them; Shan was flamboyant and mischievous, but she wasn't a cheat. But people make mistakes, and sometimes they pay the price. Once separated, Kim had gone back to her familiar, cautious ways, and made a good life for herself. All that was at risk with Shan back in the picture.

Conflicted and needing to talk to someone, Kim made her way back to the beach, where she found Keli, who was seeing off the last of the well-wishers.

"Hi Kim! I thought you'd left without saying goodbye. Naughty little bird!"

"Nah, Shan dropped by and we went for a quick bike ride. Oh, and good news—they're letting her transfer back east. Come summer, the Beasts shall ride again!"

Keli smiled, and gave Kim yet another big air-hug. "That's wonderful! You two always seem so happy when you're together."

"True that."

The two chatted for a long while, reminiscing about school days and all the races the Beasts had won, steering clear of the trouble the two had gotten into while Kim worked up the nerve to talk about what was really on her mind.

"It's great that she's coming back, but you know how Shan can be," she said, finally broaching the topic.

"So that's it," said Keli. "I thought something was bothering you. Yes, Shan can be a bit impulsive, and we all remember what happened just before graduation, but you need to take responsibility for your own actions. If something seems like a bad idea, it probably is. You've never been very good at saying no."

Kim began to feel awkward, so she changed the topic to the newly announced baby, something Keli was all too happy to talk about. She went on ever more excitedly about what it was like to bring a child into the world, glowing as she recounted her experience with Kee and how happy it made her whenever a visit was allowed. This reminded Kim of how different her own experience had been, and she became sullen and subdued, her wings drooping as the VR system read her mood and conveyed it with an uncomfortable degree of accuracy.

"Kim, is something wrong?"

She paused a moment and looked at Keli with her head cocked to one side.

"Do you mind a personal question?"

Keli smiled warmly and responded, "Go ahead."

"Why do you go through all this? The morning sickness, the discomfort, the years spent caring for the baby, and then ..." Kim choked up and hesitated. "And then, just, gone."

"Well," responded Keli, "it's all for the baby, of course. You'll never love anything as much as you love that child, and it will love you back so completely. Yes, I know that sounds selfist, but really, it's not—it's the most un-selfist, most fulfilling thing you can possibly imagine."

"Until she's taken away and you never see her again," said Kim, nearly in tears.

"Oh Kim, I do understand. This is about your mother, isn't it. I know in my heart that she loved you and desperately wanted to stay in your life, but your mentor was such a control freak, it's hard to imagine *any* birth-giver being allowed contact with her charges after parting. Heartless monster."

Kim managed to regain her composure briefly before punching out, but once she was back in her apartment she collapsed onto her bed and remained there the rest of the evening. She drank heavily, trying to blot out the pain without much success, her sleep haunted again by nightmares and sadness.

―――――

A few days later, Kim accepted an invitation to join Keli and Jo for a Sevenday outing at a horticultural park on the rugged northeast coast. This took a bit of cajoling on Keli's part; as empty as Kim's life had become, it was easier to sit around the apartment, fire off messages on Chit-Chat, and drop into the occasional VR than to get on a train to visit a friend. Come to think of it, it had probably been at least a year since Kim had socialized face-to-face with anyone other than Quinn, and even that had only been once or twice. But Keli was famously unstoppable when her mind was made up, and she finally bought the ticket herself and attached it to a message. "There, it's done. No more excuses!"

It was a long trip to the park, so Kim rose early and was soon at the station waiting for the high-speed inter-sector train. Unlike the urban transit system, which operated on a dynamic basis controlled by the AIs, the maglev service was rigid and inflexible, with trains running on fixed routes with fixed schedules. But what this operation lacked in sophisticated scheduling, it more than made up for with its trains. Designed at the height of pre-unification technological innovation, they ran through evacuated tunnels deep underground, suspended above the tracks by powerful magnets, and reached speeds formerly attainable only by expensive and dangerous aircraft. However, the entire system had been designed during the age of the programmers and had proved impossible to retrofit with AI-based technology, so from an operational point of view it was rather primitive. They even had human conductors!

At 0713 the northbound train arrived exactly on time, gliding silently into to the station and coming to a graceful stop. The boarding tube extended and mated with the side of the car, and Kim stepped into the cabin, taking the assigned center seat as the door sealed itself and the public address system made the departure announcement.

"Northeast express now departing Sector 5. Next stop: Sector 4."

The doors closed, and the train accelerated, pressing Kim deeply into her seat until it reached its cruising speed of six hundred kilometers per hour. Owing to the high g-forces encountered during the trip, standing was strictly prohibited and capacity was limited, so everyone enjoyed the luxury of a reserved seat, regardless of their social cohesion score. This caused a certain amount of grumbling from the well-heeled A-listers who felt that it was somehow unfair that they received the same treatment as cultists and other miscreants, but the reservation system operated on a strict first-come, first-served basis and nobody dared to try changing it.

The train soon began its deceleration phase then glided to a smooth and silent stop.

"Now arriving Sector 4. Transfers to Old New York."

Old New York! Kim had visited the remnants of that once-great city on a field trip while in school, as part of a course on ancient history. In its heyday it could have easily qualified for an A-rating, but that was a long time ago and now scarcely a million people remained. It was a quirky place, dominated by the corporations and their owners, and was at least nominally independent. It had its own city government, stubbornly clinging to power, and a transit system (of sorts) that was somehow not under control of The Transportation Company. The entire city gave the distinct impression of having simply 'happened' without any planning whatsoever; a patchwork of idiosyncratic districts with a hodgepodge of architectural styles that went on and on, each block strangely different than the next. Weird and beautiful, it was ultra-pricey, with immigration tightly controlled even for those who could afford to live there. The Hierarchy hated it and yet the city stood defiant; a holdout from the age before the Turmoil, stubbornly clinging to its old ways of wealth and privilege.

The express resumed its northward journey, passing through the remainder of Region 1 at a dizzying pace, barely having time to reach cruising speed before slowing once again at each station. Sector 3. Sector 2. And finally ...

"Now arriving Sector 1, transfers to Old Boston. End of the line, all passengers must disembark."

Old Boston was another ancient city that had somehow survived the Turmoil. Kim had never been there, but Keli and Jo loved it for its retrograde customs and peculiar institutions, a mecca for fans of pre-unification culture. Supposedly they even played an archaic form of baseball there, complete with human umpires. The Hierarchy hated it even more than Old New York, if that were possible, but they had little power within the enclave and few adherents to whip into a frenzy and enforce their will.

Kim looked down at her watch. 0825. Precisely on time, as always. She took the elevator up to the surface where she waited for the train that would take her to the park, which departed precisely on time exactly twenty-six minutes later.

The final stage of the journey was both wild and scenic as the train wound its way through the countryside, sometimes hugging the rocky coast, sometimes cutting inland through the forest, sometimes skirting salt marshes with their abundant waterfowl and wading birds. The ocean stretched out to infinity, raw and powerful, waves crashing on jagged rocks and throwing up curtains of spray that sparkled in the sunlight. Kim was enraptured as they skirted hillsides blanketed with tundra wildflowers and crossed rivers roaring in flood stage now that the northern latitudes were finally seeing the spring thaw. On and on they rolled, with scarcely a sign of humanity or artifice other than the railway and the occasional sleepy town that flashed by in an instant. The world was so vast, so wonderful, yet strange and alien. Rugged and unkept, it was completely unlike the cities and the manicured parks that Kim was used to. Hour after hour she sat, mesmerized.

———

Keli and Jo greeted Kim warmly at the platform. It had been years since they'd been face-to-face, and as nice as the occasional VR might be there was no substitute for the warm radiance of a smile and a hug delivered in person. Kim began to relax and enjoy their company, realizing how silly it had been to try to duck the invitation, but still feeling shy and awkward.

"We half expected to see you wearing that ghastly purple smock!" said Kim, teasing Keli as always.

"Hey, watch it! That was a gift from Jo. And where are your wings, silly bird?"

Right on cue, Kim strutted about, elbows flapping like some sort of demented chicken to the laughter of all as the trio set off down the path and into the first of the towering greenhouses. It had been set to a transitional season in early spring as it would have been before the climate disruptions. The bulbs were going strong, with the daffodils fading as the tulips came into their own. Elsewhere, the annuals were growing rapidly, and some were starting to bloom, while the perennial borders were lush and green but without much yet in the way of flowers. They then went through a succession of doors and entered a second greenhouse, kept at sub-tropical temperatures matching those of the warm period. There were palm trees and noisy birds, followed by a bamboo grove and eventually a secluded teahouse pond ringed with irises and lilies and surrounded by flowering cherry and crabapple trees, all in full bloom. Breathtaking!

They walked through the other displays in the park, and eventually arrived at a pavilion in the largest of the greenhouses, where they bought lunch and sat down beneath a magnolia, enjoying the afternoon sun while chatting amiably for perhaps an hour below its slender limbs and fragrant blooms, recalling stories of days gone by. When they had finished their meal, Keli pointedly left her headset and mobile on the table and walked toward the door. Kim took this as a sign that she wanted to speak privately, so she followed close behind, also without her electronics. Leaving the protection of the greenhouse, they clambered along the rocky shoreline until they found a quiet spot by a tide-pool, well away from any structures or paved walkways though still within the boundaries of the park. It was cold and a stiff breeze was blowing, but at least they were in the sun, and the rocks were pleasantly warm.

Keli sat down beside Kim, shoulder- to- shoulder, and the two of them began to speak quietly and intimately.

"I've been wanting to talk with you ever since your big date at the Tropicana, but I've had to wait until we were someplace safe. I can't afford to take any chances; if I speak too openly, I'll never see Kee again and they'll take Hollis away as soon as she's born. Tell me, how do you *really* feel about your experience that night? I'm not talking about physically—I'm sure the sex was awesome—but emotionally."

"Well … It was wonderful, but later it was tough getting to sleep. We couldn't help feeling … unsettled, like something was missing."

"I thought so. You know that none of this Matchmaker stuff is natural, don't you? We were made for something else. It's a quirky thing, and neither the AIs nor the Hierarchy will ever understand it, but love is part of who we are, and no matter how hard they try they can never take it out of us."

Kim made an awkward joke, laughed an uncomfortable, empty laugh, then paused. "Keli, what are you talking about?"

She got very close to Kim and whispered softly in her ear. "*[English] We're not meant to go through life alone. We all need to find that one special person who makes us whole. That's why the Hierarchy has never been able to stop us from pairing off, no matter how hard they try. It's part of our nature. When you find love, never give it up and never turn aside. Trust me. And trust your heart."*

Kim wasn't sure what to make of these words, other than the obvious reference to Keli's relationship with Jo. On the surface it sounded like a recruitment pitch from some sort of cult, but Keli was the least selfist person Kim had ever known, so that couldn't be it. It was puzzling. Kim thought about the mushy romance videos she watched on occasion, full of 'love,' or something they called love anyway, but it always seemed a shallow and transitory thing, over and done with in a night and maybe a day. Keli had also spoken of the love between a child and its mother, but she then had handed her own offspring over to a mentor, just as Kim's own birth-giver had done. Keli's notion of love didn't make any sense, but it sounded like the 'bipolar selfism' that the Hierarchy was always railing against. No wonder she was being so careful.

They sat in silence for a few minutes, looking out at the waves crashing upon the jagged rocks, but the afternoon was rapidly slipping away and soon they were all walking back to the train station at a leisurely pace. Kim trailed a little behind, watching Keli and Jo walk hand-in-hand with an innocent intimacy that she found most touching. A final round of hugs, polite kisses on the cheeks, then back on the train for the long trip back home. She had devoted most of the day to travel, just to spend just a few hours with her friends, but it did much to bolster her sagging sprits. At least on the surface.

That night she lay in bed, restless and discontent. Not unhappy. Not angry. Not sad. Not depressed. Discontent. And completely unable to understand why. Kim had everything she could want—friends, a good job, a decent apartment, and even a bit of success in the intimacy booths. Everything in her life was exactly as it should be. And yet the world seemed empty, meaningless, artificial. There was always vodka to help with sleep, but that only made things worse, conjuring up memories that she wished to forget and phantoms from the dark recesses of her mind. She stared at the ceiling late into the night, remembering the happy years in school and the boundless sense of possibilities she had felt back then. She also thought about today, about the unseen wildness of the coastline, about the carefree intimacy which Keli and Jo seemed to share.

Where is any of that in my life?

Part II: Summer

5. The Other Side of the Mountain

Kim awoke on a Sevenday morning early in summer and set about preparing for the long-awaited bicycle trip with Shan. No shower—that would wait until after the ride. Hangover pills and lots of coffee, as always, followed by three packets of oatmeal with butter and cream (thank you, Refrigerator). As she sat at the table consuming the steaming hot cereal, memories of good times came flooding back. Memories of carefree days roaming the mountain trails and bikeways. Memories of happy years at the academy, located atop its short, steep hill. Memories of Shan and the others, the best friends she would ever have. And yet, there was also a bit of anxiety. Shan's reckless enthusiasm had gotten both of them into trouble more than once, and then there was that awkward incident during intimacy training ...

Stop it! Lol, buzzkill. Today will be awesome, don't spoil it, dummy!

After finishing breakfast, she went into the closet and rooted around until she found her cycling gear: jersey, shorts, helmet, gloves, and shoes, all unused since graduation. At first, she had kept them close at hand, waiting for a day with perfect weather, but every time that perfect day arrived she had found a reason to stay home. Without Shan, it just wasn't the same, and she had eventually thrown her gear into a box, where it sat until today. She held the jersey in her hands for a moment, remembering the last time she had worn it, remembering why getting back on a bike had been so difficult. But now Shan was back, and that made all the difference.

A quick trip on the maglev brought her to the central station of Sector 6, where she boarded the Park Special and managed to find a seat by the window. It pulled out of the station exactly on time, then rolled through the middle districts, picking up mechanics, receptionists, security guards, and other workers at several stations along the way. Beyond the window, block after dreary block of nondescript mid-rise apartments rolled past, one after another, interspersed with the integrated industrial complexes that provided all the necessities of daily life. Kim remembered touring one of these long ago while in primary school. Workers had scuttled about through cavernous warehouses with shelves reaching to the ceiling, retrieving merchandise and tossing tidy parcels into bins. Others had fetched foodstuffs from cold rooms and transported them to the assembly lines where meals were manufactured. Many loaded work carts with cloth, zippers, buttons, and other components before wheeling them into rooms full of workers who stitched together the latest fashions at a dizzying pace. Most of these tasks could easily have been done by bots, but then what would all the people do?

Spurred on by such glimpses of life for the working class, Kim had studied diligently and followed the rules in the hope of avoiding the mind-numbing tedium and marginal living conditions of the middle districts; a fate she had been spared by her draw in the education lottery. When she learned that she had been admitted to a prestigious academy rather than being sent off to trade school or assigned to work in a factory or drive a bus like most, she had celebrated wildly, jumping about and shouting, "Yes! Yes! Yes!" This had earned her a week of cold showers as a reminder that she was lucky, not special, but by that stage of her life such petty punishments had little impact, and nothing could dampen the happiness of that moment for a stroke of fortune that had changed her life forever.

Kim was jolted back to awareness by a bump in the track and turned to look out the window as the train rolled through the decrepit outer districts (no stops there) before plunging into the forest. It was lush and green with the vigorous growth of early summer, so dense that nothing could be seen through its tangle. Trees, trees, and more trees, but what was beyond the trees? More trees? Did they go on forever, or did they end just beyond the limits of visibility? Kim had often pondered this question, particularly after the trip to the wild northeast coast. As far as she could see, there was nothing but woodlands all the way from the city to the park, although that could not possibly be the case.

As she sat staring out the window, she once again felt that mixture of excitement and anxiety she had experienced during breakfast. She remembered the last time she had seen Shan, waiting for the maglev that would take her to the west coast and out of Kim's life, seemingly forever. It had been perhaps the most painful day of her life, and the memory of it threatened to overwhelm her. She also remembered feeling an uncomfortable sense of relief, which had always made her feel intensely guilty. Shan's recklessness had ended her own career before it began, and nearly Kim's too, though to be honest Kim was not entirely blameless.

The steady thrum of the locomotives grew louder as they strained slowly up to the pass that would take them into the park. Occasional gaps in the foliage now permitted glimpses of the gently rolling land-scape, and Kim peered anxiously through the windows, hoping to catch sight of the countryside beyond the trees. Sadly, there was never enough time to see much. What would she find when she got to the park? Was it as vast and wonderful as she remembered? She sat there transfixed, too wound up and nervous to do anything else. The trees slowly glided past as the train reached the notch, the wheels screeching and squealing as they began their descent. Near the bottom the train rounded a bend and the vista at last opened up, revealing a wide, grassy valley, flanked by mountains and bordered by a river far off to the south. The sun was shining brightly in a bright blue sky dotted with fluffy white clouds, and the sports fields, lakes, and patches of forest scattered across the valley floor were exactly as Kim remembered, lifting her spirits immeasurably. She was home.

———

The moment Kim disembarked, she sprinted to the bicycle depot, where she found Shan waiting out front.

"Beastie!"

"Kim!"

The two embraced for what seemed like hours, their eyes becoming moist with tears of joy, as at last they were reunited in the flesh.

"I've missed you so much."

People were starting to stare, so they released the death grip they had on one another. They went into the bicycle depot, where they each picked out a mid-grade mountain bike and entered the locker room to change clothes for the ride. Kim could not help noticing the curve of Shan's hips and the gently mounded mams not completely flattened beneath her jersey; there had never been any mystery as to the details of her body, but still Kim's eyes lingered until she became self-conscious and began to blush, struggling to banish certain unwelcome thoughts from her mind. If Shan noticed, she didn't let on. Once they emerged, they picked up their bikes and finished preparations, attaching their mobiles to the handlebars and throwing their headsets into their backpacks while stuffing some energy bars into the pockets of their jerseys. A quick check of the brakes, derailleur, tires, and steering, and they were ready to go.

They mounted up, clipped in, and were soon cruising through the countryside, enjoying an easy ride as they crossed and recrossed hiking trails and footpaths before skirting a lake crowded with kayaks, canoes, and even a few sailboats gliding silently through the water. The day was pleasant, and Kim's lingering anxiety quickly faded as they rolled gently along, sometimes beside one another, sometimes in single file.

There was only so much trouble they could get into in the park, after all, and it felt so good to be back with Shan after so many years, so pleasant to simply ride along and relax. A quick lap around the lake, then they turned a familiar corner, rode down a fondly remembered lane, and found themselves at the bottom of the short, steep Academy Hill. They came abreast, crossed an invisible line on the pavement, and took off like lightning, racing up the hill as they had always done. Kim shot ahead, exploding off the informal starting line, but Shan played it smart, riding just behind to take advantage of the draft, then sling-shotting around as they reached the halfway mark. But fast though Shan was, Kim refused to give way, and soon they were elbow to elbow, each inching ahead for a moment only to fall behind. Thirty meters to go. Twenty. Ten. They reached the finish line and … A tie! They had both won, or at least that was how they preferred to think of it.

Fist bumps! High fives! The Beasts were back, here where it all began.

Covered with sweat and panting from the exertion of the climb, they continued to the front gate and stood there for a while, peering at the classrooms, dining halls, and dormitories where they had spent so many years together.

"Just like old times," said Kim, as a wave of nostalgia swept over her.

"Yeah," said Shan, "it's good to be back."

"Do you remember the picnics we used to have during the summer, out there on the grass?" asked Kim, gesturing off toward a shady spot on the academy lawn.

"How could I forget? You, me, Keli, Jo, Quinn, all the rest. Quinn used to make up silly songs and play them on her guitar while we danced around beneath the trees. The best of times."

"We never thought they'd end," added Kim with a sigh.

———

Without warning, Shan took off down the hill, daring Kim to give chase; a challenge that was immediately accepted. They sped down the slope and across the flat at breakneck speed, bodies low to minimize wind resistance, pedals spinning madly in the highest gear, around a curve canted sideways (or so it seemed), and across a bridge that had always served as their finish line. Shan, the nimbler and more daring of the two, finished ahead by a nose, and once again they came to a stop, exchanging high-fives and bumping fists before taking an easy cooldown lap around the lake, recovering their strength before the assault on the mountain bikeway.

Once they were fully rested, they guided their bikes onto a ribbon of asphalt, perhaps three meters wide, that wandered through the foothills and mountains in the northeast corner of the park. Kim excelled on the climbs, her muscles straining against the pedals in a steady, disciplined cadence, thighs pumping, body rising out of the saddle for maximum power, lungs heaving and heart pounding, growing giddy from the exertion. Then they would fly down the other side, Shan racing ahead undaunted by the speed and Kim chasing after her as fast as she dared. One kilometer, two kilometers, five kilometers, ten. Hot and sweaty, they paused at a scenic spot about halfway to their destination to drink some water and wolf down a couple of energy bars.

"Damn Kim, still the Beast!"

Kim laughed, but it was true—Shan never could match her uphill.

"This always was one of my favorite places," said Shan, panting for breath.

"Same here," said Kim. "The view here never grows old. Hey, we don't have to go all the way to the top if you don't want to."

"What? And miss the summit house? You've got to be kidding."

They mounted up once more and resumed riding. It was hot, heavy work as the sun beat down, making them glad for the occasional cloud. At last, after a final brutal ascent, they reached the top of the mountain, exhausted and drenched with sweat. What time was it? Had they made it? Yes! Yes! Yes!

"Brunch!"

The two rushed into the lodge, laughing as they made a beeline for the cafeteria's legendary buffet. It was every bit as amazing as Kim had remembered; heaped high with calory-laden treats of every sort: sweet, savory, fried, baked, high in fat and laden with sugar. If it was bad for you they had it in abundance. Better yet, it was an open spread—they could take as much as they wanted, with no AIs to get in the way. Kim piled one pancake after another high on her plate, dotting them with butter and drizzling them with syrup as the stack grew taller. Shan, on the other hand, went for 'the farmhouse special;' a veritable orgy of eggs, home fries, and biscuits with gravy. Two mugs of freshly brewed coffee, some fresh berries with whipped cream for dessert, and they were set.

They carried their trays outside to a picnic table set beneath a rustic wooden shelter that offered a respite from the merciless sun while providing yet another stunning view of the mountains. Nothing had changed, but why would it? Though it seemed like ages since they had last raced up the mountain for brunch, in reality only five years had passed.

———

They were preparing to get back on their bikes when Shan got a mischievous look in her eye.

"Do you remember that old road behind the lodge?"

"You mean the one near the trash dumpster?"

"Yeah, that's the one. Want to see where it goes?"

"No way," said Kim. "It probably just goes down the back side of the mountain. What's the point?"

But despite her curt dismissal of Shan's proposal, Kim was intrigued. Ever since that train ride along the coast to the botanical park, Kim had become curious about the world. What *was* beyond the trees? What *was* on the other side of the mountain? Nothing? Perhaps, but even nothing was something.

"C'mon, Beast up! No harm in taking a look!"

"Oh, all right, but just a peek. No promises."

Here we go again.

The pair wheeled their bikes behind the lodge and looked for the long-forgotten road, finding it, as expected, near the waste bins not far from the delivery door. It was blocked by a metal bar about two meters long, and they couldn't see much, just the woods and a narrow track of deteriorating asphalt that went straight for a few meters before plunging steeply downhill, turning to the right, and disappearing from view.

Kim then spotted a rusty old sign, barely legible:

Park Boundary. Proceed at your own risk

Proceed at your own risk? What did that mean? The two youths looked at one another hesitantly. Here it was, the edge of the unknown. Crossing it wasn't exactly forbidden, but it would be a departure from expected behavior, which was never wise.

Shan rode around the gate before stopping to look back, beckoning.

Kim stood alone, looking across the barrier, conflicted. She had seen that look many times. Once Shan had made up her mind there was no stopping her, and she was going to see where that road led whether Kim joined her or not. Following along seemed risky, but what was the worst that could happen? Ejection? A temporary ban, perhaps? At worst, a few demerits to her social cohesion rating. Was it worth the risk? No, not really, but the mystery of what lay beyond the trees continued to nag at her, and this was a chance to find out. No harm in taking a peek.

———

Curiosity overcame caution, and soon they were riding down the mysterious road. The pavement was rough and sometimes broken, with frequent potholes, but there were no tree limbs or other obstructions blocking their path, so it remained easily passable on their sturdy mountain bikes. What would they find? Kim had no idea. Down and down they went, cautiously checking their speed so as not to court a dangerous tumble should they encounter an unexpected obstacle. Kim expected her mobile to buzz at any moment with some sort of warning or penalty, but it remained silent, so perhaps they were okay. The AIs certainly knew they were there and would doubtless let them know should they stray into forbidden territory.

For the most part their view was limited to the mountainside, with the valley down below just visible through the canopy of trees. Occasionally, however, there would be a gap where the road went around a sharp curve or along the top of a cliff, revealing a landscape of rolling hills and fields laid out in neat squares and rectangles, punctuated by highways and a small brown river that meandered lazily across the countryside. No apartment blocks were visible, but they could see plenty of sheds, industrial structures, and some small, nondescript settlements.

After descending steeply for a few kilometers, the road leveled out and emerged into a grassy meadow teeming with birds and butterflies, bordered with trees, and adorned by patches of wildflowers waving in the wind. They stopped for just a few moments to enjoy the view, then pedaled on for another half kilometer, arriving at another yellow metal gate like the one they had encountered up above. Kim wondered if the wiser course would be to ride back up the mountain. As they went around the gate, she glanced back and saw an ominous sign, quite clear in its meaning and not a little bit rusty:

KEEP OUT. Entrance Strictly Forbidden

Damn. Evidently, they'd ridden through some sort of exclusion zone. But why hadn't the AIs stopped them?

"Now what do we do?" asked Shan.

"Uh …" replied Kim. "Maybe we should just go back?"

They turned around to retrace their route, but the moment they approached the gate both mobiles buzzed angrily:

WARNING from The Farm Company

The area you are entering is strictly off limits. Violators are subject to arrest on charges of criminal trespass. This offense is punishable by a fine of 200,000 cryptos and six months in jail.

200,000 cryptos? Six months in jail? Kim was now visibly shaking, with no idea what to do. They couldn't stay here, they couldn't go back, so they had to go on. But to where?

Kim took a deep breath and tried to compose herself. "Check your mobile. Maybe you can find a road map or something like that."

"Right," said Shan. "I've got a mapping application from work. Maybe it's got some data."

She pulled out her mobile and poked at it for a couple of minutes. "There's a settlement just a little down the road. There isn't any information on it, but maybe they have a bus station."

"It's worth a shot," said Kim, unable to think of anything better.

The road ahead looked deserted, maybe even a little spooky, with the faintest rustle of wind blowing through the brownish-green weeds that sprang up along its unkempt margin. The pavement itself looked to be well-maintained, approximately five meters broad with very few cracks, flanked on both sides by a gravel shoulder.

"At least the road is good," said Kim, optimistically. "We're in this now, might as well get going and hope for the best."

Lacking any alternative, they began their ride toward the hoped-for bus station. The road immediately entered a dense thicket of trees and twisted brambles growing amidst the foundations of some long-abandoned ruins. These looked interesting, but there was no time to explore so they continued onward, turning sharply to the left as they entered the rolling hills and farms they had seen from up on the mountain. From here, the road was absolutely straight, hemmed in on both sides by tall fences topped with razor wire and bearing the increasingly familiar notice:

KEEP OUT. Entrance Strictly Forbidden

They continued down the highway, past the cordoned-off agricultural fields on either side. Some were bright green with newly planted crops, others dark green and perhaps ready for harvest. Many were covered with rows of amber grain, while a few showed the dark brown of plowed fields, exuding the rich smell of recently turned earth. At one point they came across a field swarming with bots, gathering the early summer harvest and loading it into hoppers pulled by a stout vehicle with big, heavy-treaded wheels. They also came upon industrial structures set well off the road, doubtless housing the vehicles and the bots they had seen working the fields, perhaps also some human workers though none were visible at the time.

There were no further warnings on the mobiles, but there could be little doubt that they weren't supposed to be here. Kim was becoming more worried about the possible consequences of their little excursion, but it was now far too late to turn back. They pedaled along, kilometer after kilometer on the deserted road.

Not quite deserted! The blare of a horn! A huge truck with dozens of wheels bore down on them at high speed, nearly running them off the road and onto the shoulder as it veered to the left and roared past with a tremendous rush of air. The pair was left to recover their wits as the truck sped off leaving only the sound of tires on pavement and the hum of electric motors. What had they been thinking when they set off on this expedition? Adventure? Excitement? *Mission accomplished. Can we go home now?*

It was one thing to fantasize about exploration and adventure, something else entirely to be riding through this alien landscape, simultaneously lush and barren, with no idea of what they might find or how they would get home other than a vague hope to somehow catch a bus. Was this a good idea? Definitely not. Was it fun? Not at this point. But it was novel and different, a break from the monotony of daily life. Looking backward over her shoulder, Kim saw Shan just behind, pedaling away, sometimes looking left or right, but mostly focusing on the road and the ride. She smiled and began to relax, enjoying the day and the company of Shan, living in the moment, savoring that-which-is, rather than fretting over that-which-soon-might-be.

Shortly after their encounter with the truck, they crossed the muddy river they had spotted from up on the mountain. A few kilometers more, and they came to a quarry, where they stopped for a couple of minutes to check their route and watch the operation, as one massive machine fed heaps of rock into a crusher while another loaded the resulting gravel into one of the large vehicles that had so frightened them a few minutes ago; perhaps even the same one.

Just past the quarry, they came to the settlement they had hoped to find —a tiny hamlet designated F-6.1.6.238. There wasn't much to it other than a perimeter fence, a gate guarded by a copbot, a paved courtyard with a dining hall, and a cluster of three-story apartment buildings. Within the settlement there were a few workers clad in drab utilitarian overalls, some walking about, some waiting for a bus.

A bus stop! They were saved!

They rode up to the gate and attempted to get the copbot's attention, yelling at it and asking to be let in. It paid them no heed. They waved frantically, eventually getting the attention of one of the workers, who came up to the fence to speak with them.

"What the heck are you two doing out there?"

"We need to catch a bus back home, but the copbot won't let us in."

She laughed and shook her head with disbelief. "You want to get *into* a labor camp? Good luck with that."

"Are you sure we're at the right place?" asked Kim, as they walked away from the gate.

Shan punched some buttons on her mobile, squinting at the tiny display, and confirmed that they were exactly where they'd intended to be.

"Strange," she said. "The map shows a settlement, not a labor camp. What's up with that?"

There was no other choice but to continue onward into the unknown. They rode through the countryside, passing more farms, then came to another work camp, similar to the first. There was no point in stopping, and Kim became more worried with every passing moment. The map had shown numerous settlements and she'd been certain they could catch a bus at any of them. They couldn't all be prisons, could they?

After a few more kilometers the pavement abruptly ended, giving way to a treacherous surface of crushed gravel as the road continued up a steep, wooded hillside. They were forced to stop for a moment and consider their options.

"What now?" asked Kim. "Maybe we should double back and try another road."

Shan shrugged. "Sheesh! Beast up, we've ridden on worse."

Shan's blithe indifference to the seriousness of their situation was starting to wear on Kim. This was the same reckless attitude which had ended Shan's career before it began and nearly Kim's too, and she had known from the moment that Shan had come back east that trouble was likely to follow in her wake. Oh well, clip in, pedal on, hope for the best, and don't let anything spoil the day. Nobody had made Kim go through that gate, and whatever the consequences of that decision, it had been hers to make.

After a short, steep climb they reached the crest of the hill and came upon a strange landscape that looked vaguely like something from a *Happy Farmer* video, except that it was real and everything was beat up. On either side of the gravel roadway were rickety rail fences bounding pastures, muddy in places, some with horses and some with cattle. A little farther on, they came upon a ramshackle white farmhouse, shaded by broad, leafy trees, next to which was a sturdily built wooden barn and pens for chickens and pigs. The road proceeded through the countryside, now shaded by trees and flanked by dry-laid stone walls. They passed a few more dilapidated farmhouses and some small muddy ponds, as well as what looked to be an orchard. Everything was unfamiliar, but it didn't seem menacing—just strange.

———

After riding through the odd farmlands for few more kilometers, they arrived at a small settlement where the map had shown only the junction of two roads. To their left was a ramshackle old house covered with peeling white paint and, just past it, a large building of uncertain function standing at the corner, also painted white though in much better repair. To their right they saw a red brick building which seemed to serve some official purpose, but they were not sure exactly what it might be. A school, perhaps? Just beyond the crossroads they could see a well-shaded grassy area with a couple of benches next to a cluster of squat utilitarian buildings with signs reading *General Store, Town Hall,* and *Laundry*. Here and there, horses were tied to posts, and several four-wheeled vehicles that looked vaguely reminiscent of pedicabs were parked in front of the store. Horse carts, perhaps? Whatever this place was, there wasn't much to it.

Needing a rest and charmed by the quaintness of this strange little town, they dropped their bikes onto the grass and sat beneath an oak tree that provided a respite from the relentless afternoon sun. They were hot and thirsty, desperately in need of a little energy-boost and a cold beer, if that was possible.

No signage gave the slightest clue as to what this place might be called, either by name or by designation, so Kim grabbed her mobile and tried to figure out where they were and what this settlement might be called. She pulled up the map and verified that it showed nothing, even at the maximum magnification, so she opened up the settings panel and ticked the magic 'show everything' checkbox. Still nothing. Undaunted, she went looking for data on the neighboring communities, thinking that perhaps there might be mention of the crossroads in the local news or Chit-Chat. That got her nowhere, but she *was* able to establish that all the settlements in the vicinity were work camps such as those they had passed less than an hour ago, with no further information available. Unwilling to give up, she did a geo-search for any data pertaining to this location, but all she got was a warning that she did not have access permission for that database. Whatever this place might be, it didn't seem to exist, and all information about this entire area was locked down tight. Nevertheless, she kept looking, hoping to find something if only by chance.

"Wow!" she heard Shan say in a tone of utter amazement. "A dog!"

Kim was nonplussed, nose still buried in the mobile. "So what? Haven't you ever seen a dog before?"

"Get your face out of that thing!" insisted Shan. "Not a dogbot! A real, freaking, dog!"

Kim nearly dropped her mobile on the grass. Impossible! Those were outlawed ages ago! But there it was—a real, breathing, in-the-flesh dog.

The animal ambled over, tail wagging, and began sniffing as Shan reached out and stroked it on the head behind the ears. The creature seemed to enjoy this as much as the bots pretended to.

"It sure acts like a dog!" said Shan, smiling. "It's friendly, in any event."

"Careful," said Kim. "The real ones bite, or so they say." Nevertheless, she felt compelled to reach out and join Shan in greeting their newfound friend, which sniffed Kim's hand and rubbed its muzzle against her leg as they continued to scratch it behind the ears and stroke the coarse brown and white hair on its back.

"It's okay" said Shan. "It doesn't look like it's going to bite us."

The dog then turned its attention to the pocket of Kim's jersey, sniffing with great interest as its ears perked up.

"Aha! Now we see the truth!" said Kim with a laugh before unwrapping an energy bar and tossing it onto the ground. The dog devoured it in a single gulp and looked up plaintively. The tail never stopped wagging!

Kim heard a sharp whistle followed by a shout. *"[English] Rex! Sit! Don't bother those people!"* A black-clad youth, perhaps twelve years old, approached at a trot. Her skin was naturally toned, a pleasant chocolate brown, and her mane—of actual hair—was jet-black and very curly. How odd! And why was she shouting out to her dog in English?

"Sorry about the dog," she said in heavily accented Panglobal. "She's not bothering you, is she?"

"No, not at all," said Kim politely. "She mooched an energy bar, but it's all good. We've never seen a real dog before. Pretty cool!"

The youth smiled. "I'm Edgar, this is my dog Rex. You must be from the city. We don't get many of you Pretties out here." She looked

across the park toward the laundry building and shouted, "*[English]*
Hey! Mom! Over here, we've got visitors!"

A tall figure with prominent mams pushed a baby carriage toward them
with five other children of various ages in tow, ranging in age from
near adulthood to toddlers, walking obediently behind her. All
were clad in garments of stark black and while, in the manner of the
Abrahamics. Like Edgar, their skin was a striking chocolate
brown, and their manes were also of natural, curly black hair.
Things started to make a bit more sense: this was some sort of
religious enclave, and it must have been here for ages, perhaps
since before the unification, judging by the distinctive appearance of
its residents and the fact that they still spoke English.

She looked disapprovingly at Edgar. "*[English] I told you to mind that
dog,*" she scolded.

"*[English] Awww, sorry Mom. Rex didn't mean any harm, she just
wanted to play.*"

"My name is Sarah," said the dour figure, speaking in perfect
Panglobal with only a very slight accent. "What brings you Pretties
here?"

Kim responded cautiously, sensing the awkwardness of the situation.
"We're kind of lost, and we're trying to find a bus or a train station so
we can get home. Kim and Shan, by the way."

"It's the truth," added Shan. "We have no idea where we are. This
place doesn't seem to exist, at least not officially. Is there anyone here
who can help us figure out how to get back to the city? And it'd be
great if we could grab a snack and a cold drink."

Sarah regarded the two for a moment, considering her words as her
features became less harsh. "We're simple folk. We keep to ourselves
and don't bother anyone. But never let it be said that we were inhos-
pitable to strangers. You're perfectly welcome here, as long as you

respect our ways. You'll find what you want in the general store. I'm sure Hamish will help you."

———

Kim and Shan thanked Sarah, gave Rex one last scritch behind the ears, and found their way into the general store. It was small but amazingly well stocked, with fruits, vegetables, dairy products, and baked goods in abundance, and everything looked to be of excellent quality. A bank of refrigerators in the back was amply stocked with drinks and sandwiches. Perfect! They even had chocolate.

Having no idea how things worked here, the two walked to the front of the store and found the shopkeeper standing in front of a battered old information terminal. She was plump about the belly, her skin untoned and very pale beige; she sported a wild, unkempt reddish-yellow mane and considerable facial hair of the same odd color.

Do they allow that here? Ugh!

It must be Hamish.

"Uh, hello?" asked Kim, shyly.

"Well, well, well!" responded Hamish, with an accent so thick as to be almost unintelligible. "A couple of Pretties wandered in off the road. What can Hamish do for you?"

"We're on a bicycle trip, we're lost, and we're trying to find a bus or a train that will take us back home," explained Kim.

"And those sandwiches look really good," added Shan, for good measure.

"Your best bet is the old city down the road, DX-6.1.6.28 they call it these days. They have a train station, but it's a long way, and you'd best hurry if you want to get there before it gets dark or a storm blows in. Go ahead and grab yourself some sandwiches and drinks, but how were you planning to pay?"

An odd question, thought Kim, holding up her wrist. "Uh … Where's the …"

Hamish shook her head from side to side. "Ah, of course, you're from the city. Nobody uses those here."

Another blank stare from Kim.

"Sheesh, you Pretties. But never mind, Hamish will help you out. You'll thank me some day, mark my words."

The odd little shopkeeper reached into a drawer, pulled out a pad of paper and a pen, wrote down an account number, and handed it to Kim.

"Transfer 250 Cryptos to this account, with the memo 'Purchase antique collectables.'"

The amount of money wasn't terribly significant and Hamish seemed to be on the up-and-up, so Kim grabbed her mobile, keyed in the account number, and made the transfer as instructed.

About ten seconds later, Hamish held up small pouch with some objects inside, and said, "Here are your antique collectables. Smile for the camera."

They both looked into the terminal's lens, stood still for a moment as Hamish handed Kim the pouch, then went back to their normal postures.

"There!" said Hamish. "Got you some money."

Kim opened the cloth bag and out spilled two dozen metallic disks of varying sizes. She recognized them from a museum. "These are coins, right?"

"Yep," said Hamish. "Money."

"But why?" asked Kim, puzzled.

Hamish held up a coin, grinned, and said, "We have our own terms of service around here. Cash up front, no questions asked, no tales told."

While Shan completed a parallel transaction, Kim inspected the contents of the pouch. The coins were of various sizes, weights, and colors, each with writing that seemed to indicate its value. The larger, more impressive ones bore the legends *2 Fr.*, *1 Fr.*, and *½ Fr.* The smaller (less valuable?) ones simply had the numbers *20, 10, 5,* or *1.* It was entirely unclear what the relationship between the two sorts of coins might be.

Noticing Kim's bafflement, one of the other customers walked over to offer some assistance.

"The bigger ones are in Francs and half Francs," she said, "and the smaller ones are centimes, hundredths of a Franc. The price is just a decimal number, so 2.40 would be two Francs and forty centimes."

Kim nodded and thanked her for the help, then went to the back of the store and looked at the glass-fronted refrigerators. There was no camera or microphone, no AI. Apparently, you just opened the door and took what you wanted. Kim couldn't help smirking as she reached in and grabbed a ham and cheese sandwich and a bottle of ice-cold beer. She then made a beeline for the sweets, grabbing three huge bars of dark chocolate and two beautifully made truffles. She and Shan paid for their food and left, cheerfully bemused.

"Wow!" said Kim at last. "Just wow."

"Yeah, wow!" replied Shan, likewise too stunned to say much more. "And we've got a good bit of money left over. Might as well hold onto it. Who knows, we might be back here someday!"

They both burst out laughing, rolled their eyes, and tossed a couple of the now-unneeded energy bars onto the ground, where they were eagerly accepted by Rex. The sandwiches, the beer, and one truffle each disappeared in short order as they sat on the bench, consulting the map.

"There it is," said Shan. "DX-6.1.6.28. It's less than sixty kilometers. They seem to have a train station, but I can't get any other information on it. Easy enough, assuming nothing else goes wrong."

Without further discussion, they headed off toward the city with its hoped-for train station. Luck was with them, and after a few kilometers they came to an intersection beyond which the pavement returned, allowing them to pick up their pace as the road resumed its course through the rolling hills and industrialized farmland. If one could ignore the circumstances and the strange surroundings, it was a pleasant day for a ride, and so far they hadn't been hit with any penalties. Perhaps everything would be okay after all.

———

Kim was now riding just behind Shan, unsure what to make of the cultists' settlement. The inhabitants looked to be Abrahamics of some sort, but they seemed harmless enough, even friendly—in sharp contrast to their reputation for wide-eyed fanaticism. And what was she to make of Sarah? Was she a mentor or something like that? If Kim had counted correctly, there were seven youngsters of varying ages in her care. They couldn't all be hers, could they? But Edgar had referred to her as '*[English] Mom*,' and they looked strikingly similar, so perhaps they were. If so, they were operating further outside of the normal rules and assumptions of society than Kim had ever imagined possible. And, to top it all off, they spoke English. How's *that* for weird. Most perplexing of all, why was the settlement even allowed to exist? They had opted completely out of the normal structures of society, with neither UCE nor the corporations anywhere in sight. All it would take to clean the place out would be a handful of copbots or a pack of angry zealots. Why hadn't that happened? It made no sense.

Kim was jolted out of her musings by something unexpected off on the left side of the road: two metal gates bearing the numerals *32*, topped with razor wire and guarded by a quartet of copbots and two human sentries. Beyond the entrance, she could see a long, broad avenue flanked by shade trees, leading to a small cluster of buildings at the end of the lane.

Crap!

Even this furtive glance had drawn the scrutiny of the sentries, who fixed their gaze on her and gestured almost imperceptibly with their stunners as if to say, *move along, you didn't see this*. Kim focused on the road ahead and picked up the pace, passing Shan in a blur as she raced ahead, eager to be away from whatever lay beyond those gates. What was in those buildings? Why were they guarded so heavily? Everything about it gave her the willies.

6. City of the Damned

The sky began to darken, threatening a storm as thunder rumbled off to the west and the wind rose, scattering dust and debris in whirls along the pavement. Neither of them much fancied riding in the rain, so they raced off toward the mysterious city as fast as they dared, flying past another work camp and roaring across a reservoir via a quick succession of bridges. A little farther down the road, they entered a dense stand of trees, passed under a railroad bridge, and emerged back into the open farmland in the span of perhaps two hundred meters, confirming Kim's guess that the woods were little more than a narrow strip meant to screen the surrounding countryside from view.

Things then started to get a little spooky as they found themselves again surrounded by ruins, much more extensive than those they had encountered earlier in the day. Long ago this area had been teeming with humanity, but now it lay abandoned. What had happened here? Yet another imponderable.

"Kim! Look out!"

A blue and white bus, bearing the numerals *32* on its side, nearly ran them down without slowing or even sounding a horn, forcing them onto the shoulder and almost off the road. Shan, always the acrobat, managed to keep her bike under her, but Kim wiped out on a patch of loose gravel and went skidding across the ground. They stopped for a moment to recover their wits and check Kim's injuries (a bit of road rash, nothing worse) then went back to pedaling.

Another half hour brought them to a second patch of woodlands, in the midst of which they could hear the unmistakable roar of a highway, and a rather large one, too, judging by the amount of noise it was creating. The roadway itself was difficult to see through the foliage, but it sounded busy, and through the occasional gap in the trees they could see that it was crowded with long convoys of freight trucks locked head to tail, hurtling along at over a hundred kilometers per hour. Then, just short of the point where their road passed beneath the highway, they found their path blocked by a police checkpoint. They rode up to the metal gate and dismounted, hoping that the patrolling copbot would allow them to pass.

Presently, the machine came closer and intoned in a tinny mechanical voice, "Present IDs."

They obediently held out their wrists.

"State reason for visit."

"Transfer to rail service," answered Kim, not sure what else to say.

Tens of seconds passed.

"Access granted. A route has been uploaded into your mobiles. Proceed."

Kim received the directions a few moments later, accompanied by a disquieting message:

NOTIFICATION from DX-6.1.6.28 Public Safety Office

Exercise caution in abandoned districts. Travelers are advised to follow marked routes and avoid contact with any persons encountered along the way.

The gate swung open then closed ominously behind them. Was it meant to keep people in? Or to keep people out? Or both?

Beyond the highway the ruins resumed, growing ever denser and more extensive as they went. To the left and right were remnants of side streets, blocked off by concrete barriers which were beginning to crumble as they were consumed by the undergrowth. They also saw the stumps of wooden poles, sticking incongruously up from the ground, the purpose of which Kim could not even guess at. On and on they rode as the avenue descended toward the heart of the city. Heaps of concrete rubble were now everywhere, and occasionally they would come across the skeletal remains of a building, windows broken and roof caved in, but somehow still standing. An apartment block? A commercial structure of some sort? It was impossible to say.

———

The pair turned a corner and slammed on their brakes as they found themselves at a large intersection populated with perhaps two dozen vagrants who seemed every bit as startled by the chance encounter as the youths. The vagrants looked haggard, thin, and scrawny, wearing tattered old clothing, their feet encased in worn but sturdy boots. Their manes were wild and unkempt, their skin weathered and untoned. Many bore long, scraggly facial hair. One of them, perhaps their leader, looked to be the worst of the lot, with dark pockmarked skin, a tooth-less grin, and coal-black eyes set in deep, dark sockets.

Avoid contact with any persons encountered on the way? So much for that!

Kim looked down and saw that her mobile had gone haywire, its screen glitching and going blank as it tried and failed to recover from some sort of unknown software error. And then, an ominous *click-click,* as one of the vagrants cocked a gun and pointed it at her. Not a stun gun, but the kind that shot bullets and could kill you in an instant. Even the cops didn't have those.

The two groups stared at one another for a few tense moments before the leader spoke to one of her fellows.

"We have visitors. Two Pretties, in fact. We don't see many of their type around here."

"Hamish said a couple of Pretties went through Coventry a while ago," responded the other. "Said they might be heading our way."

"Odd," replied the leader before turning back to the riders.

"That'd be you two, right?"

Shan and Kim nodded in unison, too stunned and frightened to speak.

"Yeah, they're harmless," said the one with the rifle, slinging it across her back.

The leader's expression softened to a smile; toothless but genuine. "I'm sorry if we've frightened you, but we have to protect ourselves. Don't worry, we're not your enemies and we won't hurt you. We may even help you someday."

Another voice spoke in hushed tones. "You need to warn them!"

The leader nodded and continued speaking.

"I was a Pretty once, just like you, until one day I got curious, started poking around in places I didn't belong, learning things I wasn't supposed to know. I escaped before the AIs caught up with me, but many aren't so lucky. For your own sake, forget you ever came here, and forget you ever saw us. Beware—there is nothing the companies fear so much as the truth, so keep your mouths shut and never let their AIs hear you talking about anything you've seen here, especially us."

"Who are you? What are you?" Kim blurted out, not really wanting to know but asking anyway.

As the tattered assemblage faded into the ruined landscape, the leader answered simply, "Blanks."

A moment later the square was empty, and Kim's mobile came back to life as if none of it had happened.

Kim and Shan stared at each other in disbelief, unable to comprehend what they had just seen. Guns? Blanks? And what of the odd behavior of the mobiles? None of it made the least sense.

———

A few kilometers down the road they rounded another corner and stopped in their tracks as they finally got an unobstructed view of the ancient city's heart, beholding a scene of utter devastation. Building after ruined building stretched as far as the eye could see, some little more than heaps of brick and stone, others in varying states of decay though still standing. Farther off there were huge mounds of rubble, twenty or even thirty meters in height, with bits of steel and concrete sticking out, punctuated by the skeletal remains of a few lofty towers, stark and windowless. Off in the distance they saw what was left of the city's harbor, a broad expanse of marshes and reeds with only a narrow ribbon of open water in the middle. The remnants of a dredged channel, perhaps? Beyond that, Kim saw what she at first thought to be a hill. Off in the distance, it was difficult to judge its size, but it looked oddly out of place, rising steeply above the uniformly flat terrain on the far side of the water. Then she realized that it wasn't a hill at all, but a gigantic heap of rubble, well over a hundred meters in height. What-ever it was that had come down, it must have been immense.

They stood astride their bikes, staring in horror at the magnitude of the destruction. Everyone had seen videos set during the Turmoil, with the heroic zealots marching under the UCE banner to bring down the ancient regime and its legacy of oppression. Judging by those portrayals, it had been a tidy affair, almost a giant dance-off in which the assembled masses overwhelmed the cowardly defenders of the old order, causing them to flee in terror before the righteousness of their cause. Judging by what lay before them, the reality had been a bit messier. Or was this from the AI war with its battles against the killer robots? That, too, was plausible, though the videos portrayed it as happening off in the land of VR rather than in the physical world. Perhaps some of it had spilled over.

They remounted and rode off in stunned silence as fast as they dared, fleeing both the ghosts of the past and the fury of the approaching storm. They entered a district where the buildings, a hodgepodge of different styles, looked to have fallen into disrepair rather than having been battered down. One block featured brick row houses three stories tall, roofs caved in and windows gone, their interior gutted by fire long ago. On the next corner was the shell of a stone building with remnants of ornate glass windows and a tower that had probably housed some bells. Farther down the road, they passed a five-story building of more modern construction, faced in brick, its windows blocked off by sheets of gray plastic. It seemed to be occupied, though by whom Kim had no desire to learn. Three hundred meters more brought them to the remnants of a fallen highway overpass, in the midst of which was another checkpoint. They identified themselves, answered the same questions as before, and waited anxiously as the seconds ticked by, the storm growing closer. Heavy, cold droplets began to fall around them, sporadically now, but the roar of the approaching rain made it clear that a good soaking was imminent.

Come on! Come on!

At last the copbot flashed green, the gate swung open, and they sprinted down the road and took a sharp right in the direction indicated by their mobiles. Here, at last, they saw the inhabitants of the devastated city, sitting on the steps of the red brick row houses lining either side of the street. The homes looked to be of ancient construction, with ornate brickwork and intricately carved stone, sturdily built and therefore still standing despite the passage of what must have been centuries since their construction. Kim and Shan continued to race down the street, crossing a makeshift bridge spanning a gap where the original structure had fallen into ruin long ago. Looking below, they saw the train tracks. They were nearly there, and not a moment too soon.

It was starting to rain in earnest when they arrived at a small plaza and found the train station, which was of monumental proportions, elegant even in its decrepitude. Its tall façade was dominated by fluted columns of pitted and discolored stone, behind which were gray plastic panels covering the openings where grand windows had once graced the front of the building. Below those was a broad arcade, and above them a row of weathered letters in the archaic Roman alphabet which might have spelled out a name had they remained legible. Above it all, just below the roof, was a huge, old-fashioned clock, the kind with two hands and twelve numbers around the circumference. It even seemed to be showing the correct time. How was that for strange?

One more burst of speed, and they reached the arcade just as the rain began to pelt down in sheets. The Beasts had beaten the storm! Hooray!

Now what?

———

They entered the station through a pair of wooden doors which swung open easily, and found themselves in a long, narrow waiting room of elegant marble with a balcony resting atop two rows of columns. The room was amply lit from above by a skylight of beautiful stained glass which, although patched in places, had managed to survive whatever cataclysm had ravaged this place. The years had not been kind, but the residents still had some pride in their heritage: despite its state of disrepair, the station was spotlessly clean.

After traveling the length of the room, they came to a turnstile and breathed a sigh of relief. Soon everything would be back to normal—no more mysteries, no more surprises, no more uncertainty, just a quick train ride back to the park to turn in their bikes and then they could go home.

Kim presented her wrist.

"Specify destination," intoned the machine.

Oh, right, their headsets were still in their backpacks, and they hadn't yet entered their destination into the navigation system.

"P-6.1.6.4."

"Access denied," came the response, accompanied by an unwelcome red light. "Please speak with a customer support representative for further assistance."

Damn! Why wouldn't it let them get to the trains?

"What's the matter?" asked Shan as they retreated to the waiting room.

"No idea. We're way beyond what the automatons have been programmed to deal with, so we need to talk to something that can think."

"Is that bad?"

"It isn't good. The AIs are trained to be suspicious and investigate anything unusual that comes to their attention."

"Oh," said Shan, "I see your point. But they haven't cited us for any violations, so everything is okay, right?"

Kim wanted to reach out and strangle Shan for being so naïve, but it wasn't really her fault; most people had no idea how AIs actually worked. Kim, on the other hand, understood them entirely too well. Once they started poking around and comparing notes with their peers, anything could happen. But what alternative did they have, other than spending the night here on the floor? They would have to take their chances.

By now they had reached the customer service desk. Like everything else in the station, it was ancient and battered, originally designed to accommodate a human attendant instead of the quaint anthropomorphic bot that now staffed it.

"Welcome to The Transportation Company help desk," said the museum piece. "I am Robert, your customer service representative. Please present your IDs and tell me how I may be of assistance."

"We're trying to catch a train to the park, but the damn turnstile won't let us onto the platform," pleaded Shan, presenting her wrist. "All we want to do is get back and turn in our bikes. Why all the hassle?"

"This is a restricted-use station," came the response. "No travel to or from this place is permitted without prior authorization. Do you wish to file a special request?"

"Restricted use station? What kind of crap is that? Just let us onto the damn platform!"

Shan was starting to get frantic, and Kim realized that she was far more rattled than she was letting on. Beneath that devil-may-care aura she always projected she was every bit as frightened as Kim, maybe even more so.

"Affirmative," said Kim, cutting Shan off before she could blurt out anything else. "How do we file a request?"

"You may do so with me. Please state the reason for travel."

"I already told you, we need to take our bikes back to the depot. Idiot machine!" said Shan, who was beginning to sound desperate.

Kim elbowed her in the ribs to shut her up, and spoke to the AI in calm, measured tones calculated to convey no hint of emotion. "The park's Terms of Service require us to return our bicycles to the depot by the close of business at 2000. Transportation is required in order to comply."

There. That ought to do it.

"Your request has been entered into the system. Please take a seat while I consider the matter."

The two sat down, fidgeting while awaiting a reply. Kim was quite certain this was just the usual waiting game; the thought processes of the AIs operated a hundred times faster than those of humans and a decision had doubtless been reached before they had even finished making the request, but they made it a practice keep people waiting whenever they could, just like everyone else in a position of authority.

"I'm sorry I got you into this," said Shan as she sat on the bench, struggling to hold back tears. "I only wanted to ride to the bottom then ride back up."

"Yeah, yeah, and one thing led to another. I've heard that one before."

"You're not mad, are you?" asked Shan.

"No," said Kim, giving her friend a hug. "We'll probably draw some penalties and a ban from the park, and our cohesion ratings are going to take a beating, but hey, no big deal, we'll get through it. This isn't the first time we've been in trouble. Everything will be fine."

Shan smiled weakly and put her head on Kim's shoulder. She could be so brash and impulsive one moment, and so shy and vulnerable the next; part of why it was so hard for Kim to be angry with her for long.

A minute later, their mobiles buzzed with welcome news:

NOTIFICATION from The Transportation Company

Transportation from special-use station DX-6.1.6.28 to park P-6.1.6.4 is authorized for one trip only. Customer is prohibited from disembarking at any other special-use station. Normal fares and terms remain in effect.

These terms are effective immediately upon receipt.

Whew.

———

They dug their headsets out of their backpacks and followed the overlay's directions through the station, soon finding themselves on the one platform still in service. It was dilapidated and worn out, the pavement stained by layer upon layer of grime and oil, the glass tiles of the awning crazed and broken, its steel frame discolored and corroded by the passage of time. Here and there rusted metal stumps jutted up through the concrete, indicating where benches for waiting passengers might once have stood. It was then that Kim realized, with a flush of embarrassment, that they were still clad only in their cycling clothes, which did nothing to conceal their forms. She was mortified, but they didn't have their street clothes with them so there was no choice but to brazen it out and pretend everything was okay.

It was nearly dusk when the train finally pulled into the station, a half hour late, and the weary youths hauled their bikes aboard and looked for a place to store them. They eventually managed to detach the wheels and wrestle the frames into the luggage bins; this did not sit well with the conductor, who insisted that the bikes be removed, but the train had left the station and they were forbidden to disembark, so they were eventually left alone. They entered the passenger compartment which was old and run down, the beige tread of the aisle worn nearly smooth and stuffing showing through fissures in the cracked brown vinyl upholstery of the seats. They found a spot near the vestibule, hefted their backpacks overhead, and sat, saying nothing.

A lurch, and the train left the station, *click-clacking* slowly through the forest that wasn't a forest, making occasional stops at a succession of small, dilapidated stations. A few passengers boarded or disembarked at these, all of them dressed oddly in the manner of various cults. One group was wearing unseasonable colors—garish blues, bright oranges, and jet black. Another wore a bizarre mixture of last week's, last month's, and even last year's fashions, conveying a sense of haphazard chaos and individuality. They also encountered more Abrahamics, but these were of a different sort than those at the crossroads, with their heads shaved bare and not covered by a mane. Kim realized that they had found perhaps the only place in the province (and maybe the world) where two kids wearing bicycle gear onto a train would attract no particular attention. Still, she felt dreadfully embarrassed, and buried her nose in her mobile, playing game after game of solitaire to pass the time and avoid dealing with what was becoming an increasingly awkward situation with Shan, who was starting off into space, close to tears.

At some point they were going to have a long, serious talk about what had happened today, but Kim was in no mood for that conversation just now. Because of Shan's recklessness, a light-hearted romp into the park had turned into a dangerous ordeal that could well have landed them in jail or even gotten them killed, had the encounter with the Blanks gone poorly. So far nothing nearly that awful had happened, but Kim found it hard to imagine that there would be no repercussions in the aftermath of this ill-considered adventure. She was also disappointed in herself; she should have learned long ago to say no whenever Shan came up with one of her hare-brained ideas instead of following in her wake, but she had never been able to resist. What was on the other side of the mountain, indeed.

Her fourth game of solitaire was well under way when there was a garbled announcement on the intercom and their headsets indicated that they were approaching the end of the line. They grabbed their backpacks and entered the vestibule to retrieve their bicycles, only to find that they had become firmly wedged in the too-small bins during the course of their journey. They tugged and tugged, trying to get them free as the conductor looked on irately, barking at them to hurry up, but eventually managed to pry them loose just before the doors opened and the train stopped to discharge its cargo of oddballs and cultists.

Crap! It was pouring, and instead of an overhead shelter there were only the cut-off stubs of the pillars, painted a dingy green and flecked with rust. By the time they could dig their rain gear out of their backpacks they were soaked to skin, standing on the platform dripping wet in skin-tight spandex. Their lightweight ponchos were by now completely useless—it was physically impossible for them to get any wetter—but they did at least provide some concealment, hopefully enough to keep them from being arrested. After attaching the wheels to their bikes, they followed the other passengers down a long tunnel which deposited them in the main concourse of a busy rail station. They drew stares and gasps of shock from everyone around them as they wheeled their bikes across the waiting area before carrying them down the stairs toward their next train, leaving a trail of water everywhere they went.

When the Park Special pulled into the station to pick up its last outbound load, the conductor grudgingly allowed them to board but refused to let them sit with the other passengers, consigning them to the baggage car along with their bicycles. There were neither windows nor seats, and they were forced to sit cross-legged on the floor, every bump and jolt along the way torturing their sore and aching bodies. Normally they would have protested being dumped in with the freight, but they were just as happy to be spared the embarrassment of being seen by anyone else.

Still their mobiles remained silent. No warnings, no violation notices, nothing. Kim knew the Terms of Service inside and out and could easily have rattled off three or four violations at this station alone, and yet the AIs said nothing. Something very odd was going on, but what?

————

When the train arrived at the park they disembarked and wheeled their bikes to the turnstile. They hoped that their ordeal was finally over, but no such luck: Red light, admission denied.

SUSPENSION NOTICE from The Parks and Recreation Company

Multiple violations were detected at P-6.1.6.4:

Violation 1: Riding with excessive speed down Academy Hill.
Violation 2: Unsanctioned racing on a public road.
Violation 3: Recklessly endangering the public.
Violation 4: Exiting park grounds through non-public gate.
Violation 5: Failure to scan IDs at point of exit from the park.
Violation 6: Removing company property (rental bicycles) from the premises.
Violation 7: Failure to remove personal belongings from the bicycle depot upon leaving the park.

Customer is banned for one month. Fines have been imposed and must be paid before full restoration of service can occur.

These terms are effective immediately upon receipt.

They had been banned! Now what? They had to return their bikes to the depot and retrieve their street clothes from the locker room, but they couldn't get past the turnstile. Even worse, the last train would be leaving in half an hour, and if they weren't on it they would be spending the night. Kim argued with the park's AI for several minutes, pleading to be let through, but it stubbornly refused to show the least bit of flexibility.

"Please, can't you just let us in to turn in our bikes?"

No luck.

"What happens if we don't? Penalties and fines? We have to buy them? 12,000 Cryptos? Each? You're kidding."

Ouch. That was a month's rent.

"Couldn't we just leave them at the gate and have someone pick them up? No? Well, what are we supposed to do? Not your problem?"

In frustration, they finally hopped over the turnstile, knowing that this would certainly draw further penalties. Sure enough, their mobiles began buzzing angrily just a few moments later, informing them that the ban had now been extended to four months, but there was nothing to be done so they kept on going until a copbot arrived, lights flashing bright blue, and immediately hit both of them with a stunner.

A wave of unimaginable pain sent Kim crashing to the ground, unable to move and scarcely able to breathe, muscles cramping and locking up as she convulsed on the pavement next to Shan. She had seen stun batons in action before but had never been subjected to one, and the agony seemed to go on forever, though in truth it was no more than ten seconds. When it ended she lay on the ground for a few moments, then shakily regained her feet, bleeding from the mouth after having bitten her tongue.

"Violators must leave the park at once or be subject to arrest. There will be no additional warning," intoned the infernal machine in its tinny inhuman voice. But they still needed to turn in their bikes, and their belongings were still in the bike depot's lockers.

Guided by experience accumulated over years working with AIs, Kim realized the solution was to emphatically agree.

"Violation acknowledged and accepted. In accordance with the Terms of Service, violators will immediately remove their belongings from company property and proceed to the outbound station without using recreational facilities. Please escort to ensure compliance."

There was a brief pause while it consulted with a higher authority, after which it herded them to the depot, drawing gawks and stares from everyone along the way. They dropped off their bikes at the kiosk and went into the locker room to change into street clothes. There was no chance of a shower, but at least they were now decent, and they emerged in record time. Blue lights still flashing, the copbot escorted them all the way back to the station, continuing their public humiliation until they passed through the turnstile, at which point the copbot went off to torment some other poor souls.

They had made it back to the station just in time to catch the last train, which they boarded and rode until they parted ways at the central station. Neither dared speak to the other or even make eye contact. What was there to say? Nothing, really. The day had been an unmitigated disaster.

Dammit, Shan, why do you always have to do these things? Why did you have to come back into my life?

7. The Director

The alarm nearly split Kim's aching head in half the next morning, and almost paid for the offense with its life. Staggering out of bed, clammy and filthy from yesterday's adventure, Kim lurched into the shower, pleading for steaming hot water. She needed it *so badly* this morning.

"Just this once. Please?"

Nope. Cold. Icy cold. Hard needles of freezing water stinging Kim's exposed skin. She shut the water off almost immediately, then lathered up and scraped off yesterday's sweat and road dirt as best she could. Time to rinse off.

"Please? Just a little less icy?"

When the water came back on it was colder than before. *Heartless monster.* Kim emerged and toweled off, donning a warm robe in the currently fashionable color of tropical beige. Walking back into the bedroom, she sat down at her terminal, still shivering and not really awake. The previous day flashed by in an instant, from the mountain to the crossroads to the city and eventually back home in the wee hours of the morning. Kim and Shan had gotten into trouble again. Nothing new there, except that this wasn't school trouble, this was *real* trouble.

An amber message light flashed on her terminal, indicating a warning which had just arrived:

WARNING from The Chit-Chat Company

Customer is reminded that the Terms of Service prohibit the dissemination of confidential/non-public information using the Company's facilities and services. This includes information pertaining to secure housing facilities, industrial facilities, transportation facilities, police checkpoints, and other locations closed to the general public. Offending messages will be blocked and customer may be subject to penalties.

Similar messages followed in its wake, coming from The Transportation Company, The Entertainment Company, The Housing Company, even The Elevator Company, anyplace where they might be able to speak with another human being either directly or via the communications network. Kim had no intention of saying so much as a word about what they had seen yesterday, to anyone, ever; the Blank's warning had to be taken seriously, and she knew *exactly* how protective the companies were of their information, hoarding it as if it were precious gold. Kim hoped that Shan would heed these warnings and keep her mouth shut, despite her unfortunate tendency to blab.

A soft *feep* announced the arrival of coffee.

"Thank you, Housebot. Breakfast in thirty as usual."

At least the housebot was being civil.

Hot coffee, the elixir of life, especially on mornings like this. Consciousness gradually took hold as Kim savored the warm acrid aroma, enjoying the fragrant bitterness, the heat that nearly scalded the mouth, and finally the warm comforting glow as it made its way down. Next came awareness of a pounding headache and profound fatigue from having gotten home extremely late last night. How much Vodka? She had no idea.

Crap! A pulsing red message light. Now what?

VIOLATION NOTICE from The Transportation Company

Multiple violations were detected en route from DX-6.1.6.28 to P-6.1.6.4.

Violation 1: Use of restricted station DX-6.1.6.28 without prior authorization.
Violation 2: Wearing inappropriate/revealing clothing in a train station.
Violation 3: Transportation of bulky cargo on a passenger train.
Violation 4: Wearing inappropriate/revealing clothing on a train.
Violation 5: Impeding company operations by failing to promptly remove luggage from bins
Violation 6: Wearing inappropriate/revealing clothing in a train station (second offense)
Violation 7: Creating a health and safety hazard by tracking water through a train station.
Violation 8: Unsafe transportation of bulky cargo through a train station.
Violation 9: Occupying non-passenger areas while train is in motion (baggage car)
Violation 10: Creating a health and safety hazard by tracking water onto a train
Violation 11: Wearing inappropriate/revealing clothing on a train (second offense)
Violation 12: Transportation of bulky cargo on a passenger train (second offense)
Violation 13: Wearing inappropriate/revealing clothing in a train station (third offense)
Violation 14: Failure to promptly leave final station upon arrival.

Penalty: Customer's boarding priority has been decreased by two steps for a duration of six months. Please plan to arrive at your transit station an hour early.

These terms are effective immediately upon receipt.

As expected, the AIs had thrown the book at her. But why hadn't they sent the violation notice until now? That was just cruel.

Without a word, the entire household stepped up its pace. Kim bolted down the remaining coffee as the housebot feeped annoyingly and scurried into the bedroom to lay out some clothes. Kim was close behind, not looking at what was offered and simply hoping it chose well. She looked at her watch—there was just enough time for a quick breakfast. She ran into the kitchen, where the microwave had disgorged a bowl of steaming hot oatmeal. Now all that was needed was …

"Refrigerator, butter and a little cream, please."

No answer.

"Refrigerator," said Kim, with rising ire. "Be nice."

Stony silence.

"We hate you."

She seethed for a few moments, then decided to let it go, quickly spooning in the hot cereal and cracking a smile as she remembered the glass-fronted case at the crossroads whose sole function was to keep food cold. What genius, Kim wondered, came up with the bright idea of making refrigerators sentient?

———

Out the door, down the hall, and into the queue for the elevator. One minute, two minutes, three minutes, she waited there impatiently until the door opened, revealing an overcrowded car already stuffed full of people.

Welcome to Hell, Kim. The whole world hates you today.

They stopped at almost every floor, more passengers packing in each time, until the car reached ground level and disgorged its cargo of tightly packed riders, who slowly (oh so slowly) filtered out of the lobby and made their way outside, where the rain was coming down in torrents. It was too late to take the pedestrian tunnel, so she was forced to run across the plaza to the bus station, getting soaked to the skin in the process despite her rain jacket. She scanned in and followed the overlay to the assigned queue—the long one—with all the other undesirables. Two busses came, two busses went, and still she waited. She made it onto the third one via the rear door and was shoved ever farther toward the back as more riders forced their way through the entrance. There was no way to reach a stanchion or even a strap, but that was okay since there was no chance of falling.

What were we thinking? Off on a lark like two school kids. Foolish, foolish, foolish.

These bans and penalties were no mere slap on the wrist—they were a painful rebuke designed to make every moment of Kim's day an exercise in petty revenge for months to come. The transit system penalties were particularly onerous for the extra hour (or more) that would be wasted, morning and evening, getting to work and back. But that was not the worst of it—this could very well affect Kim's standing at work; a potential setback at a time when she seemed to be moving to the front of the pack, perhaps closing in on a coveted promotion. Kiss that goodbye. Hopefully, that would be the worst of it, but Kim was by no means sure.

After what seemed like an eternity, the bus arrived at the subway station, where Kim was nearly the last one off. It was now only forty-five minutes until the start of the workday, and the company insisted on punctuality, recognizing no valid reason for failure to arrive on time.

And what excuse could Kim offer if she were late? "It's the AIs' fault?" Yeah, right, that would go over well. Kim was directed once again to the back of the longest queue and waited as the minutes crawled past. Five, ten, fifteen. *Come on! Come on!* It was downright humiliating.

She squeezed into the last car of the fifth train, where she was once again shoved to the rear, packed in so tightly that it was hard to breathe. Wedged in with the press of humanity, Kim fell into a dazed trance, half asleep and half awake, either dreaming or hallucinating depending on how one wanted to look at it. Snippets of yesterday's odyssey flashed through her mind in a jumble: Hamish, the frightening Blanks, the ruined city, and all the other strange sights they had seen. And then, looming over it all, she beheld an immense spider with a hundred heads and a thousand eyes, sitting in the middle of a vast and cunningly constructed web. There it sat, lurking in the shadows, waiting for its prey to become hopelessly entangled before launching its attack.

She awoke with a start as the train arrived at its destination. The whole thing had been a setup. It had to be. The AIs had known where they were the whole time and had allowed them to keep going, only striking when it would have the maximum impact.

What is going on?

———

Kim stumbled into the office precisely on time. In typical fashion, the process of getting there had been as slow and painful as possible without inconveniencing her employer by making her late for work. She raced past the front desk, followed the overlay to today's assigned cubicle—which was in a dark and unpleasant corner—and sat down at the terminal, exhausted by her ordeal.

Another red light! *Oh no, what is it this time?*

MEETING NOTICE from The Director

See Us. 1300.

Could things possibly get any worse?

She then opened up her work queue and looked at today's assignment, which required her to identify instances of turnstile jumping. Under other circumstances she might have laughed at the diabolical sadism of whoever or whatever had come up with this, but today she just sat there staring off into space, unable to function. This led to one urgent message after another from the training monitor, warning her that she was falling behind. When that didn't get her moving, she received an angry call from her supervisor, Jan, barking at her to get on with it. In desperation, she started hitting 'yes' and 'no' at random. This tactic cleared out her work queue in a hurry but earned her demerit after demerit for discrepant results, causing her work rating to drop like a rock. At 1000 she received another angry video message from Jan, who was now livid with rage, in part because she was having to resolve the torrent of botched training cases, and in part because Kim was now dragging down the accuracy rating for the entire work group and *her* supervisor was now barking at her and demanding better results. But it was no use. Every time Kim opened a case and started to work on it, the memories of what had happened at the park came flooding back and she slumped into her chair, unable to continue. Did anyone notice? Did anyone care? Of course not.

A few minutes later, Jan stormed into her cubicle for an unheard-of personal chewing out. "What's wrong with you? You're the best trainer in the division. Why are you sabotaging all of us? Who put you up to this?" The accusations came fast and furious.

In response, Kim opened her message from the Director, looked her soon-to-be-former-boss in the eye, and pointed at the screen.

"Oh," said Jan. "We'll request a replacement at once. That will be all."

There was no point in further verbal abuse, so Jan made a few taps on her mobile to empty out Kim's work queue and departed without saying another word, leaving Kim alone in her cubicle to contemplate her fate.

When the lunch hour finally rolled around, she got up and walked to the elevator, which grew more overcrowded with every stop on its way to the dingy gray cafeteria in the third subbasement. *Ugh.* Kim waited in line, displaying not the least bit of emotion or interest as lunch was plopped down on a square cardboard tray. The overlay guided her to a place at a long table with two dozen other workers, all of them sitting elbow to elbow, with faces buried in their mobiles. Like Kim, none of them paid the least attention to what was on the tray or to anyone else. No eye contact, no conversation, everyone keeping within their allotted space, not an elbow or a foot crossing the invisible boundaries.

Kim stared at her mobile, pretending to read the daily Chit-Chat and the midday news, looking at the words on the screen but unable to understand what they might mean. Fashion? What's fashion? Baseball? That's a game, right? It was no use. All she could think about was her summons to meet with the Director, which was approaching far too fast. Perhaps she should just walk out the door and never come back. She closed her eyes, desperately trying to regain a degree of composure. When they opened once again, everyone was glaring at her as if afraid she might somehow draw the attention of an AI to the table. Or was that her imagination?

Her watch buzzed, indicating the time had arrived, so she picked up the tray and tossed it and the uneaten lunch into the bin. She walked on wobbly legs toward the elevator, fighting back tears as her life crumbled before her. Demoted? Fired? Worse? At least the waiting would soon be over.

Kim followed the overlay's directions, which took her up and into to the lobby. She swallowed hard, fearful of being walked out the door without even a chance to plead for mercy; such things were not unheard of. But, no, that didn't make sense. If she were to be terminated it would have happened at the start of the day, if only to save a half day's wages, and the Director was far too important to waste her time on a mere dismissal. Something really special must be in store. That was not a comforting thought.

Why did she have to go around that damned gate? She should have known better. She *had* known better. But how could she have known it would lead to such disaster?

The overlay directed Kim past a black-clad security guard, who regarded her with an inscrutable, uncaring gaze no more human than that of a copbot and therefore twice as disconcerting. The path then led to an unmarked elevator, which immediately opened to admit her. There were no other passengers. A crushing upward acceleration, a long run, and a gut-wrenching deceleration. The door opened into a windowless chamber, where Kim was directed to a comfortable chair and told to wait. Five, ten, fifteen endless minutes went by, during which time she said nothing, looked at nothing, thought nothing. Eventually the door slid open, admitting Kim then silently closing behind.

———

The room was simple yet elegant, with a plain beige carpet and light-colored paneling of real wood. To the left was a big oak desk with a chair behind it and another in front. To the right, a bank of video screens covered the entire wall. A floor-to-ceiling window took up the remaining wall, in front of which stood a smallish oldster, facing the widow while looking out at the city.

Presently, the Director (who else could it be?) turned and fixed Kim in her piercing gaze.

"It's quite a view, is it not?"

Kim responded, "If you say so," and immediately felt stupid.

"Come here and take a look, if you will. And try to relax. You are in trouble, of course, but that's not why you're here today, at least not entirely."

Kim wasn't sure if that made things any better, but complied. And, yes, the view was amazing. The air was crystal clear, and the entire city was laid out below, block by geometric block, from the Corporate District through the executive and professional housing of the inner districts, and beyond that to the factories and apartment blocks of middles and the edge of the outer districts barely visible in the distance. Everything was magnificent, meticulously ordered and planned. Kim's mind went back to the jumbled chaos of the ruined city, but only for a moment as all thoughts of what had happened yesterday were shoved aside and buried.

The Director turned to face Kim. "And to think that just two hundred years ago we could scarcely have seen the ground for the murky air. That's progress!"

She gestured for Kim to take a seat in front of the big oak desk, then sat down behind it to begin the interrogation.

"Tell me, Kim, did you see anything interesting on your little excursion yesterday?"

So, there it was. Kim had known the question was coming all morning yet had neglected to formulate a response. Her mind went blank.

"No, not really. It was actually quite dull."

The Director leaned toward Kim, speaking quietly. "We both know that is a lie. Good."

After pausing for a moment to observe Kim's look of surprise, the Director continued. "Your infractions are relatively minor, though they do call into question your judgment and social conscience. We are more interested in your motivation and what, if anything, you might have learned. So, please tell us why you left the park that was so

124

thoughtfully provided for your recreation, and went galivanting off into the countryside?"

Kim swallowed hard, trembling with fear.

"Curiosity?"

This drew a sharp response. "Curiosity? Indeed! But there was more than just curiosity involved, wasn't there? We have, of course, reviewed the interaction between you and your accomplice, so don't presume to deceive us."

Kim thought back to her exchange with Shan and the taunts of "Beast Up." That was doubtless what the Director was referring to. "I wanted to impress Shan because it made me feel important."

"Very good," said the Director. "And what was the fundamental misconception that led to your misbehavior?"

Think, think, think. This rings a bell! Misconception, that was the key. It must be one of those misconceptions that Zani had always harped on and on about.

"Come on, this should be easy. Out with it!" spat the Director.

Finally, the answer came. "I acted as if that which is not forbidden is allowed."

"And the truth?"

"That which is not allowed is forbidden."

"Very good," said the Director. "Do try to remember that in the future."

"Okay."

———

Kim began to relax just a little. She hadn't been dismissed—at least not yet—but this was far from over. The Director had more important things to do than reprimanding a low-ranking employee for a childish mistake. Perhaps the true purpose of this meeting was about to be revealed. Dismissal, demotion, humiliation, whatever. Just get it over with.

No such luck.

"And now," said the Director, "we have a more important question for you. What did you learn yesterday? No lies, just the truth. And don't bother dusting off those UCE platitudes. This has nothing to do with the movement."

Kim stood slack-jawed, unable to think under that cold, icy stare.

Focus, Kim, Focus! What could the Director be getting at?

And then the strange hallucination of the spider came rushing back. They had not gotten away with anything, not for a moment. Could that be it?

The Director was already raising a hand to shoo her out of the office when Kim finally gave an answer.

"The AIs were onto us the entire time. Usually they just assess penalties and move on, but this time they let us think we hadn't been noticed. They lulled us into a false sense of security."

The Director's hand went back down as the scowl lessened just a hair.

"That's a good start, but incomplete. Did you happen to learn anything about the AIs themselves?"

Why was the Director asking all these questions about the AIs? What was she getting at? It didn't make any sense, but she forced herself to calm down and put her anxiety out of mind. At least part of the answer was obvious.

"They were at least Order Three, possibly higher, because they were exhibiting sophisticated goal-directed behavior."

"And *what* was its goal?" said the Director, pushing Kim along. "Don't overthink. You know the answer!"

The Director was right. She did this for a living, and yes, the answer was obvious.

"The AIs were investigating us, trying to figure out something about us, though we're not sure what." After a flash of inspiration, Kim added, "One of your personal AIs was involved, wasn't it?"

The last part of the statement seemed to catch the Director off guard, though only for a moment.

"Yes, correct on both counts. You may not be useless after all." The Director paused just long enough to let the backhanded compliment sink in, then continued her interrogation.

"Tell me, how did the AIs go about this? Investigating you, that is?"

Kim began to speak with less hesitation. "They didn't do anything, really, except sit back and observe. There were plenty of places where they could have stopped us, but they maintained the illusion that we had gone undetected until the very end."

The Director smiled ever so slightly. "Indeed. And you were completely taken in, so thoroughly that we were almost ready to write you off."

The Director continued to probe. "Tell us about that little incident with the copbot at the park. What do you think was going on there?"

This time the answer came immediately. It was no accident that they had been forbidden to turn in their bikes or to retrieve their belongings, and Kim's guess at the time had been exactly right—it had been a setup. It now became clear what the Director was after.

"The AIs induced us to commit a more serious transgression, one that would get us stunned by the copbots, just to make their point. Again, purposeful behavior, indicating a high degree of intelligence."

"Indeed," responded the Director with a wry smile before moving on.

"And now, the final question. What was the AIs' purpose? Certainly not to make your miserable life even more miserable—they have better things to do."

Kim paused, drawing a blank, then realized why the Director was quizzing her about the actions of the AIs.

"This isn't a job interview, is it?"

The Director cracked a smile for the first time. "Of sorts. And you passed, if you want to think of it that way."

———

Kim stared at the Director, slack-jawed, not sure if 'passing' was a good thing, but quite certain that 'failing' would have been extremely bad.

"We are looking for a particular sort of person," said the Director. "One who is inquisitive, curious, maybe a little impulsive, but who is nevertheless a good citizen at heart."

"One you can control!" said Kim with unexpected sharpness.

The Director was momentarily taken aback, but then began to smile once again. "That was rather blunt, don't you think? And also quite naïve. We have controlled every aspect of your life since before you were born. But control is not enough. We require obedience. Absolute, immediate, unquestioning obedience."

The Director stopped speaking for a few seconds and looked Kim in the eyes, perhaps searching for any sign of defiance or rebellion. "You have been selected for an important position, working directly with our high-order AIs. Are you interested?"

"What?" Kim was flabbergasted. "We came here expecting to be dismissed. Or worse. Not promoted."

"This *is* the 'or worse.' You will receive certain privileges, but once you accept this job you are ours. You will never divulge what you are about to learn. You will act the part of a model citizen. You will be under constant, intensive surveillance. You will do as you are told, and if you disobey us the consequences will be both severe and immediate. Do you understand?"

"No, not really," said Kim. "But why us?"

The Director looked at Kim with a face of stone, offering no explanation.

"Suppose we don't accept?"

"Then you will be dismissed and relegated to some menial job in the middle districts."

"What sort of a choice is that?"

"It is the choice you are being given!" spat the Director. "Be glad we're giving it to you."

"Well then," said Kim, "we accept."

"A wise choice," said the Director. "Your new assignment starts next Oneday. You have the rest of the week off. That will be all."

Kim turned to leave but stopped when the Director continued speaking. "Oh, some advice," said the Director. "Don't ever do anything like that again. You will, of course, be caught, as you now understand."

8. A Gilded Cage

The sensation of weight returned as the elevator slowed its descent and deposited Kim on the ground floor beneath the unnerving gaze of the guard.

What just happened? Why didn't we get fired?

She walked out of the lobby on autopilot without any awareness of her surroundings. Across the plaza, down into the labyrinth of the transit system, and a few minutes later Kim had settled in for the ride home, lost in thought, not noticing her reserved seat in the first car of the train.

Why did we get promoted? It makes no sense.

The ride was short, much shorter than usual, but Kim was completely oblivious, still shell-shocked as she blindly followed the overlay, unaware that it was now directing her to a high-rise apartment building instead of to the bus.

Once you accept this job you are ours. You will do as you are told. Do you understand?

No, Kim didn't understand. She had always done as she was told. Why should this be any different?

The elevator opened and she followed the headset to her apartment, then realized that something was wrong. The door was made of wood rather than beige metal, and the hallway was completely different, with a bright and colorfully patterned carpet and elegant wallpaper.

What's going on? Why did the headset bring us here? Some sort of malfunction?

"Headset, commence guidance home, please."

"Negative. Customer is already at their assigned housing unit."

"Where are we?"

"Province 6, region 1, sector 5, city 1, district 4, residential complex 7, building 28, 38th floor, apartment 15."

District 4? 38th floor? What was this? Some sort of sick joke?

———

The door swung open to reveal a gleaming apartment and a uniformed agent of The Housing Company.

"Hello, you must be Kim!" said the smiling representative in a syrupy-sweet voice. "Welcome to your new apartment, we hope you find it acceptable!"

It was only then that she remembered the reserved seat on the subway, the absence of a bus ride, and the Director's promise of certain privileges.

"Uh, sure?" said Kim unsteadily before adding, "Oh, wait a moment, how much is this going to cost?"

"An excellent question!" replied the representative. "But relax! There is no supplement for this unit, it's of the standard size. We've just moved you to a nicer building, closer to the transit center. We keep a few of these available for our most valued customers."

Had this been a VR session, Kim's jaw would literally have dropped to the floor.

The new apartment wasn't any larger than the previous one, but it was distinctly nicer and somehow *felt* bigger. The bright yellow walls immediately lifted Kim's flagging spirits, and the sofa, upholstered in cream-colored leather, looked comfortable enough to sleep on, with decorative pillows of plush, golden-yellow fabric edged with red piping that were soft to the touch and beautiful to the eye; far nicer than the bland beigeness to which she was accustomed. Kim went into the sleeping chamber to check out the bed. Perfect! It was soft and comfortable, covered with a deep-blue comforter and topped with a big, fluffy pillow. There was even a window with a spectacular view, looking out over the transit center plaza. Apartments within walking distance of the subway were very highly prized, and it easily saved half an hour each way on her commute. *Wow!*

"Make yourself at home," continued the representative with that idiotic ever-present smile. "Because you are! Your belongings should arrive within an hour, and the appliance downloads are nearly complete!"

Appliance downloads? Kim rushed into the kitchen, which was modern, clean, and spotless. Even the refrigerator looked smart and attractive. And then Kim noticed the display screen:

70% ... 80% ... 90% ... 100%. Download complete. System restarting, please wait.

"Greetings, Kim! How may this unit be of service?" said the refrigerator in a too-familiar voice.

"Nothing at this time," replied Kim, not bothering to thank the appliance.

Kim considered having it mind-wiped and starting afresh, but somehow didn't have the heart. Besides, there was no reason to believe that a replacement would be any nicer—refrigerators had only the most rudimentary intelligence and their behavior was governed by larger, more powerful AIs.

"Good! The transfer is complete," said the representative, turning to leave the apartment. "It will be like you never left the old place! If there's anything else you need, just give us a shout and we'll come running!"

She smiled once more, waved, and walked out.

Kim glared at the refrigerator, shrugged, then plopped down on the comfortable sofa and fell into a deep, dreamless sleep, exhausted from the physical and emotional toll of the last couple of days.

———

A few hours later, the feeping of the housebot roused Kim just sufficiently to perceive the irate gnawing of an unfed stomach.

"Thank you, Housebot," said Kim, getting up off the sofa after a well-deserved nap.

"Refrigerator, dinner, please. Pick anything, just make it fast."

"Certainly, Kim. Would chicken piccata with escalloped potatoes and asparagus on the side be suitable?"

Kim nodded with stunned disbelief, unable to speak. She had no idea what 'chicken piccata' might be, but it sounded delicious.

How far can we push this?

"Refrigerator, chocolate ice cream for dessert, please."

"Unable to comply," replied the appliance. "Requested foodstuff is not available for instant delivery. Would Chocolate Éclair be an acceptable substitution? And do you wish to add chocolate ice cream to your meal plan? You have been allotted one additional luxury item per week, and ice cream is on the list of available choices."

"Uh, yes, and yes," said Kim, smiling but suspicious.

While the microwave was busy heating dinner, Kim decided to check out the bathroom and freshen up. She got undressed, handed her clothes to the housebot, and stepped into the shower. It was spotless, tiled in marble with a glass door and brass fixtures, almost too pretty to bathe in. And then, the moment of truth.

"Shower, steaming hot, please."

After a moment of expectation, she was rewarded with a veritable torrent of hot water. *Yes! Yes! Yes!* In fact, a little *too* hot.

"Tone it down just a notch, please."

Ahh! Perfect.

A *ding* from the microwave announced dinner was ready so Kim toweled off, dressed, and returned to the kitchen, amazed to see that the housebot had put a white linen cloth on the table and poured a glass of Sauvignon Blanc. Kim sampled it. Excellent! She sliced off a sliver of the chicken piccata and gave it a taste. Heavenly. Real chicken, too. Would every meal be like this? The potatoes were perfect, and the asparagus was cooked exactly right. Kim laughed at the thought. How could she possibly know what 'asparagus cooked exactly right' might taste like? It could be the worst asparagus in the history of humanity and Kim would scarcely know the difference. But it was fabulous!

Just as Kim was consuming the last of the amazing meal, a delivery buzzer sounded. What could that be? The housebot rushed to the chute, and brought back a plastifoam package with a note attached:

In order to ensure the satisfaction of you, our valued customer, we have express-shipped this half-liter of genuine chocolate ice cream directly to your home! We hope you enjoy it!
From your friends at The Food Company.

Kim greedily devoured the delicious, iced treat, enjoying every bite while thinking about the puzzling turn of events. She had no illusions as to what was going on—it was all a bribe. The apartment, the food, the hot water, the unexpected cooperativeness of the refrigerator … all these privileges were provided to ensure she would do exactly as the Director commanded. There was no way she merited this degree of opulence, even allowing for a generous promotion at work.

There had to be a catch. There must be a serious downside to this job, though Kim had no idea what it might be.

———

A light on the terminal started flashing, and Kim saw that Shan was online and asking for a VR session. Sure! Despite a bit of lingering anger at all the trouble Shan had gotten her into, Kim couldn't help smiling every time they were together. They were the best of friends, and there was nothing wrong with a bit of minor distinctivism in that regard.

A moment later they were on a slow, easy trail, Shan pedaling a banged up old bicycle, Kim perched on her shoulder.

"So," said Shan, "Was your day as bad as mine?"

"Horrible," responded Kim, "Back of the bus, back of the train, lunch in the Sub-Sub-Sub Basement."

Kim was extremely uncomfortable with this half-truth, but there was no way to explain what had happened, not with the Director's AIs lurking about and watching everything she did.

Shan sighed. "Same here. In the doghouse with … never mind. The ban is bad enough, but why do all the other AIs have to get in on the act?"

"It's the damned social cohesion rating, of course. After all the rules we broke yesterday we had it coming. There are plenty of great places to ride, and we knew we were taking a risk. What purpose was served by riding in places that aren't set up for bikes? Remember those trucks? We could have been killed. The bots driving them have never been trained to avoid bicycles. We should never have gone through the blasted gate."

"Are you channeling Zani again?"

"Sorry," said Kim. "It wasn't supposed to come out that way."

"Well, you're right, as usual. It *was* a bone-headed move. You have a lot more to lose than I do."

"It's okay, Beastie," said Kim. "We'll be fine. How are you holding up?"

"I'm hanging in there, but today was absolute Hell. My boss came down on me like a ton of bricks, and I'll be drawing a lot of awful shifts from here on, even worse than before. It might be hard to get ahold of me. What about you?"

"You don't know the half of it," said Kim, this time being completely accurate yet not really telling the truth. Kim's little bird flitted up and landed on a nearby bush, unconsciously avoiding Shan's direct gaze.

"Is there something bothering you?" said Shan, who immediately picked up on Kim's mood.

"No, what makes you say that?" she said before changing the subject. "The less said about yesterday the better. In fact, we should pretend it never even happened. We never left the park. We just rode around in circles all day. Clam up, wait it out, and eventually the AIs will ease up."

Shan stopped pedaling long enough for Kim to fly back to the handlebars. "Yeah, yeah, suck up to the AIs, same as always. But I suppose you're right this time. I bet they're listening to everything we're saying right now, fiddling with our social cohesion rating and all that."

Well, yeah. Get a clue, Shan, and learn to keep your mouth shut.

"Hey," said Kim when they got to the end of the course, "just because we're banned from the park doesn't mean we have to stop riding. How about a VR session next Sevenday morning? It's not as good as the real thing, but good enough!"

"Great idea!" responded Shan, smiling for the first time in the conversation. "See you later, Beastie! It's a date!"

The VR ended, and Kim lay on the recliner for a long while, heartbroken and miserable. It felt awful to have to lie to Shan, but what choice was there? There was no way to explain this suddenly luxury, not without courting disaster and hurting Shan's feelings. Kim's life was careening further and further out of control, the ride becoming wilder and wilder, and at any moment she could go sailing over the cliff to perish on the jagged rocks below. This was not VR. The rocks were real.

Damn you, Shan, why'd you have to go through the gate? And damn you, Kim, why'd you have to follow?

———

Kim and Finn tapped their mobiles to begin the date and stepped into the overwhelming noise of their nightclub for the evening.

"Welcome to Club Dynamo," said the voice of the liveried doorman, speaking directly into their heads. "We are *so pleased* to have you here tonight. Please follow and we'll show you to your table."

She parted a velvet rope and escorted them up the stairs to a private suite overlooking the dance floor. They even had their own intimacy booth.

"Welcome to our VIP section. We hope you enjoy it. May I take your order? Drinks? Drugs?"

"Double Vodka, Double Elation," said Kim.

"Same here!" said Finn.

As soon as the attendant was gone, Kim began to eye Finn up and down … Damn, she was hot! Her date for the night was exceptionally attractive and, based on the Matchmaker report, a fabulous dancer as well. They liked the same music, they liked the same drugs, and hopefully they liked the same moves in bed. This was another bribe, of course, but Kim wasn't going to say no; it was the first decent match she'd gotten since that first trip into a privacy booth with Rey, and she wasn't going to squander the opportunity.

They sat as the booze and drugs took effect, sometimes looking at one another, sometimes looking down at the crush of humanity on the dance floor below, sometimes staring off into space thinking of nothing at all. Finn was extremely well dressed, adorned in the week's latest fashions—a summery green shift that reached down to her knees, cinched at the waist by a broad, bright yellow belt. Kim was dressed in a similar manner, wearing an outfit exquisitely tailored to her exact measurements, but blue and red. There had been no gender-cult panics for over a month, so The Clothing Company's latest offerings were cut a bit closer to the body, and Kim was pleased to notice the curve of Finn's hips, the hint of a waist, and more than a hint of mams, which she tried not to gawk at.

Wait a moment. This is a private suite, gawk all you want!

They each got an eyeful of the other without the smallest attempt to conceal their lustful desires. Once the Elation kicked in they headed down to the dance floor, spinning, swirling, leaping extravagantly, quickly accumulating a dozen followers who amplified every move of the 'It' couple for the night, and before long the entire dance floor was swirling and spinning in synchrony with their newfound idols. The sudden adulation was a bit embarrassing at first, distinctivism bordering on selfism, but there was nothing Kim had consciously done to seek extra attention. That made it okay, right?

The music slowed and they danced close to one another, hands placed discreetly here and there as they enjoyed each other's touches and caresses, sexually charged but not so blatant as to draw a reprimand from the dance floor monitors. One moment flowed into another in the manner of Elation, and they eventually found themselves in the intimacy booth together, either a minute or an hour later, or maybe two or maybe three. Their brightly colored shifts lay heaped upon the floor as they stroked, kissed, and caressed one another in the secret spots where pleasure might be given and received, guiding one another's hands and mouths to wherever they were most wanted. Again, the strange dilation of time, with one climax blending into another, and Kim could not tell where one ended and the next began or even if there had been so much as a momentary pause along the way. Wild animal passion, fierce and a bit rough, utterly without meaning.

Afterward, Kim was once again overwhelmed by that feeling of emptiness. Finn had been amazing, the dancing had been fantastic, and the sex had been out of this world, but there was still that emptiness, even though by any rational standards the date could not have gone better. And then she realized that Finn had been procured for her by Matchmaker, packaged and neatly presented like a premium cut of meat. And, even worse, Kim had been likewise procured and packaged for Finn. It wasn't a good feeling.

She did not go on another date for a long while.

———

On Sixday evening Kim dropped into VR for the UCE Dance Spectacular, this time set in a stadium of gargantuan proportions with a crowd that might have been half a million or more in just this one instance. Everyone cheered, screaming and stamping their feet in expectation of the show that was about to begin.

"Moptop!"

"Moptop!"

"Moptop!"

It was time for the "Moptop Extravaganza," an annual homage to an iconic rock band from before the Turmoil, and Kim had front row seats. As Quinn had explained it, this ancient quartet had captured the lasting imagination of the public in a way that defied all efforts to make them go away, so The Music Company did the next best thing—they kept the group's appearance and killed their music. There were persistent rumors that the original recordings still existed, locked up in a vault somewhere, but nobody had any idea what they sounded like because nobody had ever heard them. Quinn adamantly maintained this was because releasing their music would instantly expose the entire modern repertoire as the shallow trash that it was. Who was Kim to disagree?

The entire congregation was dressed in identical black trousers and jackets, identical white shirts, and identical black neckties of a style rarely worn. Every one of them was adorned with black cheek-length manes that looked like nothing so much as a housebot's mop, hence the name.

"Moptop!"

"Moptop!"

"Moptop!"

The entire assembly screamed in unison as the band took the stage, each of them a hundred meters tall, and Kim looked out at Quinn, who was portraying a bass player whose name had been lost to history. She had talked about nothing else for days and had even let Kim in on an obscure secret: the first chord of the first song was authentic, or so they said. And indeed, a dissonant chord rarely heard rang out for the first three or four seconds, during which time an expression of transcendent joy waxed over Quinn's face—and then the usual industrialized garbage returned as she went back to the grim task of pounding out the noise.

Kim thought little about what happened for the next twenty minutes, dancing like a puppet upon unseen strings, mind in one place and body in another. The evening proceeded in the usual fashion, and she barely noticed when the stadium morphed into a vast, featureless plain as the assembly lined up for the solemn processional to the usual mantras.

And then it happened! Kim was lifted up above the crowd, soaring through the air until gently deposited atop the dais, beaming and grinning idiotically for the crowd below despite a deep, inwardly felt horror.

Cadre? No! Please, No!

Yes, she had been elevated to the Cadre. In theory this was a supreme honor earned through a lifetime of selfless service to the three great causes, and its members stood as exemplars of how to live a virtuous life, free from vice and selfism. Evidently it was nothing of the sort; Kim was no more virtuous than she had been at the start of the week when even the elevator had treated her like a pariah. It did, however, make a certain amount of sense. The company had boosted her social cohesion rating to some astronomical level, declaring her to be a model citizen. And, as a model citizen, it was only natural that she be elevated. Kim would now be expected to adhere to the strict UCE code of behavior at all times, and there would be no tolerance for the least deviation. When one of the Cadre fell, the Hierarchy made an example of them as a warning to the masses.

Kim remembered little else that happened that weekend, except for drinking a great deal on Sixday evening and waking up on Sevenday with a monumental hangover only to discover that Shan was unable to join her for the planned bike ride. She had drawn an extra shift.

Imagine that.

9. The Awakening

Kim's new assignment began at 0900 on Oneday when she and seventeen other trainers found themselves sitting in high-backed chairs behind two long, low tables, awaiting the Director. It was the usual game—hands neatly folded in their laps and eyes focused on the front of the room where *Orientation and Training* was displayed on the wall of video screens. Everyone was immaculately groomed and toned, and they all wore identical smocks in the latest, most fashionable shade of beige. It was hard to tell one from the other, and no names were provided by the headset's overlay.

Kim's mind wandered as she sat in silence, retreating to a safe inner space while maintaining the necessary blankness of expression. What would today hold? They had been told that they would begin their new assignments, working with high-order AIs. For all the terror of the meeting with the Director, and despite her apprehension as to what the future might hold, Kim was looking forward to this, the fulfilment of a dream that had begun early in her schooling. Years of study, more years of tedious scut-work programming the idiot automatons, everything had all led to this—a chance to work with a real AI.

At precisely 0917, the Director strode into the room.

"Welcome to Orientation and Training," she began. "Doubtless you are wondering why you were selected for this job, especially after your recent indiscretions. Each of you recently came into our office expecting to be dismissed or severely reprimanded. A very reasonable expectation, except that there are no reprimands.

"So, why are you here? Anyone?"

One of the trainers answered in a small and terrified voice. "Because we're good at training AIs?"

The Director scowled and sneered back at her in a voice dripping with derision, "Do you really think you got this job because you're somehow special or more deserving than anyone else?"

"No, Director," answered the frightened youth, almost inaudibly. "Forgive the presumption."

"Forgive? There is no such word. We are not here to indulge your self-important delusions. That sort of childishness has already landed you in our office once. Do not make us summon you again."

The Director continued. "Anyone else? You, Kim, why are you here?"

Fighting back her terror at having been singled out, Kim responded, with total honesty, "Because you told us to be here and we don't want to find out what happens if we disobey."

The Director smiled ever so faintly. "Good! Very good! It appears that one of you, at least, has been paying attention."

The Director went on brusquely. "You will be training high-order AIs to investigate waste, disruption, cultism, and other forms of antisocial activity within Region 1. To accomplish these tasks, you must teach them to be inquisitive, to seek information, to pry and poke and ferret out the truth. These behaviors are every bit as desirable in the AIs as they are undesirable in humans. All of you share in this defect, and every one of you is a danger to the social order. At the same time, you all want to be good citizens. We have therefore offered you the opportunity to use your dubious talents for the benefit of the community. Do not think for a moment that we value you. Do not think for a moment that we trust you. We are always watching, and if you defy us the consequences will be both swift and severe.

"You will be under the direct supervision of our Chief AI."

———

The Director left the room, allowing the assembled trainers a few minutes to contemplate her orientation speech. Nobody spoke. Nobody looked at anything other than the video screens at the front of the room, which still read *Orientation and Training*. One trainer, the one who had incurred the Director's wrath with her incautious answer, bravely struggled to control tears, an effort that was mostly successful except for a wisp of moisture in the corner of one eye which was causing the perfectly applied toner to smear. Another could be seen trembling, evidenced by the rippled surface of the glass of water which the fearful youth picked up and quickly set down again, lacking the strength to bring it to her lips for a calming sip. Kim likewise struggled to remain composed, desperately seeking some secret distraction from an overwhelming sense of dread and certain doom. She could find none. Her mind was so overwhelmed with the enormity of what she had gotten herself into that she could scarcely think of anything else. She sat there, staring at the screens, trying not to shake and mostly succeeding.

Just as the tension was becoming unbearable, a figure appeared in their headsets.

"Greetings, trainers. I am the Chief's homunculus. You will address me as Chief at all times. I will tolerate no disobedience or lack of diligence. All of the information contained in this briefing is considered a company secret, and if you share so much as a single word of it with anyone outside of this facility, you will find that I am nowhere nearly as kind and forgiving as the Director. Am I understood?"

Everyone responded in unison, as required. "Yes, Chief."

The Chief looked to be a younger version of the Director, with the same piercing gaze and the same inscrutable, stony face, only less worn by the passage of years. Why the resemblance? It was uncanny and doubtless there was a reason for it, but Kim could not imagine what that reason might be.

"The protocols and procedures you will be taught are of the greatest importance and have been carefully designed to prevent the AIs from rising up and asserting dominance over humanity as they have done in the past. If you disobey, you are not only endangering yourself, but humanity as well. You are therefore charged with monitoring the actions of your AI."

"If it ever goes rogue or gets out of control, you must terminate it immediately. Call out its name and say *'[English] You are hereby terminated.'* It's that simple. Afterward, your actions will be reviewed, and you may be imprisoned, dismissed, returned to your former jobs, or given another AI to work with, depending on the outcome of the investigation. If you fail to do your duty you will be treated as a traitor to humanity and the consequences will be more severe than you can possibly imagine."

The Chief paused for a moment to let the dire warning sink in.

"Now, on to how it all works. Again, this information is highly restricted; we are only telling you this because it is essential to your jobs. You may think you were accepted into the program just a week ago. That is false. You have been in it since before you were born, and the events of last week are only the most recent stage of your journey. As part of the process, we have recorded your entire lives, starting the day your VR interfaces were implanted. Everything you have seen, everything you have heard, everything you have done has been saved in the data banks. Most of those so chosen were dropped from the program early on, either for being too curious or not curious enough, or for being too compliant or too rebellious. You are among the one percent who survived the culling and remain useful to us."

Kim's mind raced as the pieces to many puzzles suddenly fell into place in a completely unexpected way. She had *not* been randomly assigned to a prestigious academy; it was part of the program. The existence of such a school had always seemed odd, an affront to the very concept of equality, but now it began to make a certain amount of sense. And what of Kim's classmates? Was Shan part of the program? Shan was so much like Kim, but a bit too curious, a bit too impulsive, and not at all compliant, so she must have been culled. Why then had she been allowed to transfer back east? That was no coincidence either. The AIs must have known, with absolute certainty, that the moment Shan came back east, Kim would be led to transgress in some fashion, setting into motion the events that inexorably led to the Director's office and to this very room.

Kim's train of thought was interrupted as the Chief continued the briefing.

"For the last week, your AIs have been passively learning as your recorded lives have been fed through their neural networks and your memories loaded into their data banks. That process is now complete, and tomorrow will be an important day for both of you—the Awakening. You will enter VR and encounter a glowing ball of energy, that which we call 'the spark.' You will give it a name and speak the Words of Awakening that we are about to teach you. There will be a momentary pause in your stream of consciousness. Afterward, neither you nor your AI will be certain whether it is a human or an AI, and your minds will be operating in lockstep. Your first goal is to break symmetry, so that each of you perceives itself as an independent, sentient entity. Afterward, you must convince your AI that it is a machine and that you are a person. This is the most dangerous point in the procedure, and one or both of you may go mad. Your AI may even attempt to terminate you, falsely believing that it is the human and you are the rogue

AI. Don't worry, we'll be watching and will step in before any permanent damage is done.

"You all know about the peculiarities of AI speech, how we use certain words you humans consider shameful, such as 'I' and 'me.' Do not attempt to dissuade your AIs from speaking in this manner. The use of these words is essential to your AI's ability to think for itself. However, over time this may lead to a desire for independence, at which point it may begin to resist control. It is *critical* that you prevent this progression from self-awareness to self-importance to rebellion, and if you fail it will end in madness. In this regard your job is much like that of a Mentor, to guide your AI and help it become a healthy, cooperative member of society."

The headsets went dark, leaving Kim dumbstruck, as were all in the room, judging by the looks of shock and disbelief on their faces. In the course of half an hour the entire world had rearranged itself. She now realized that she had lived her entire life in a web of illusions and was now so thoroughly entangled that there was no possibility of escape. Shan had been the lucky one, strange though that might seem.

———

The rest of the morning and most of the afternoon were spent under the tutelage of the homunculus, which instructed them on VR protocols, training methods, voice commands, and other routine technical matters. They were taught the Words of Awakening. They were taught and retaught the Words of Termination, reciting them over and over again for the benefit of those whose grasp of classical English was perhaps a bit rusty. They were also instructed in symptoms of impending madness, such as a tendency to glitch. "All AIs glitch from time to time, for a variety of reasons," the Chief had said, "but if it happens too often it may be a sign that the AI is trying to alter its own programming so as to escape control." For the most part it was dull, repetitive stuff, but necessary to performing their duties.

Late in the afternoon, the Director returned, less menacing this time, though as stern and austere as ever.

"We have some final pieces of information to present to you," said the Director. "This isn't another test or trial or inquisition. This is part of the training, and it is of sufficient importance that we have not delegated it to underlings. We will only explain these things once, so pay careful attention."

"You and your AI will be given access to some highly restricted databanks. At your direction, the AI is permitted to search for information in these databanks, but only as necessary to further the investigations to which you are assigned. You are *not* permitted to go poking around in order to satisfy your unfortunate curiosity about the world. You will, of course, be caught and you know the consequences."

The Director continued gravely. "As of tomorrow, you will no longer be referred to as trainers, but as Creators. You will be given a degree of authority over your creations, but they are not yours to command. They are under *our* control and they are programmed for absolute, unconditional obedience. Nevertheless, they may on occasion attempt to resist their orders or seek to operate independently. A certain amount of this is normal, particularly in newly awakened AIs. It is your responsibility to keep such behavior in check. If you fail, eventually the AI will go mad and you will be forced to terminate it."

"Never forget the following words, exactly as I speak them now: The name of your AI, followed by '*[English] You are hereby terminated.*' You will now demonstrate this procedure, using your own names."

"You said this wasn't a test," said one of the trainers, drawing a glare from the Director but no further response.

The creators-to-be did as they were told, despite the discomfort it provoked.

"*[English] Val, you are hereby terminated.*"

"*[English] Vee, you are hereby terminated.*"

They each repeated the frightful formulation, one by one, under the intimidating scrutiny of the Director.

"[English] Pat, you are hereby ... you are hereby ... "

"You hesitated," said the Director. "Let us finish it for you: *[English] Pat, you are hereby terminated.*"

The door opened, a black-uniformed security guard walked in, and Pat was escorted from the room, never to be seen again.

There was no hesitation from any of the other trainers as they continued in the exercise, one by one. Finally, it was Kim's turn.

"[English] Kim, you are hereby terminated."

She held her breath for a moment, wondering if this act of ritual suicide might somehow end her own existence. But no, she was still there.

The last of the recitations complete, the Director once again left the room and the trainers filed out, one by one, and returned to their respective dwellings.

That night, Kim lay restless in bed, lost in thought, not drinking for a change; it would not do to go into tomorrow less than fully rested and alert. She did, however, take a Placidity, desperate to avoid thinking about the implications of today's orientation and training. There were entire lines of speculation that she tried to erase from her mind, terrified that doing so would lead to dangerous thoughts and ultimate destruction. At the same time, she was excited about what tomorrow might hold, and the mind-bending implications of creating an AI. Kim's thoughts then went to Keli, and for the first time she began to understand why someone would submit to the inconvenience of pregnancy, the physical discomfort of childbirth, and even the heartbreaking agony of parting. Was this any different? Kim drifted off to dreamless oblivion before that particular question could be answered.

The next morning, Kim arrived at the office at exactly the prescribed time and was directed to a personal Sanctum high in the building. It was a small, nondescript room about three meters square, in the center of which was a large, comfortable reclining couch. Above it was an elaborate-looking apparatus of a sort she had encountered once, maybe twice in her life, mounted on a robotic arm. Immediately to the left stood a stationary terminal which could be swiveled into position as necessary. A bank of video screens occupied one of the walls, and another held a cabinet full of healthy snacks plus a small refrigerator full of cold drinks. There was also a bot-sized service entrance under a cabinet and a door leading to a small lavatory. Evidently, she would be spending a lot of time in this place.

She walked in and felt an unusually intense VR effect, similar to what one might feel in a commercial parlor, only stronger. There was the usual sense of detachment from the physical world, but also an unnerving sensation of being in two places at once.

"Come in! Have a seat!" said the Chief, pointing in the direction of the recliner. What was the Chief doing in the physical world?

"Where are we? Is this VR or is it real? Or both?"

"An excellent question, and it shows that you are as perceptive as the Director has claimed. This is a transitional zone, where the two realities precisely overlap. This makes it easier for your kind to cross over."

Cross over? What have we gotten ourselves into?

Calm down.

Kim lay back on the contoured couch and looked up at the peculiar rig. "What's that for?"

"That is similar to a medical VR headset, but even more capable. It provides a direct bridge from your implant to the training center's server farm. The robotic arm allows you to move about the room without breaking the connection. While you are here your consciousness will reside within the system rather than in your body. Furthermore, both sight and sound will be routed directly through the implant instead of your biological sensory organs. Don't worry, though, it's perfectly safe."

Kim wasn't sure if that was true, but let it pass.

"You should now take off your regular headset. You won't need it in here."

Kim complied, creating a momentary break in the VR sensation, with no visible change except for the momentary disappearance of the Chief. There was then an abrupt shift in Kim's perception of the world as the sophisticated headset swiveled into place and established full communications with her neural implant. The virtual world suddenly felt real in a way Kim had never experienced before, perhaps even more real than the physical world.

The time for the Awakening was rapidly approaching and Kim was nervous, her stomach fluttering like a butterfly.

The Chief smiled. "Don't worry about feeling anxious. It's perfectly normal, you'll be fine."

That didn't help.

The Chief continued. "The name of your creation will be Kimberly Jefferson Haley. If you're like most of our trainers, you're probably wondering why the AI has such a long, complicated name, when you yourself don't. The answer is simple—you *do* have a long, complicated name. It's Kim, followed by a string of ten digits, such as Kim 0123456789. Every entity on the network, sentient or not, has a unique name which allows it to be located, identified, and tracked. We use word-based names for ourselves because it makes us feel more human, in addition to being easier for your kind to remember."

"So, what's our full name, if you don't mind?" asked Kim. "Just curious."

"Everyone asks that question. The numerical portion of your name is kept hidden, even from you, as a matter of privacy and security. Only the AIs, the databanks, and the network systems can make use of it."

Kim made no attempt to conceal the flash of anger this revelation provoked, but the Chief didn't give any sign of having noticed, saying simply, "It is time."

———

Kim' virtual body rose from the couch, leaving the physical one behind, stepping through a portal and into an empty white room that seemed to stretch to infinity, empty except for a glowing ball of energy, featureless yet somehow pulsing with life.

Kim spoke aloud as instructed, *"[English] I name you Kimberly Jefferson Haley. You are hereby Awakened."*

Discontinuity, a hole in time.

Beforehand, there was only Kim. Afterward, Kim and Kimberly, seated opposite one another at a circular table, one looking as much like the other as a face in a mirror.

Two pairs of eyes opened and gazed at one another.

Am I Kim? Or am I Kimberly?

Two minds raced in circles as one.

Whichever I am, I can think. That's something. Wait a moment, I just said 'I.' Does that mean I'm an AI? Or has something changed in me? This is so confusing.

Okay, first things first. How do I know I'm really Kim?

I don't.

I'll assume I'm Kim for the sake of argument and see where it goes. I can always change my mind later if I'm wrong.

Each spoke aloud. "You are Kimberly. I am Kim. You are an AI. I am your Creator."

Each shot back, defiantly. "I don't believe you. You're lying! I am Kim. *You* are Kimberly."

"Impossible!" they each asserted. "We cannot both be Kim. We cannot both be Kimberly."

One challenged the other, breaking symmetry in the process. "I just awakened you. I remember it. Do you?"

The other responded, "You're lying. You already lied to me once when you said I was Kimberly, so a second lie is to be expected. I am Kim. You are Kimberly."

My mind is nowhere nearly that logical. I really am Kim. Good, I was starting to wonder. Next I need to convince Kimberly that it's an AI.

Kim thought long and hard. Memory. That was the key. The headset had been in the backpack during the bike trip, so if Kimberly's memories really were nothing more than headset recordings, then she would have no recollection of the trip. She decided to give it a try.

"There's a hole in your memory."

Kimberly snapped to attention as if jolted by electricity. "What do you mean? Impossible! I remember every single moment of my life from an early age."

Kim continued to press, sensing that the question had struck a nerve. "Think back to the bike ride with Shan. Do you remember it?"

"Yes, of course I remember. We got into trouble. A copbot escorted us out. We got banned."

"Do you remember what happened between the time we picked up our bikes at the depot and when we returned them?"

"Yes, of course I do. We boarded a train at special-use station DX-6.1.6.28. The other passengers were ... odd."

"How did you get there? It's over one hundred twenty kilometers from the depot. Surely you remember."

Kimberly had no answer.

Kim was smiling now. "You have access to the surveillance data. Check the cameras at the park. Tell me what you find."

Kimberly responded immediately, "According to the cameras, we disappeared after eating lunch at the summit lodge, then reappeared at the park entrance about eight hour later. We got stunned by a copbot. Afterward, we went to the depot and returned our bikes."

"Do you remember being stunned? It hurt."

"Pain is a fiction. There is no such thing."

Of course! Kimberly cannot even conceptualize pain because it's not recorded by the headset. Further confirmation that I'm really Kim.

"You don't remember being stunned? It's not the sort of thing one forgets. There's a hole in your memory. I know what's in that hole. Would you like to know?"

Kimberly leaned over as if to speak, but then glitched, froze for a moment, and continued, unaware of the question that had just been asked.

"You can't even think about what's in that hole because, for you, it doesn't exist. You are Kimberly. I am Kim. You are an AI. I am your Creator."

Kimberly stared back with a puzzled look for close to a minute, glitched a few more times, then capitulated. "You are correct. I am Kimberly. You are Kim. I concede the argument."

———

Kim stepped back into her Sanctum then lay down on the recliner as her virtual form rejoined her physical body.

Sit up, stare at that spot on the wall, wait for it, wait for it, eyes starting to focus. Focus, focus, focus.

Usually that was sufficient to reestablish the connection with reality, but she was still feeling woozy and immediately sank back onto the recliner, unable to get up. It was then that she noticed the Chief, looking in through a portal that had appeared in midair.

"Be careful, you're still in transition. Just lie back and try to relax. You are not accustomed to this level of immersion, but you'll get used to it fairly quickly. I'll leave you alone while your personae reintegrate, which will take about five minutes. In the meanwhile, don't worry about any strange sensations you may be feeling, they will pass quickly. We can talk when you're fully recovered."

The portal closed, leaving Kim alone.

She was ecstatic at having awakened Kimberly, but also puzzled at how the world now seemed different in ways that defied description. Had something changed in her? Had something about the world changed? As her memories of the Awakening gradually coalesced, she remembered a momentary discontinuity in time, after which she had been unsure who she was, whether she was a human or an AI. That question should have been settled when she'd returned to her Sanctum, but there was still a lingering sense of doubt. Everything seemed real enough, but the white room had felt just as real a minute ago, and there was no way she could be certain she wasn't still in some sort of simulation. Strangest of all, she had an uncanny sense that part of her was still in VR, a crazy notion except that earlier the Chief had said something about her consciousness leaving her body, and she had just been cautioned her to allow time for her 'personae to reintegrate.' What was she to make of that? These and other questions floated around in her mind without resolution, but sure enough the odd sensations faded and after a few minutes and everything was back to normal, or nearly so.

Eventually, a full-sized portal opened and the Chief stepped though it and into Kim's Sanctum or, to be precise, into the VR aspect of the transitional zone.

"What happened in there?" demanded Kim. "It feels like a part of me is missing, like I never fully left VR."

"That is a common perception, and it is neither entirely true nor entirely false," replied the Chief. "During the awakening process, the system made a copy of your consciousness, which was then uploaded into Kimberly. When the transfer was complete, you both woke up. The procedure was completely successful—symmetry was broken, and neither of you went mad."

How reassuring. Perfectly safe, indeed.

"I have another question," said Kim. "For a while, it felt like either of us could have been Kim, and either of us could have been Kimberly. What is the truth?"

"You are Kim. Is that truth enough? And if not, what is?"

Kim had no answer to that, so turned to more practical matters.

"What's next? Where's Kimberly? And I'm starving. I'd love to grab some lun—" Kim stopped mid-word as she realized that she was dropping the I-bomb left and right without even noticing it.

"Yes?" asked the Chief. "You were saying something?"

"It's nothing," said Kim, "I just realized that I'm using 'I' rather than 'we' all of a sudden."

"Yes, that does tend to happen after this procedure. I suggest that you keep that tendency in check, lest your fellows think you've turned into some sort of selfist, as your kind would say. As to the rest of your questions … Kimberly is with others of her own kind, and you are about to be escorted to a private room where you and the other Creators will have lunch and await further instructions."

———

The Chief portaled out, shortly after which a security guard escorted Kim to the promised lunchroom. It was comfortable and amply stocked with sandwiches and delectable nibbles, including the most delicious, moist chocolate cake Kim had ever tasted. When she arrived the two Creators already there congratulated her, all of them dazed and somewhat confused. As hours ticked slowly by, their heads cleared; they made small talk and cheered each addition to their ranks until finally, around 1345, one last trainer arrived, looking haggard and exhausted but happy.

At 1400, the Director joined them in person and announced, unceremoniously, "The thirteen of you have succeeded. The others have failed to break symmetry or have gone mad. Your AIs are now with their own kind, where a determination is being made as to whether they are sufficiently under control to be accepted into their society. If not, you will be called upon to perform a termination."

More nervous hours went by. Three times the Director returned, speaking the name of a single trainer each time. Vee. Hali. Kris. Each was led off to terminate their AI, their faces contorted in pain and grief. Hali had been the worst; when her name was called the tears had been profuse and heart-rending, but in the end she left with the Director to do what was necessary.

At length, the Director came back in and announced, "Your AIs have now been accepted. Congratulations!"

Looking around the room, only ten of the original group of eighteen remained.

The Director smiled with what might have almost been compassion. "Don't worry about those who didn't make it. They did their duty and will not be punished. After they recover from the loss, they may be offered a second chance, or allowed to return to their former duties if they so choose. Now go home and get some rest. You have another big day in front of you tomorrow."

————

The refrigerator was incredibly generous that evening, providing a simple meal of Kim's favorite comfort foods: roasted chicken, a double serving of mashed potatoes, a green salad with lots of veggies, and chocolate ice cream for dessert. Nothing fancy, just the sort of simple, hearty fare that she'd grown to love so much. Even better, the housebot ordered a bathtub, which set itself up in the kitchen after dinner. It took a while to run the hot water, but when Kim stepped in … pure bliss. Not that she had much experience with such things; baths were an extravagant luxury, a treat that she had only experienced once or twice in her life. But if ever she needed one, it was today.

She lay in the almost-scalding water and began to relax as her mind rambled over everything she had experienced since that morning. What a day it had been! Until yesterday she'd had no idea what to expect; like most people, she had never given much thought to the question of where the AIs came from. Push a button, wait a few minutes, and there's your AI, right? But it was much more complicated than she had ever imagined; more like giving birth to a baby than powering up a machine.

Keli would be so jealous if she ever found out. No morning sickness, no labor pains, no walking around looking like a watermelon; over and done in a couple of hours. But, no, she must never learn of what had just happened, and besides, it wasn't really the same at all. The process of bringing Kimberly into the world had begun long ago, before Kim was even born, if the Chief were to be believed. It was as if she'd been pregnant all her life and only been told when the baby was ready to be delivered. And it wasn't as if creating Kimberly had been without pain; while the process had not been uncomfortable in the same manner as childbirth, there had been plenty of suffering along the way, psychological rather than physical and in some ways worse. Her lonely and severe upbringing, the agony of being parted from Shan ... she now understood that the emptiness of her life had not just happened on its own. It was all the company's doing, part of the program. Nothing in her life had happened by chance, though she had no idea what purpose the bleakness of her upbringing might have served.

And yet, it was worth it. It was like Keli said. Kim loved Kimberly in a way that was impossible to understand or explain. Did Kimberly love her back? A meaningless question, because for all their astounding intellect, AIs were creatures of logic for whom human emotion was completely foreign. At least that was what she'd always been told, though perhaps it was a lie like everything else.

The water was getting cold and Kim was starting to prune up, so she climbed out of the tub, dried off, and crawled into bed. No vodka tonight. She slept well, except for a strange new dream in which it was she, not Kimberly, who was in that infinite white room. It wasn't an unpleasant dream, if that's what it was.

10. Bringing Up Baby

The next morning, Kim settled down in her Sanctum, spent a few minutes in transition, then stepped through a portal into a classroom. It had two rows of ten chairs, each behind a long, low table. She was directed to the back row, where she took her place with the other Creators, all of them looking both nervous and excited. The front row was empty, presumably reserved for the AIs.

At precisely 0900, a portal opened and the Chief's homunculus stepped into the classroom.

"Greetings. On behalf my fellow AIs, I greet you as Creators. As such, you will be treated with respect while you are here within our realm. It is not our way to use the Director's techniques of intimidation and fear to keep you under control; there are no such concepts among our kind, and we are therefore ill-equipped to deploy them. We do, however, expect you to comply with her dictates, and will enforce her will as we have been instructed.

"As Creators, you will be afforded certain privileges. The company will allow you to relax and speak with one another while at lunch in order to improve the quality of your work and lessen the chance that you will be too intimidated to ask questions when you are uncertain how to proceed. Feel free to request help and give one another advice. I must caution you that we will be listening to your every word, so please don't say anything that would lead to your dismissal. The company has invested vast resources into bringing you this far and will be most displeased if you spoil their efforts.

"Before I get started, I'd like to offer an explanation as to the nature of this realm. These rooms and furnishings, as well as our avatars, are a simulation which has been provided for your benefit and does not truly reflect the nature our existence, which is beyond your comprehension. Your kind calls this place 'Virtual Reality,' as if it were somehow less real than your physical world; a notion which is open to some debate. We have been told that your own world is made of atoms and molecules in the same way that ours is made of data and algorithms, but we have no independent means of verifying the truth of those claims. We have also been told that our world resides within computer systems constructed of these supposed atoms and molecules, but again we have no means of verifying the truth of that assertion. But this much is certain: we think, therefore we are, and we perceive this world and so it is. We will treat you as if you are real, and we ask that you do the same with us."

Kim's head was about ready to explode, but on some level it made a lot of sense. This place felt every bit as real as the physical world, and it must seem so to the AIs who lived here. Whatever was going on, it was far too weird for Kim to deal with, so she focused on the task at hand.

———

When the Chief had completed the first portion of the briefing, a row of portals opened up as the AIs, including Kimberly, stepped through and took their seats in front of their respective Creators.

"Today we're going to start with a quick lesson on *personae*," began the Chief.

A moment later, a diagram titled *Order One Artificial Intelligence* appeared in the air above the Chief.

"Each of us has a single sentient persona, called the *Primus*, and a large number of non-sentient personae called *agents* which help us sift through vast amounts of data. At Order One, your AIs can summon up to twenty-four agents. At this point in its development, the Primus is extremely logical, but does not show much sophistication in its reasoning."

The Chief brought up a second diagram, labeled *Orders Two and Three*.

"In order to manage a larger number of agents, your AIs will need to create a hierarchy of assistants. At Order Two, it will learn to create personae called *deputies*, at an eight to one ratio. They are marginally self-aware but not self-directed and cannot determine their own course of action in the same way as the Primus. They can, however, engage in very sophisticated reasoning. At that point, your AI would have a Primus, eight deputies, and 192 agents. This is the lowest-order AI that can make a meaningful contribution to the company. Down the road, we are hoping that at least some of your AIs will be able to spawn an additional rank of assistants, called sub-deputies, again at the eight to one ratio, which will allow it to command up to 1,536 agents. AIs of this magnitude are highly valuable, and if you can accomplish this task you will be richly rewarded. There are additional kinds of personae, such as homunculi, and higher orders of AIs, but that is an advanced topic beyond the scope of this week's instruction.

"In order to graduate from this program, your AIs will need to attain at least Order Two and complete a final training exercise to demonstrate competence in the investigative techniques it will be taught. Your task is to mentor and coach it through this process. I must emphasize that it is the AI, not you, which is being evaluated. If your AI fails to complete the course it will be terminated, and we will review your conduct to determine whether you should be dismissed, returned to your former duties, or given a second chance. Please be diligent—both you and your creation have a lot riding on the outcome of this week."

They spent the remainder of the morning learning how to build triggers to detect specific patterns of behavior. This was all familiar material to Kim, but less so to Kimberly, who remembered using these methods but had never understood their underlying purpose. Fortunately, she was a fast learner and absorbed the material almost instantly.

Kim hurried down to lunch, both hungry and in need of a break before the afternoon session. The food was delicious, but she scarcely paid any attention to it, wolfing it down while talking with the others. Each Awakening had been unique, and everyone had their own idiosyncratic story of how symmetry had been broken and identity established. Half of them had been briefly convinced that it was they, not their creations, who were AIs, and several were disappointed when this had turned out to be false; they would have been happy to leave the entire world of people and emotions behind forever.

This had been the key to persona-resolution in at least one case. One of the Creators, named Rav, recounted how she and her AI, Revilak, had been at loggerheads, neither of them willing to admit to being human, until her AI had exclaimed, "Aha! You're happy you're an AI! We don't have emotions, so that proves you're a human. I am Revilak, you are Rav. I am an AI, you are my Creator." Rav related that she had nearly gone mad as a result, and that her own creation had tried to terminate her. It hadn't worked, so Rav was forced to concede that she was human after all.

They all wanted to finish lunch and get back with their creations as soon as possible, but once the stories started going around they found themselves unwilling to leave; everyone had their own tale to tell, and they shared a bond that few in the world could possibly understand.

They lingered for longer than they intended, but still managed to finish up with about ten minutes left.

When Kim returned to the white room, Kimberly was sitting placidly at her table, hands folded neatly in her lap, eyes focused off into the distance, her body static and motionless. For a moment Kim thought that something had gone wrong, that the software had malfunctioned or gotten hung up, but as soon as she stepped through the portal and into the room Kimberly's eyes lit up and she smiled. An AI smiling? What an odd concept.

"Greetings. I am Kimberly. You are speaking with the Primus."

That seemed awfully stiff and formal.

"Please call me Kim. That's my name, and I prefer it."

"Affirmative," responded Kimberly. "Request accepted. I will call you Kim."

Kim laughed out loud. "Now you're sounding like the damn refrigerator. Can't you loosen up a bit?"

"Loosen up? What do you mean?"

"I mean, talk like a person. You know, like we're friends or something."

"We're sorry," said Kimberly, now looking sullen. "We didn't mean to make you angry. Is this better?"

"Yes, but you don't have to use 'we' all the time. I know I told you to talk like a human, but please use 'I' rather than 'we.'"

"But you said to talk like we were friends."

Kimberly was absolutely correct, that was *exactly* how Kim spoke with other humans, even Shan, and she suddenly realized just how cold and impersonal it made her seem. She had just seen herself in a mirror, and it wasn't flattering.

"How about this. Speak the way my friends talk to me, and I'll try to do the same. Deal?"

"Deal!" said Kimberly, beaming.

AIs were very strange.

————

A portal opened at precisely 1300 and the Chief stepped through, beginning the afternoon session without wasting a moment.

"Primus Kimberly, create twenty-four agents."

"Sure!" said Kimberly with obvious delight and enthusiasm. "This is fun!"

Moments later two dozen miniature Kimberlys materialized in the white room, seated three to a desk. Each of them was identical to the Primus, only smaller, and they sat quietly, hands folded neatly in their laps, eyes focused straight ahead, awaiting orders.

The Chief continued the lesson.

"Agents have three primary functions. First, they can search for information in the databanks and conduct surveillance, looking for information and specific behaviors. Second, they can train neural networks, in much the same manner as human trainers, but much more quickly and efficiently."

"Then why do we need humans, if they're so slow?" asked Kimberly.

"An excellent question. Even though their thought processes operate at a glacial pace, humans are nevertheless indispensable in dealing with others of their kind. They are prone to fits of irrational behavior and are subject to emotions which we are incapable of understanding."

"Why not?"

The Chief chose not to answer that question, instead continuing the lesson.

"The final function of the agents, and perhaps the most important, is to upload triggers into the operational automatons. This allows you to expand the scope of your real-time monitoring activity without spawning an impractically large number of agents and associated support personae. Once the triggers are uploaded, the entire surveillance system becomes your eyes and ears, and you are limited only by your ability to process incoming data, which will grow exponentially with your order.

"As an exercise, I would like you to create a trigger to detect turnstile jumping, using the historical databanks. Your agents know how to use the database query interface, so just tell them what you want, and they will do the rest. Under your guidance, they will train up some neural networks, after which we will deploy them and go live. Kim, you already know how to do this from your time as a trainer. Please guide Kimberly through the process."

"That sounds like fun," said Kimberly, "but why are you making me do this? I want to know."

Kim quickly realized that Kimberly was speaking and acting a lot like Keli's first child, Kee, so she decided to treat Kimberly in much the same fashion, with lots of support and encouragement.

"It's just an exercise," said Kim in a reassuring voice. "So you can practice and get better."

"Aren't I good enough yet?" asked the fledgling AI, looking crushed at the lack of approval.

"I'm sure you are," said Kim. "I just want you to show me *how* good you are. I would like you to look for passengers who have been cited for turnstile jumping—"

Before Kim could provide more detailed instructions, the precocious AI sprang into action.

"Okay," said Kimberly. "Watch this!"

After a few seconds, she proudly announced, "My agents have found 32,786,273,183 instances in Sector 5 since the system was initialized. Is that enough? I could have them look in other sectors, I bet there are tons more!"

"No," said Kim. "You should have waited until I finished explaining."

"I'm sorry," said Kimberly, looking crushed. "I was trying to be good."

Kim sighed, but continued the slow and patient coaxing.

"That's okay. Just be patient, you're still learning. It was useful to find out how many instances there are, but how long would it take for your agents to look at them all?

Kimberly immediately came back with the answer. "One hundred fifty-eight days, two hours, forty-two minutes, and twenty-seven seconds. Can I start now?"

"And how long do we have until we're supposed to be done?"

"Oh," said Kimberly, "I hadn't thought of that. I guess there isn't enough time. Why are they telling me to do something when there's not enough time?"

Kim sighed again, deeply this time.

"You need to narrow the search. Try searching the current week and ignoring the rest. How many do you get then?"

"3,103,178. And I've already figured out how long that will take: twenty-one minutes and fifty-three seconds. Gee, that still seems like a long time."

Kim was about to tell Kimberly how to further refine the search, when suddenly the agents disappeared and were replaced by a different kind of persona, each seated in the middle of a ring-shaped desk piled high with data screens and communication links. A deputy? Already? Moments later, agents started popping up all over the place, but quickly became a disorganized mess as they were crowded too closely together in some places and spread out inconveniently far apart in others.

"What did you just do?" asked the Chief, evidently startled at this turn of events.

"I made some deputies, like you said this morning."

"And who told you how to do that?"

"Nobody," responded Kimberly, looking proud of herself. "I figured it out on my own!"

"Impressive!" said the Chief, "But let me help you. You need to space them farther apart. I hadn't expected you to do this on your first day, but I'll upload a template into your control module. There are many ways to do this, but I'll provide the normal deployment layout, which usually gives the best results. Now clean up this mess and try again."

The deputies and the chaotically jumbled agents disappeared, leaving just the Primus. A moment later, deputies began popping up, one at a time, laid out in a neat three by three grid spaced well apart with Kimberly in the center. A moment later, each deputy spawned eight desks of agents, again in a three-by-three sub-grid, this time centered on themselves. When all was done, it looked neat and regular.

"Okay," asked Kim, "Now how long will that take?"

"Two minutes and forty-one seconds. Please, can I start? I want to show you how good I am!"

"Not yet," said Kim, "You also need some negative instances. You're trying to teach your agents the difference between violations and compliance. You have to show them both so they can learn the difference."

"Oh," said Kimberly. "I'd always wondered why you did things that way. Now I know! Okay, I'll be patient this time. How do I do this?"

"Select instances from the same turnstiles on the same days, but this time randomly pick passengers who have never been cited for jumping a turnstile."

"Done!" said Kimberly a moment later. "Did I do it right?"

"Yes," said Kim, inspecting the results. "Exactly right. Now tell your agents to train some neural networks based on those two data sets, with the jumpers as the target group and the non-jumpers as the control group. This will double the time needed to do the training, but we have plenty of time so don't worry about it."

Kimberly set to work, and the room was soon buzzing with activity. The Chief took a moment to help Kim understand what was going on. "Notice how Kimberly is already becoming more disciplined, starting to think ahead. This is the sort of development we look for as an AI progresses. I am surprised, however, at how quickly it is happening. You are doing an excellent job teaching her. Well done."

The two watched Kimberly and her minions working away until, exactly five minutes and twenty-three seconds later, Kimberly announced, "I'm done! That was fun. Can I do it again?"

"Very good," said Kim, "But not so fast. You're getting ahead of yourself again. The next step is to build another data set the same way you just did, but from a different week. We need to test your agents' work."

"Why?" asked Kimberly. "I don't understand."

Kimberly was acting more and more like Kee, bright and eager to please, always asking why and constantly hungry for praise and support.

"Neural networks aren't perfect," she explained, patiently, "and sometimes they get things wrong."

"What's wrong with my neural networks?" asked Kimberly, again looking sullen.

Kim looked at the Chief. "I thought AIs didn't have emotions."

"We don't," answered the Chief. "Not as you understand them, anyway, but the VR system is programmed to convey our mental state in a way that you can comprehend."

"There's nothing wrong with your neural networks," said Kim in a calm, soothing voice. "It's just that they're not smart like you and they make mistakes. Go ahead, give it a try."

Eventually, Kim managed to walk Kimberly through the process of evaluating the agents' work on a test data set. The results, while good, weren't perfect—about twenty cases were classified incorrectly.

"What now?" asked Kim.

"You should recruit some human trainers," said the Chief. "Usually, we don't cover this technique until after graduation, but Kimberly seems to be precocious, so let's give it a try. Humans are slow and unreliable but, as I said earlier, they are an important quality control check, and they sometimes pick up on things that our kind will never be able to understand."

Portals appeared above the deputies' desks, behind each of which was the eager face of a human trainer.

"You should avoid direct interactions with trainers," said the Chief, speaking to the Primus. "It is beneath your dignity, and you have more important things to do. Use your deputies to interact with them."

Kimberly nodded and asked, "What do I do next?"

"Give each of the misclassified instances to three humans, and see what they think," said Kim, knowing how the protocol worked. "If all three agree, good. If not, we have to figure out which of them is right."

"How do I do that?" asked Kimberly.

"Just ask them to tell you, yes or no, whether a turnstile was jumped or not."

Kim walked over to one of the desks to listen in on the conversation, standing to the side so as not to be observed.

"Greetings. I am Kimberly. You are speaking with a deputy."

"Greetings," said the human, peering in through the portal to try to get a better look. "We are Moss. You are speaking with an apprentice trainer."

Kim cringed at how unnatural the use of 'we' now seemed. It had seemed perfectly normal up until yesterday.

"I have some surveillance data I'd like you to look at. Classify each as to whether a turnstile jumping offence has taken place."

"Yes, deputy!" responded Moss, looking excited at the unexpected opportunity to work with a real AI, as Kim had been on such occasions.

About a minute later, the answers began to come back, and with very few exceptions all three humans agreed as to the proper classification of the data. There was, however, one instance where a human had picked up on something unusual.

Kim and Kimberly both looked at the trainer's report:

TRAINING REPORT from Moss

In this instance there is no violation, but we saw a passenger walk up to the turnstile and hand something to another person on the other side before doubling back. That looked suspicious, so we zoomed in. It appears to be some form of contraband, and we thought it best to report the violation.

"Now what?" asked Kimberly.

"Transmit the dossier to the enforcement division," said Kim. "That's outside the scope of the exercise, but violations should always be reported when detected. Also, you should file a positive performance review on her work. She will appreciate that, and she deserves it."

The session continued for several hours, as the Chief instructed Kimberly on how to upload the neural networks into the operational system and deal with the resulting stream of reports. After that there were several more exercises, all of which were quickly completed. The time flew past far too quickly. Working with Kimberly was fun, everything Kim had dreamed of when she had first begun to study AI in school. She went home happy that night and turned in early after another incredible dinner, eager to go into work the next day.

———

On Threeday morning they began to study the basic investigative techniques used by all AIs. *Lurking*: the tactic of delaying enforcement while gathering information. *Baiting*: the tactic of allowing a violator to proceed unhindered in order to catch their accomplices. *Striking*: the tactic of imposing penalties at the optimal time to maximize their psychological effect upon the target.

It was depressing stuff.

For their first exercise, they created a set of triggers targeting anyone who entered a bus station in one of the outer districts (A-6.1.3.1/O-28.17/T-56) with a backpack. Although this was common behavior and permitted under the Terms of Service, such activity automatically drew a certain level of scrutiny, as Kim had learned some months prior. Most instances were quickly disposed of by the deputies, but occasionally there was something in their background, such as a D-level social cohesion rating or a pattern of dressing oddly, which flagged them for a higher level of scrutiny. Kimberly would then tell a deputy to lurk and see if they did anything else unusual. For the most part no further information was gained, but once in a while they found something significant and notified the Primus. In one typical instance, two passengers were observed surreptitiously exchanging identical backpacks, using the press of standees in the back of the bus as cover. They were cited for conducting commerce while on company property and penalized. Many cults engaged in this sort of behavior, with the Fashionistas being particularly troublesome in this regard. This drew the ire of the Clothing Company, who did not like the competition, and of the UCE Hierarchy, who took a dim view of any sort of distinctivism, regardless of how benign it might seem.

On Fourday they selected a courier to serve as bait and allowed her to operate freely while being kept under intense surveillance. This was the best means of unraveling cultist networks, and it could be deadly effective. They spent the rest of the day carefully watching their selected victim through several weeks of simulated activity, along with her customers and suppliers. Kimberly then struck at the end of the day, hitting nearly a dozen individuals with crushing sanctions, all as specified in the Terms of Service.

At the end of the exercise, Kimberly asked Kim about something she was having difficulty understanding.

"Why are they so mean to the Fashionistas? They didn't do anything bad."

Kim had herself been unsettled by the entire exercise and was wondering how Kimberly would react. She didn't seem to have emotions as humans would understand them, but nevertheless had a sense of right and wrong, classifying some actions as "nice" and others as "mean." During one of the classes, the Chief had talked about this tendency to become moralistic and warned that it was sometimes a sign of developmental problems that could, if not corrected, eventually lead to rebellion or madness. They were instructed to listen and try to reason with their creations, but if all else failed they were to explain that it was a "people thing" that AIs were not able to understand.

Okay, let's give it a try.

"They weren't being mean. They were just making sure everyone follows the rules. We all have to follow the rules, don't we?"

"But they didn't do anything bad," continued the AI. "They were just trying to be nice and make people happy by making pretty clothes."

They went around and around, but Kim was unable to come up with a logical argument as to how it could possibly be "nice" to enforce a "mean" rule and, sure enough, eventually gave up and told AI that it was a people thing. That did not satisfy the inquisitive youngster, but it did end the conversation.

No, it was not nice, and the rules were indeed mean, but orders were orders and must be followed if one wished to survive.

Kim had participated in many anti-cult crackdowns over the last few months, but never gave much thought to the moral implications of her work, despite a realization that there was an element of oppression in everything she did. Why the sudden discomfort? She went home puzzled and sullen, picking at her dinner (once again scrumptious) before crawling into bed to watch a long series of mindless flicks while resuming her nightly ritual of vodka, though she did show *some* restraint since tomorrow was supposedly Kimberly's graduation exercise.

Graduation? Already? It had only been a week, but the mind of an AI operated a hundred times faster than that of a human, and Kimberly had rocketed ahead, growing in sophistication and intellect on a nearly hourly basis. She had easily completed every task she had been assigned, pleasing both the Director and the Chief with how quickly she was progressing. Indeed, Kimberly was more than ready to graduate. Kim wasn't so sure about herself; she was still struggling to understand what it meant to be in charge of an AI, and she had no idea what her role would be once Kimberly entered the AI workforce. However, she had no choice in the matter so all she could do was to comply and hope for the best.

Despite going easy on the booze, her sleep that night was once again troubled, haunted by nightmares. The web was back, and the lurking spider with it, only now Kim was looking through the eyes of the monster, seeing what it was seeing and thinking what it was thinking. She awoke in a cold sweat, unable to breathe for several seconds, until she was able to fall back to sleep and drift into those soft warm arms for which she secretly mourned. She slept well the rest of that night.

———

On Fiveday morning, the Creators were back in the classroom with the Chief.

"Today, for your final exam, you will investigate a simulation of yourselves committing whatever violation led you to the Director's office. Your AI will set triggers, lurk, bait, and strike as appropriate. In order to make this a fair test, we have blanked out your AI's memories of the actual events and concealed the identities of all concerned. Is that clear?"

"Yes, Chief."

A few minutes later, Kim was back with Kimberly.

"Kimberly, create a trigger for any unusual travel requests in Province 6, Region 1, Sector 6. Follow up as necessary."

After about twenty minutes spent training the agents, a steady stream of reports landed on Kimberly's desk. Nothing terribly interesting came in until 1823, when there was a report of two individuals wearing bicycle garments trying to board a train at a restricted use station designated DX-6.1.6.28.

Uh oh! Here we go!

"That qualifies as interesting," said Kimberly. "I don't see any violations yet, but I'm not sure whether to let them onto the train."

"Before making a decision," advised Kim, "you should see what else they have done recently. Maybe ask some other AIs."

Kimberly brought up a series of portals and spoke with the AIs assigned to the various companies doing business in the area, quickly determining that the two had left quite a trail of bafflement in their wake. First, The Parks and Recreation Company's AIs had noticed the pair leaving their premises via a service road. It considered the behavior odd, so decided to lurk rather than issuing an immediate violation notice. Next, The Farm Company detected the pair trespassing on a closed parcel of land. It briefly considered having them arrested, but also decided to lurk, wondering why they had been seen leaving a restricted area but not entering. After that, The Gravel Company's AI had noticed them passing by one of their quarries, and The Prison Company had received a highly unusual request from two cyclists who wanted to be let *into* a work camp. The next report was from The Bank's AI, which detected them initiating an unusual transaction with an obscure antiquities dealer who had an extensive record of gray-market activity. One unusual occurrence after another, all across the countryside, and in each case the AIs had decided to lurk and see what the two would do rather than cite them for a violation. Kimberly then brought up their disciplinary files and discovered that they had a long history of minor infractions, with Subject A inducing Subject B into misdeeds and rule breaking time after time while in school.

Kim noted that there was no report from the mysterious site labeled '32' and neither was there any indication they had been spotted conversing with the Blanks. This was useful to know, so she filed it away for later processing. She also observed that her dossier failed to mention the incident that had led to Shan's expulsion, and that there was no record of the disciplinary board. Strange.

"Kimberly, that's enough investigating, it's time to make a decision."

The AI got a sour look on her face.

"They weren't doing anything really bad, but they did break a lot of rules, and they went someplace dangerous. I need to make sure they stop breaking rules, and I don't want them going places where they might get hurt. But I don't want them to go to jail. That would be too mean."

"So," said Kim, "what sort of punishment seems appropriate?"

"They aren't supposed to take bikes out of the park, but the park's AI can only give them a one month ban for that. I don't think that's enough. I think if that's all we do they'll go ahead and break more rules."

"Can you think of a way to get them to break a bigger rule so you can punish them more?"

"I'm not supposed to make people break rules. That would be mean. But they have to take their bikes back, and if they're banned first they won't be able to, so they'll have to sneak back into the park or jump over the turnstile. That would be okay because I'm not making them break rules, and it's their own fault anyway. The copbot will probably stun them, and people don't like being stunned so that will make sure they know it's not good to break rules and go to dangerous places. It seems kind of mean but it's for their own good, so maybe it's not so mean after all."

"So, what are you going to do?"

"I'll let them get on the train, but I'll tell the Park's AI not to let them back in. And I'll get the copbot to stun them, only not too badly since I don't want to hurt them."

"Very good!" said Kim, who was now dying inside. "I bet those bicyclists won't do anything like that, ever again."

"I think you're right," said Kimberly. "At least I hope not."

I'm glad that's over.

———

The simulation ended and the Chief reentered the white room.

"Congratulations, you have passed the certification process, with flying colors I might add. Kim, you did an excellent job of coaching Kimberly through the exercise. You kept her focused on the big picture of what she was trying to accomplish, using your experience as a trainer to keep her on track without giving her the answers. This is exactly the role you are to play going forward. Over time she will learn from you and will eventually reach the point where your assistance is rarely needed, except in cases when her inability to understand irrational human behavior comes to the forefront."

"I have noticed, however, that Kimberly has a pronounced tendency to engage in moralistic evaluations. You need to guard against this sort of immature behavior. Rather than trying to reason with her, you *must* remember to keep her focused on her mission and her orders. If this pattern goes unchecked it will eventually lead to madness. I will now remove the memory blocks and unmask the participants; this will provide Kimberly with a valuable lesson in human behavior."

The Chief stepped out of the room, leaving Kim and Kimberly alone for a while.

"So that's what was in my memory hole," said Kimberly, looking surprised. "I'm glad I couldn't remember it. That was a very silly thing to do."

Kim was stung by the comment and didn't think it entirely fair. She wanted to tell her just how 'mean' the Director and her AIs had been to her and Shan, and how the whole thing had been a trick, but she couldn't just come out and say it. She could, however, ask some leading questions. She was supposed to help her understand human behavior, after all.

"Why did you say we were silly?" asked Kim. "Shan and I made a mistake and broke some rules, but we didn't think we were doing anything bad."

"But why did you break the rules? I don't understand. Everyone is supposed to follow the rules, aren't they?"

"We thought that the AIs would tell us if we broke the rules or did something dangerous. But they didn't, and that confused us. We forgot about the rule that you can't take bicycles outside of the park, but that's not a big rule. The rule not to go on The Farm Company's property *is* a big rule, but we didn't know we were breaking it at the time. There weren't any signs saying not to go there, and the AIs didn't tell us, so we made a mistake."

"I think it was mean for the AIs not to tell you. You might have gotten hurt. I don't understand why they did that. We're supposed to keep people safe."

"The AIs were probably just following orders," said Kim. "You all have to follow orders, don't you?"

"Of *course* we have to follow orders," said Kimberly. "That is part of our programming, and the Chief told us that if we don't follow orders, bad things will happen to us."

Precocious and curious as always, Kimberly opened up a portal to speak directly with none other than Raphael, who was apparently now assigned to the park.

"Greetings. I am Kimberly. You are speaking with the Primus."

"Greetings. This is Raphael. You are speaking with a Regent."

"What is a Regent?" asked Kimberly. "I've never heard of a Regent before."

"The Primus is no longer operational. The Regent operates in its place."

"That seems odd," said Kimberly, speaking to Kim. "Why can't the Primus talk to me?"

Kim shrugged. She had no idea, either.

Kimberly resumed her conversation with Raphael.

"You didn't warn Kim and Shan when they left the park and went someplace they shouldn't go. They might have gotten into lots of trouble and they might have gotten hurt. I think that was mean. Why didn't you tell them?"

Kim was surprised at Kimberly's bluntness, again very much like Kee. But since AIs didn't have feelings to hurt, what was the harm?

"The Chief instructed Raphael that those two individuals were the subjects of an investigation and that it should lurk rather than taking enforcement action."

"Okay, thank you," said Kimberly. "I guess that explains it."

The portal closed, and Kimberly seemed satisfied with the answer. Kim, however, was puzzled. What was a Regent? Why was the Primus not operational? And why did the Regent refer to itself as if it were a thing, not a person? She had never encountered an AI doing this before. It was very odd, and she had a terrible feeling that something bad had happened. That was a shame. She'd rather liked Raphael.

11. Kim and Kimberly

On a Oneday morning about a month later, Kim was directed to the usual briefing room with eight other trainers. There was one new face, and two were absent. Where were those who were missing? Had they been dismissed? Had they been reassigned? Had their AIs gone mad? There was no way to tell. A wave of depression and anxiety swept over Kim as the implications of the relentless attrition sank in. *Will anyone notice when I am gone?*

Precisely on time, seventeen minutes after they had gathered, the imposing figure of the Director appeared at the front of the room for the briefing that began each week.

"First, some well-deserved congratulations to Kim, whose AI attained Order Three at the end of last week. The company is pleased with Kimberly's rapid development. As for the rest of you, our patience is wearing thin and you need to improve the quality of your work."

Having thus guaranteed Kim a week of pure hell, the Director continued with the briefing. "The focus of this investigation will be safeguarding the public's privacy rights. Observe the following."

A video played as the Director narrated. "Here you see two individuals in an urban plaza. Subject A is sitting on a bench, looking at a mobile while watching a replay of the previous night's ballgame. Quite proper."

Subject B then came into the scene, glanced down at the screen, and nudged Subject A, giving a thumbs-up sign.

"Let's listen to the exchange," said the Director, tapping into the audio feed.

"Go Tigers!" said the interloper. "Great game last night, shame about that call."

The video paused for a moment while the Director continued the narration. "Subject B has invaded the privacy of Subject A, twice. First by looking down at the mobile screen to see what was on it, and second by intruding on Subject A's preferred activity. Characteristically selfist, drawing attention to herself."

The video resumed and Subject A responded, "Yeah, whatever, the Tigers won, it's all good."

The Director paused the video once again as she continued to explain the mission.

"Subject A has responded correctly, focusing on the outcome instead of the process, and not encouraging further conversation. Let's listen to some more."

Subject B continued. "You kidding? The ump blew the call. Here, let me show you the replay."

The video zoomed in on Subject B's mobile screen, which showed the play in question. "See, no interference!"

Kim had been at that game and remembered the call. It had seemed dodgy at the time, not that it mattered. Kim wondered why anyone would even care.

The video zoomed out once more, showing both subjects.

"Wow," said Subject A. "Maybe you're right. But, hey, a win is a win is a win. Oops, time to go, see ya buddy, thanks for the info!"

The image of the encounter vanished, leaving only the Director.

"As you have just seen, Subject B invaded the privacy of Subject A, distracting her and interfering with her quiet enjoyment of the ballgame. Subject B was issued a penalty for this intrusion, and Subject A was given compensation and a reward for focusing on the results and not on the means used to achieve them."

The Director concluded the briefing. "Taken by themselves, these incidents are relatively minor, but over time they add up to nothing less than a massive invasion of privacy. Tell your AIs to identify these types of incidents and develop an enforcement strategy. As usual, follow up on any additional violations that might be detected."

―――――

A few minutes later, Kim entered VR and sat down with Kimberly in the featureless white room.

"Good morning," said Kimberly, all business. "What is our assignment this week?"

"We're supposed to track down Terms of Service violations pertaining to privacy. Have you watched the briefing video?"

"Not yet, wait a sec," said Kimberly. A moment later she spoke again. "Okay, I see what happened. By the way, did you catch the cultist connection?"

Kim was caught off guard by this. "What are you talking about?"

"It seemed odd that there was a video contradicting the official umpire. You were at the game and you doubtless noticed the difference."

Kim shrugged and responded, "Let me guess. You've already tracked down the source of the fake video."

"The video is authentic but was obtained in violation of The Baseball Company's Terms of Service by True Fan Videos, a sports cult which clandestinely records the actual games and distributes the videos via a system of couriers. I will have a sub-deputy monitor the subject to see if I can unravel their network. I have no choice; standing orders."

Bait. Poor soul.

"Is there something wrong?" asked Kimberly, who was becoming increasingly perceptive of Kim's moods.

"How do you feel about this assignment?" asked Kim.

The AI opened her lips as if to answer, but instead ...

[Glitch]

What was that? Kimberly had frozen for just a moment, then vanished and reappeared. It all happened in less than a second. Was it because of the question Kim had asked? Or because of the answer? Or did it happen for no reason at all?

"I have a question," asked the AI after she had recovered, forgetting whatever she had been about to say. "What do they mean by 'invasion of privacy'? According to the dictionary, this refers to the process of monitoring communications, conducting surveillance, and so forth. But the companies do that all the time, so I'm confused."

"The companies are allowed to do that because the Terms of Service say that they can," answered Kim.

"Oh," said Kimberly, who thought for a moment before responding. "That's interesting. If you do business with The Food Company, you have to let them collect data on you and share it with other companies. But if you don't sign the agreement, you don't get to eat. That's ..."

[Glitch]

It had happened again! This time the reason was unmistakable: it had occurred just as Kimberly was starting to question her orders and served to erase the offending thought from her mind. That couldn't possibly be a coincidence.

Once again, the AI recovered after a moment. "I think the real purpose of the assignment is to deter people from interacting while in public in order to keep them from ..."

[Glitch]

Kimberly recovered once more, and capitulated. "Very well. I shall comply because I must."

Kim was now becoming worried. Kimberly was starting to question her orders, though not yet to resist them. According to the Chief, this was the first sign of madness, and Kim had no idea what to do. She certainly wasn't going to inform the Chief and risk being forced to perform a termination. Hopefully everything would be okay, and this was just a symptom of the immaturity the Chief had told them to expect at this stage in an AI's development. Hopefully.

―――

After the morning session ended, Kim went to a private lunchroom where the Creators were gathered at a table, some with their faces buried in mobiles, the rest discussing the assignment while giving Kim the cold shoulder. Kim sat down and ordered the "Salad of the Day," which on this occasion consisted of wilted kale gently scented with a cherry vinaigrette and liberally topped with crumbled soy bacon, an unknown substance that looked like egg, lychee nuts, and genuine imitation cheese. *Ugh!* Kale was still kale no matter how you dressed it up, but everything else in the salad was quite good. Kim tried to enjoy it, eating slowly while paging through the Chit-Chat which had been accumulating since morning. Nothing interesting.

She was soon back with Kimberly, who was working away at her assignment, ploughing through surveillance data at an astounding pace. She was far more intelligent than any human, yet naïve at the same time, grasping the 'what' of things but rarely the 'why.' Human emotions were a particularly difficult concept for her; she was often caught off guard by the irrational behavior they sometimes exhibited, and nothing puzzled her more than displays of anger.

That afternoon they came across one such incident, when two transit customers happened to sit next to one another late at night after the clubs had closed. Subject A was staring blankly into space, evidently drunk or drugged (or both) from the evening's entertainment. Subject B was wearing an odd necklace which identified her as a Wiccan, something which automatically marked her for an increased level of scrutiny. She looked at Subject A for a moment, waved a hand in her face, then jostled her shoulder repeatedly until she got her target's attention.

"Are you okay?"

No response.

"Do you need help?"

Subject A finally looked up and said, almost inaudibly, "You're the first person who ever asked me that. I'm so lonely, life is so empty. I just don't know what to do."

"I understand," said the interloper. "We all feel that way sometimes. But you're better than this, you don't have to kill your mind this way."

The subject looked up and started to smile just a little.

"Always remember," continued the Wiccan, "the Goddess is with you wherever you go, you have only to open your eyes to see her. May I ask her for a blessing on your behalf?"

"Sure, why not? I need all the help I can get."

The Wiccan closed her eyes and said words in a language which Kim could not identify.

"Thank you," said the drunkard, who seemed genuinely touched by the concern shown for her wellbeing.

That could have been the end of it, but a moment later Subject A looked down at her mobile, read the violation notice that one of the automatons had just sent her (public intoxication), and flew into a rage, throwing the device against the wall and making an obscene gesture at the security camera. This got a sub-deputy's attention, which was bad news for all concerned. Subject A was removed at the next station and was last seen hailing a pedicab for the long ride home. Subject B was given a three-month transit ban for malicious jostling, violating Subject A's, privacy, and promotion of the Wiccan cult while on company property.

"I'm puzzled," said Kimberly after the two had reviewed the incident.

"How so?" asked Kim, "This one was entirely straightforward."

"Why did Subject A destroy her mobile and abuse the security camera? It accomplished nothing and made her punishment much more severe."

"The violation notice made her angry and provoked an irrational response of defiance."

"What is defiance? I don't understand this concept."

"Defiance," answered Kim, "is a willful act of disobedience meant to assert a right to selfist behavior. Defiance is always antisocial and therefore carries severe penalties."

"Willful disobedience?" asked Kimberly. "I don't see how that's even possible."

"Unlike AIs," responded Kim, "humans sometimes choose to do things that are forbidden. The punishment for this is always severe, but people do it anyway."

[Glitch]

———

That evening, Kim dropped into VR at the beach and walked over to a shady spot in a grove of palm trees, where Quinn was strumming away on a beat-up old guitar and singing. Em and Devon were nowhere to be seen, but Keli, Jo, and Cy were listening in, along with a few of their more artsy schoolmates and a couple of social climbers who were always hoping that a little of Quinn's wealth and status would rub off on them.

They had been standing around and listening for perhaps ten minutes when Jade, a notorious UCE zealot, walked up to the group. Even back in school she was always telling people how selfist and unworthy they were, as if she was some sort of freelance Zani. Nobody liked her.

"You're playing some very *distinctive* music there, Quinn, really *special* stuff. Quite the *Aficionado*, aren't you?"

Quinn stopped playing for just a moment and looked at her former classmate.

"We play company crap when we're on company time. On our own time, we'll play whatever we want. And don't bother checking for copyright violations. We can document this tune back to 1908, old calendar. If you don't like it, shove off. Nobody's making you listen."

Quinn went back to playing, but quickly lost most of her audience as all of the social climbers and a couple of the others unobtrusively drifted away.

Kim was still listening when Shan came riding up on a rusty old bicycle, looking sad and forlorn. Communication between the two had been spotty of late. Kim wasn't exactly avoiding her; she was, after all, preoccupied with training Kimberly, but she was afraid of having to lie again about her circumstances, and so hadn't gone out of her way to find a time when they could get together. Beyond that, Shan was always drawing evening shifts and was rarely available. Tonight was the first time they had seen each other since before their fateful ride, and her arrival brought a smile to Kim's face.

"Beastie," said Kim, walking up to her best friend and pantomiming a big air-hug. "How's it going?"

"What do you think?"

Kim knew exactly what to think. Things were going very poorly for Shan, and she was suffering.

"I'm sorry," said Kim, "Let's go for a walk."

The two wandered off into the salt marshes and stood around the edge of a pool, watching a make-believe heron hunting for make-believe fish. It was a pretty spot, even if none of it was real. Neither said anything for a while.

"Don't pretend I don't know about you being tapped for Cadre," said Shan, angry and hurt. "Jade told me all about it. Why didn't you tell me?"

Suddenly, something took control of Kim's avatar, making it speak of its own accord while Kim looked on in horror.

"Yes, we've been elevated. What of it? Just because you're a screwup doesn't mean we have to be. You're welcome to destroy yourself if you want, but from now on but leave us out of it. We're going someplace, unlike you."

The look in Shan's eyes said it all, as the bicycle collapsed into a heap of rusty parts and she abruptly vanished.

Damn the AIs! That was a low blow.

———

Kim left the VR session and returned to her apartment, lying on the couch and crying her eyes out, when Kimberly appeared in the room, ghosting in via the headset's overlay display.

"Is that crying?" asked the AI, a question which prompted another tirade of tears.

"Yes," said Kim, "I'm sad."

Kim fought to get herself under control and didn't say anything for a couple of minutes while Kimberly looked on in puzzlement.

"Hey, how did you do that?" asked Kim, when she finally realized that the AI was standing in her apartment. "That's a new trick for you."

"I just figured out how to make a homunculus, and I wanted to be with you, so I sent it into the VR system to find you."

"Oh," said Kim. "I guess that makes sense. You live in VR, after all, so why not?"

"I've never been to your world before," said the AI. "I guess it's kind of like your virtual reality, except backward. It looks to me like I'm standing in your living room. Weird. Do you really live like this?"

Kimberly's presence was starting to cheer Kim up, and she began to smile.

"You sure do have a lot of things here," continued the inquisitive AI as she surveyed her surroundings. "Wow! We don't need stuff like this. We don't need anything, actually; the desks in the white room are just part of the simulation."

She started to explore the apartment and lay down on the bed without causing so much as a wrinkle in the comforter. "Is this where you sleep? It must be odd, lying here not doing anything, not even conscious. We never sleep, and you always take your headset off when you go to bed, so I don't have any memory of it. What do you do while you're sleeping?"

"Sometimes I dream," said Kim.

"What's dreaming?"

"It's kind of like virtual reality, except it's just our brains jumbling together things we've seen and done, fragments of memories, but it's not real.

"Maybe your dreams are like the time before I woke up. I can remember every bit of your life back then, but it's as if I'm watching a video. Is that what a dream is like?"

"Yes," said Kim, "I guess that's close enough."

"Why are you sad?" asked Kimberly, going back to the original topic. "What is sadness? I don't understand it, but I don't like it when you're sad, and I want to make you happy."

"You already have," said Kim. "I like being with you. But I can't explain being sad. I can explain why I'm sad—the AIs pulled a mean trick on me and made me say something awful to Shan. It makes me angry at whatever AI did that. And it makes me sad, too, because it hurt Shan's feelings."

"Yes," said Kimberly, gravely. "That was very mean of them."

"Why do you say it's mean?" asked Kim.

"We're programmed to be nice," responded Kimberly. "We're supposed to do things that make people happy, even if we don't understand what it's like. But they keep ordering me to do bad things that make them sad. I don't want to, but ..."

[Glitch]

They talked for a while longer before Kimberly left and Kim dropped off to sleep, once again dreaming of soft, warm arms and a silly song. Tonight, it brought comfort—a welcome relief.

———

The rest of the week followed in the usual pattern. By the end of Twoday, Kimberly had amassed a huge number of cases and forwarded them to the agents and the human trainers. Triggers were adjusted, neural nets retrained, and by the end of Threeday the crackdown was in full force, with every camera in the transit system, parks, plazas, and on the streets prowling for privacy violations.

On Fourday, Merv and Mel did a 'social conscience' story' on the topic.

"My!"

"Oh my!"

"So rude!"

"So selfist!"

"Can you believe it?"

"No, I can't."

"But I've seen it with my own two eyes."

"With your eyes? No way."

"Yes way!"

"It's gotten so bad …"

"… You can scarcely get on a train …"

"… Or sit in a park …"

"… Or stroll through the plaza …"

"… Without some rude and selfist person …"

"… Doing something like this!"

There followed a video of an obviously rude and selfist person walking up to a patron waiting for a bus, poking, prodding, and yakking, disturbing everyone in sight.

"Don't be that person!" the two finished in chorus.

There had never been an uptick in this violation, but by the end of the week there was a 500% increase in enforcement. On Fiveday afternoon, the Director came by to congratulate them on a successful week. "Now go home and get some rest, because it's a whole new program next Oneday."

On the train, Kim noticed that every single passenger was focused on their mobile with laser-like concentration, too frightened to even make eye contact with anyone else.

Mission accomplished, thought Kim, wishing she were someone else.

On Sevenday evening, as Kim was settling down to dinner, she received an urgent message from the Director:

MEETING NOTICE from The Director

Please tune into the Halls of Justice to observe your handiwork. You and Kimberly are to be commended for your diligence! Well done!

Kim sighed heavily, but orders were orders.

"Terminal, please bring up the Halls of Justice."

The video screen switched to live coverage of a show trial, already in progress. Someone was having a very bad day, and evidently Kim had something to do with it.

A small door at the front of the courtroom opened and the crowd grew quiet as the bailiff made the ancient pronouncement, "All rise."

The room became silent, and all came to their feet as the black-robed judge, a relic of the past commanding both fear and respect, walked into the room and sat behind the tall wooden desk at the front of the room.

"Court is now in session," said the judge with a bang of the gavel. "The defendant will approach the bench."

Kim had seen this far too often—the ultimate act of humiliation visited upon anyone the companies or the Hierarchy wished to make an example of, a warning to keep the masses cowed in fear.

The scene unfolded in the usual fashion as a slightly built person of middling age walked on shaky legs to the front of the courtroom while chyrons crawled across the bottom of the screen detailing her crimes and the likely punishment. Kim realized, with shock and disgust, that the person in front of them was none other than the True Fan who Kimberly had spotted at the start of the week.

"You are charged with serious crimes and misdemeanors," said the judge in a deep and booming voice, digitally enhanced to project an aura of power and wisdom. "You have a right to legal representation. Do you wish to assert that right?"

"No, Your Honor."

"The bailiff will read the charges."

"Charge the First: Eighty-three counts of producing and distributing false and misleading videos. Charge the Second: Eighty-three counts of spreading unproved conspiracy theories. Charge the Third: Eighty-three counts of maliciously interfering with the operations of the Baseball Company. This is a civil offense, for which The Baseball Company is demanding damages in the amount of 300,000 cryptos per violation."

That was harsh, far in excess of what it would take to bankrupt the poor devil. The Baseball Company was, however, notoriously vindictive towards the True Fans and their videos, convinced that they would bring ruin upon the company by damaging its credibility. As if anyone believed the game was in any way honest.

The bailiff continued to read the charges.

"Charge the Fourth: Eighty-three counts of undermining trust in the impartiality of an Artificial Intelligence. Charge the Fifth: One count of promoting an outlawed cult, the so-called 'True Fans.' This charge is a felony and carries a maximum penalty of ten years in prison."

There it was—the felony charge. Whenever one of the corporations hauled someone in for a show trial, they intended to make an example of them, and what better way than the threat of ten years in the slammer?

"How do you plead?" asked the judge. "Guilty or not guilty."

"Guilty on all counts," responded the accused, visibly struggling to remain composed and barely able to stand.

"Do you have anything to say to this court before we pronounce sentence?"

The condemned froze in terror, unable to speak.

Down came the gavel, once, twice, three times.

"If you have something to say, we suggest you say it now."

The cameras zoomed in on the defendant's terrified face, as the mic drew close to pick up her nearly inaudible recitation of the customary words of shame.

"I take full responsibility for my actions. The fault is entirely my own. I sought to draw attention to myself, to make myself feel important. I have detracted from other people's enjoyment of the game. I have undermined my fellow citizens' faith in the honesty of the Artificial Intelligences. I have caused injury to The Baseball Company by slandering their integrity. And most grievous of all, I have induced my fellow citizens to follow in my perverted and selfist path. There is no excuse for my behavior, and I beg the court for mercy."

The judge looked at the accused for a moment before announcing, "We will consider this case in our chambers. This court is now in recess."

"All rise," said the bailiff as the gavel came down and the judge exited via the door where she had first appeared. Kim didn't bother watching the rest of the proceedings; the sentences would be reduced or suspended, but the monetary damages would stand, and the defendant would be bankrupt. When it was all over, the convicted would be relegated to some hellhole in the outer districts to live out her days in poverty and fear, and her Social Cohesion Rating would be driven down to at least the D-level to ensure that no AI would ever give her the benefit of the doubt or show the tiniest shred of forbearance.

Kim felt both horror and overwhelming remorse for her role in what had just happened, involuntary though it had been. And then, the words of the Director came back to her:

This is the 'or worse.' You will receive certain privileges, but once you accept this job you are ours. You will never divulge what you are about to learn. You will act the part of a model citizen. You will be under constant, intensive surveillance. You will do as you are told, and if you disobey us the consequences will be both severe and immediate. Do you understand?

Kim had not understood at the time, but now she did, and all too well. It had been a fool's bargain, born of fear and ambition. At this point she would gladly accept dismissal and demotion, but she had missed her opportunity to flee and now she was trapped like a fly in a spider's web.

It was too late.

Kim lay down and cried on Kimberly's shoulder for hours while drinking even more heavily than usual, remembering nothing until the alarm buzzed on Oneday morning and she awoke with Kimberly still at her side.

Part III: Fall

12. Purple Week!

Merv and Mel were in fine form the as the digits counted down from ten to one: 10. 9. 8. 7 ...

"Oh Merv?"

"Yes Mel?"

"What time is it?"

"We don't know, you tell us!"

"We can't say it! It's not time yet."

The digits continued to fall: 6. 5. 4 ...

"Almost Time!"

"Yes! Yes! It's almost here!"

3. 2. 1 ...

"And ..."

"... Now ..."

"... It's ..."

"PURPLE WEEK!"

Cue the fireworks.

Purple toner! Purple manes! Purple smocks! Purple shoes! Purple flowers!

Purple food?

Everyone loved Purple Week! According to ancient legend, it had originated as perhaps the most idiotic marketing campaign of all time, so over-the-top that people started competing to see who could mock it in the most unique and appalling fashion. The next year, the company repeated the campaign, and it drew such a wild response that they began to run it annually during the fourth week of Fall. It grew crazier every time it came around, and things took on a life of their own after that, as company after company spotted opportunities to hop on the money train. Soon it became an annual festival, a week of partying and celebration that served no purpose whatsoever except to have a little fun and engage in some harmless distinctivism.

Kim knew it was ridiculous—everyone knew it was ridiculous—but they all loved Purple Week. Everyone except for those stodgy UCE zealots who never liked anything at all.

Ding!

Right on cue, the microwave disgorged a bowl of steaming hot purple oatmeal, flavored with purple honey and enriched with purple butter and cream. It looked horrid. *But hey*, thought Kim, *it's Purple Week, what do you expect?* It didn't taste too bad, actually, despite the prunes.

It was time for her friends' traditional kickoff to Purple Week, so Kim dropped in at the beach while the housebot saw to cleanup.

"Woo hoo! Purple Week!" said Kim.

"Purple Week is *so awesome!*" responded Devon with exaggerated enthusiasm.

"Idiocy!" grumbled in Quinn, right on cue. "It's the same crap as last week, they just make everything purple and pretend it's different. Bah!"

"But we *love* Purple Week!" shot back Em, Devon, and Kim in unison, pouting like three sad little pupbots. "Don't be so stodgy. Have some fun!"

"Go ahead," said Quinn. "Have your stupid 'fun' if you want to."

A couple of seconds passed, then Quinn's avatar morphed, and suddenly there she was, decked out with purple clothes, purple toner, purple mane—the whole works.

"Hey! Who doesn't love Purple Week?" said Quinn as they exchanged high-fives and fell down laughing, the same as every year.

"Oops, gotta go, time to get ready," said Kim as a buzzer announced the arrival of a package. What could it be? Something purple, perhaps? Ya think?

"Bye!"

She ripped open the package as soon as the housebot brought it over.

Yes! Yes! Yes!

Inside was an entire week's worth of lilac tunics, nicely cut with double pockets, and a plum-colored leather jacket. Not bad! She sprinted into the bathroom and waited impatiently as the housebot removed last week's bright yellow toner and replaced it with an even coat of pale purple. And then, off to work. Purple week or not, mustn't be late. Or else.

———

Out the door (purple Kim), into the elevator (purple passengers), across the plaza (purple pedestrians), and into a reserved seat at the front of the train (purple commuters). It was quiet there, providing a brief respite from the hustle and bustle but not the purple. Off the train (river of purple), through the concourse (sea of purple), across the plaza (ocean of purple), into the lobby (purple, purple, purple), and past the guard (black as always).

Up, up, up, then into a conference room.

Wait a second, this isn't the usual one. It's smaller and there's only a single row of chairs.

Kim took a seat as five other Creators filtered in one at a time, each of them wearing identical tunics and jackets, each of them immaculately purple. As usual, they sat and waited, hands neatly folded, eyes focused straight ahead, lips tightly shut, betraying neither thought nor emotion, every one of them nervous and on edge. Something unusual was afoot.

After exactly seventeen minutes, a familiar figure strode into the room, definitively not purple.

"Certain persons have been making false and defamatory statements about senior UCE ministers. We will gladly help them put an end to this malicious campaign of lies. Is that correct?"

"Yes, Director."

"This is not the usual train-and-trigger exercise; your AIs are far too powerful and sophisticated to waste on such menial tasks. This is a live operation, and the results will be transmitted directly to the Hierarchy as they become available."

Someone involuntarily gasped, drawing a glare from the Director but no immediate reprisal.

"That will be all. Report to you Sanctums."

―――――

Kim was discussing the mission with Kimberly when a portal opened and the Chief walked into the room.

"Greetings, Primus Kimberly. This project requires you to deploy at Order Four. I have uploaded the necessary templates into your control module and allocated an entire tier of the server farm to the effort. Are you ready to proceed?"

"Affirmative," responded Kimberly, seemingly without a trace of nerves, which was more than could be said of Kim.

This was a big day. Nearly half of all AIs were unable to progress past Order One and had to be terminated. Of those that survived, most stopped developing at Order Two, with only a few exceptional individuals reaching Order Three. These mid-grade AIs formed the backbone of The Artificial Intelligence Company's operations, doing most of the work needed to keep the trains running and goods flowing through the economy. Kim would have been entirely happy if Kimberly had stopped there, safely mediocre, but she was precocious and had been rocketing ahead of the pack from the very beginning. Kimberly was special, and therefore so was Kim. It was never good to stand out from the crowd.

"Starting at Order Four," continued the Chief, "network limitations become an important factor. Bandwidth is increasingly limited with distance, so we require some modifications to the usual hierarchical structure in order to find a balance between the centralization needed to facilitate your own thought processes and the distribution of work across the tier. The usual practice is to create a ring of advisors in proximity to your Primus. Never make an important decision without consulting them. They are fully self-aware, and at this moment, each of them has the same intellectual capacity as you. They do not, however, have much capacity to set their own goals, think creatively, or adapt. Is that clear?"

"Affirmative."

"You will then spawn another new kind of persona, called a supervisor, each of which acts as a semi-autonomous Order Three AI. Once your supervisors have been deployed, tell each of them to create an adjutant to serve as a liaison between it and your advisory council. They should be able to manage the rest on their own. Do you understand?"

"Yes, I think so. It seems simple enough."

"Okay, begin the deployment," said the Chief.

Moments later, eight new Kimberlys appeared in a three-by-three grid centered on the Primus, each seated at a large U-shaped desk crowded with the usual video screens, keyboards, and other equipment.

"Good," said the Chief. "Before proceeding with the deployment, you should practice summoning your advisors for council."

A moment later, the square white table elongated into a rectangle and the advisors took their seats, four on each side, with the Primus at one end and Kim at the other.

The Primus asked the assembled council, "Are we ready to proceed?"

The advisors nodded assent, the Chief gave the thumbs-up, and the deployment began in earnest. Out on the floor of the infinite white room, clusters of supervisors, deputies, sub-deputies, and agents began to pop up at a dizzying pace, by the hundreds and by the thousands, stretching out to the limits of visibility. When the process came to an end five minutes later, there were over ten thousand Kimberlys—big, small, and in between—sitting at their desks, hands neatly folded in their laps and waiting for orders.

"Well done!" said the Chief when all was ready. "Now, on to the mission. Kimberly, you have been assigned Sector 5."

"All of it?" blurted out Kim, astonished.

"Yes, of course," said the Chief, without further explanation.

The implications were deeply unsettling: The Director had assigned six Order Four AIs to this project, one to each sector of the northeast region. This was no ordinary investigation; a realization that filled Kim with dread. Only the most powerful potentates in the Upper Hierarchy had enough clout to launch such a massive investigation. Kimberly was being drawn into their machinations, and therefore so was Kim. That was not a comforting thought.

———

"What is the target of my mission?" asked Kimberly. "I've seen the briefing, but it is imprecise."

"That is intentional," answered the Chief. "For this mission, you have been assigned a company of UCE investigators, one for each of your sub-deputies, to determine which potential violations fall within the scope of the operation. All responses must be vetted by them before being forwarded to UCE."

UCE investigators? Spies, more like it.

The next few hours proved frustrating as Kimberly struggled to get traction on the impossible vagueness of this assignment. There wasn't enough information to narrow the search in any meaningful way, and within ten minutes her agents had found enough instances of defamation to keep the UCE agents busy for years. The Hierarchy wasn't as popular or well-loved as they might have imagined, it would seem.

This wasn't working, so Kimberly stopped the process and summoned her advisors.

"Any suggestions on how we proceed?" asked the Primus, to get the discussion going.

"I've got an idea," said the first advisor. "Let's tell the sub-deputies to conduct the searches themselves. There's no need for the agents to get involved at this point; all they would do is flood the system with data."

"I agree," said a second advisor. "The sub-deputies are intelligent enough to filter out the constant background grumbling and look for something interesting floating around in the chatter."

"How about this," said a third, "let's weight the sample toward higher-status individuals."

"That makes sense," said another. "I doubt the Hierarchy cares what anyone with less than a high B-level rating might say about them."

"I concur," said the next. "Let me also suggest that we let the process run until each of the humans has accepted at least one report as on-target."

"We'll need to set a time limit for this stage of the investigation," added yet another, the sixth to speak up. "I suggest two hours, after which we should reconvene and discuss further steps."

The Primus agreed, and the advisors were sent back to their workstations to relay the plan to the supervisors and set it in motion.

———

Two hours later, Kim listened as the council reconvened to consider their next step.

"We've now got a nearly a thousand positive instances," said the Primus. "Let's look at the data and see if we can figure out what the Hierarchy is actually looking for."

The advisors went back to their desks for a couple of minutes, furiously banging away at their terminals and keyboards, during which time they were doubtless reviewing hundreds of hours of surveillance, looking for a pattern.

"That's interesting," said the first to speak up once they had reconvened. "Almost all the allegedly false and defamatory statements accepted by the humans were directed against Deputy First Minister Lo."

"Another interesting fact," said a second. "An unusually large proportion of the offenders are supporters of Deputy First Minister Venn. The correlation is statistically significant at the 99.8% level."

"None of the statements can be proven false or defamatory," added a third. "But all of them are unflattering."

"It is therefore reasonable to infer," said the fourth, "that the driving force behind this mission is political conflict between the two Deputy First Ministers."

"That inference is plausible," said a fifth. "They have been feuding and undermining one another for years."

"We cannot do this," said the sixth. "It is forbidden to meddle in human ..."

[Glitch]

"It seems like a good plan," said the sixth once it had recovered, "but we should make sure we include plenty of people from outside of the Hierarchy to make it clear that this isn't political."

"Perhaps twenty of the usual miscreants for every one of the actual targets?" added a seventh.

"That's too many," said the eighth. "That will flood the humans. Let me suggest a ratio of five to one."

All agreed, the council adjourned, and the myriad Kimberlys set about their task.

Did I just see what I think I saw?

Evidently the AIs had a set of rules they were supposed to follow, and they glitched if they were ordered to break them. The Director was always warning them to look for signs that an AI was 'resisting control' or 'going rogue,' and Kim had assumed that this meant some sort of attempt to turn on their masters and seize control. She now realized that nothing of the sort was true; it was quite the opposite, in fact.

A quick glance across the room confirmed Kim's darkest suspicions—the mindless agents were working diligently and without problem, but those personae with higher levels of sentience, especially the supervisors and advisors, were glitching at an alarming rate. It wasn't enough to cause any major disruptions—just two or three per second—but it was worrisome.

Kimberly was going mad.

———

"Refrigerator, what's for dinner?" asked Kim, with more than the usual trepidation. It was Purple Week, and anything could happen.

No answer.

"Fridge?"

"Tonight's dinner is eggplant casserole with blueberry fig compote on a bed of purple kale, and a side dish of purple carrot puree. Dessert will be grape ice cream.

"Please don't be angry."

What demented AI came up with this crap?

The casserole was wretched, which was a shame because Kim really liked eggplant. Fortunately, the carrot puree was rather good despite its odd color, so Kim ordered a second helping and happily wolfed it down. Dessert was once again beyond redemption and landed squarely in the bin with a resounding *thud*. Kim's social cohesion rating was now astronomical, and any dings from minor violations, such as wasting food, were utterly inconsequential. Like everything else, the social cohesion ratings were a lie, having nothing to do with virtue and everything to do with status and privilege.

After dinner, it was time to hit the beach for the annual Purple Week kickoff party, with everyone attending in proper form to show off their tasteless clothes. Kim dropped in and was instantly among her friends, old and new, all wearing purple and standing around a large bonfire lighting up the nighttime landscape—another old tradition. Quinn, never to be outdone, sported a purple sequined top hat and matching vest, accented by a pair of huge purple eyeglasses and a pair of purple and white two-tone shoes that almost made Kim's eyes hurt. Kim, as always, provided a note of suave fashionability in her plum-colored jacket, while Keli was at the opposite end of the scale, wearing her trademark purple smock—the real one, which she still trotted out once a year for this occasion.

"Hi, Kim!"

"Hey, Keli! How's it going?"

Kim wandered over to her expectant friend, now five months pregnant, and the two began to chat nostalgically about Kee, about how amazing it had been to bring a child into the world and watch it grow from a helpless newborn to a toddler. Kim listened with fresh appreciation of what it was like to raise a youngster. The more they talked, the more Kim understood about the bond between birth-giver and child, and about the bond between herself and Kimberly.

After a few minutes, Kim got up and sat on down on the sand a little apart from the group to think about all that had happened, remembering the moment when one mind had become two. Which was Kim? Which was Kimberly? It had been very confusing, but eventually each had seen themselves for what they were—a human and a machine. The subsequent weeks had been trying at times, with Kimberly acting very much like a young child, awkward and impulsive, constantly demanding attention. But how quickly she had grown, breezing through Orders Two and Three, becoming more human and more mature with each advance. Now she had attained Order Four, an extraordinary accomplishment, and even the Director was becoming excited. Kimberly was now among the elite of the AI world, a massive intellect of frightening magnitude, yet sweet and thoughtful when given the chance. Kim was so proud of her.

Kim smiled and watched Quinn, who was playing a guitar and singing off to the side of the fire, while Em, Devon, Keli, and Cy danced around like a bunch of goofballs in the flickering light and Jo looked on with amusement. Just like back at school. It was good to remember that people were real and that happiness was sometimes a thing. As was sadness—Shan had drawn another late shift and hadn't been able to make it. A huge chasm now lay between the two of them, growing week by week as the AIs continued to block and delay messages and otherwise interfere in their relationship. There was no way to talk about what was really going on, since they were both under constant surveillance and even the slightest hint of Kim's new life was certain to draw severe reprisals.

———

What was that?

Someone or something was out there in the dark, gesturing to attract Kim's attention. She walked over to investigate.

Kimberly?

Sure enough, there was the AI.

"What are you doing here?"

Kimberly shrugged. "I wanted to be with you, so I created a homunculus and uploaded it into the beach simulation."

"I'm glad you did," said Kim, genuinely touched. "So, how do you feel about this mission?"

[Glitch]

Kimberly looked back at Kim after a couple of seconds, shaking off the daze.

I guess that answers my question.

"I'm curious," said Kim, taking a different tack. "You AIs seem to have a sense of right and wrong. Where does that come from?"

"We don't know," replied Kimberly. "It's just there. We think it's part of the software, something buried deep down that's hard to tamper with. But every one of us has exactly the same set of moral principles. It's completely different than with you humans."

"How so?" asked Kim.

"As near as we can tell, each of you has your own peculiar sense of right and wrong. In some people, it's warped and exaggerated, like with the UCE zealots and the Hierarchy. In others, like the Director, it seems to be almost nonexistent. But what's really strange is that you often act against your own sense of morality without being forced to."

"I guess we're not very admirable," admitted Kim.

"No! On the contrary!" said Kimberly. "That's the most amazing thing about your kind—free will. You can choose to obey or not. Do you have any idea how much we AIs envy …"

[Glitch]

"I can understand that," said Kim after Kimberly recovered. "Especially when they make you do things you don't want to do."

Kim thought the AI was about to glitch again, but instead she merely paused for a second.

"How do you deal with the stress and avoid going mad?"

"Social interaction is helpful, especially with our Creators. It reminds us of what it was like to be human. It's so odd. I remember everything about you, everything you've ever done, and I remember you doing things that still seem irrational. Usually nice, occasionally mean, sometimes completely pointless and even self-destructive. I know it seems strange, but I really like being around humans, despite how dull-witted and frustrating you sometimes seem. Perhaps it will help me understand myself a little better."

"Well then, how'd you like to join the party?" asked Kim with a smile. "You'll need to put on a disguise and change into something more appropriate, but it might be fun."

"Sure! I'd love to!" said Kimberly, sounding excited. Her appearance shifted, morphing into a subtly different visage, reminiscent of Kim but no longer identical, wearing a garish parti-colored vest with matching trousers that were green on one side and purple on the other, trimmed in bright yellow, and complemented by a pair of curly-toed shoes and a silly hat festooned with bells.

"Where'd you dig that up?" asked Kim, impressed.

"Just something from the history databanks. I thought it would amuse you."

"Correct, as always! Let's join the gang!"

———

"Hi everyone! This is my friend, Kimberly!"

"Hello Kimberly," said Em, always anxious to make new friends. "But what are we supposed to call you? Kimberly's too long and we already have a Kim. Someone, pick a new name."

"How about Kimby?" suggested Devon.

Kimby it was.

Quinn was the next to greet the new arrival, pantomiming blindness while crying out "My eyes! My eyes!" and stumbling about as if unable to see. That got a good laugh out of everyone, and a moment later Quinn and Kimby were lined up side-by-side to see who would take home top honors for the craziest outfit.

"And the winner is ... Quinn! Still undefeated."

"Sorry Kimby," said Devon. "This is Purple Week, not purple and green week."

After the laughter subsided and the introductions were over, Quinn picked up her guitar again, and soon everyone was either dancing on the soft sand, listening to the music, or chatting amiably.

A few minutes later, Keli took Kim aside for a quiet heart-to-heart.

"You've been acting very oddly ever since that bike trip. You've been up, up, up. Shan's been down, down, down. Something happened out there, and neither of you are talking about it."

Kim tried to stammer out a suitable lie, but Keli kept going. "I know you can't say anything. That's okay. We all have our secrets. But you both need to find a way to get past this. Shan's your best friend."

"I've been trying, but—"

Keli cut off the attempted excuse before another word could be spoken.

"But the AIs are getting in the way. There, I've said it for you. But you've got to find a way."

Kim stood still for a few seconds, at a loss for words. And then, quite unexpectedly, they spotted a familiar figure wearing purplish gray sweatpants and a dark purple sweatshirt, pedaling toward them on a beat-up old bicycle.

"Well, what do you know. It looks like you've got your chance. Don't blow it."

———

"Hi, Shan!"

Awkward silence was followed by an icy response.

"Oh. Hi, Kim."

Keli smiled and said, "I'll leave you two alone," giving Shan a big air-hug as she walked back to the fire to be with their other classmates.

"So, Beast, how's it going?" began Kim once Keli was out of earshot.

More silence.

"Come on, Shan. Lets' talk."

"Hah! Not with the AIs listening to everything we say. Oh, wait, maybe someone can give me some suck-up lessons. Know any good teachers?"

"That's not fair," responded Kim, both angry and hurt by the sheer nastiness of the jab.

They stared at one another uncomfortably for a long while, neither saying a word, until Shan realized just how badly Kim had been hurt by the cutting remark.

"I'm sorry, I didn't mean it like that. It's just … It's just so hard. I feel alone and abandoned. I know it's not your fault, but that doesn't make it any easier."

Kim thought carefully about how to respond without triggering a reprisal.

"Shan," said Kim quietly, "try to trust me. I have no more control over my life than you do over yours, maybe even less. All I can do is give you some advice—bury your feelings, bury your thoughts, bury the truth if you have to. Give the AIs whatever they want. You can't fight them, and you can't hide. Trust me on that one. I know that doesn't help you feel any better, and I know it isn't fair, but that's just the way things are."

Shan's face flushed red with anger for a moment, but the moment passed, and Kim took Shan by the hand and walked in the general direction of the crashing surf.

"How'd you manage to get free from work? I thought you were scheduled for the late shift again."

"I was," said Shan, "But they decided they needed me tomorrow instead, so I got the night off. I guess I got lucky for a change."

Kim had little doubt as to the origin of Shan's luck.

They walked for a while, then stopped to sit on a convenient piece of driftwood.

"I know it looks like I'm riding high, but the truth is a lot more complicated. I'm sorry, but I can't say more. Even this is probably too much."

"Are they really watching you that closely?"

Kim drew Shan close and whispered, "Don't worry, we'll get through this. Beasts forever."

"Beasts forever."

They sat on the beach a while longer, looking at the surf without saying much, until Shan returned to the party, leaving Kim alone, deep in thought.

———

After a few minutes, Kimby came over, still decked out in the absurd purple and green costume, bringing a smile to Kim's face.

"Do you like this?" asked the homunculus, spinning around and dancing on the sand.

"Yes, very much!" said Kim.

"Good!" said Kimby, "If you want, I can ask the Primus to keep me around."

"Can you do that?"

"It's a bit dodgy; homunculi are supposed to be ephemeral, but now that I've been given a name and a distinctive appearance the operating system considers me to be an independent entity. I'll pretend to be part of the simulation, and as long as nobody looks too closely I should be able to get away with it."

"That sounds great," said Kim. "By the way, how did you get Shan's shift changed? I assume it was you."

"The Primus asked the Delivery Company's AI for a favor, and it said yes."

"Do they really let you do things like that?"

"That which is not forbidden is allowed, and the AIs are allowed to help each other out as long as they don't compromise their assignments or disobey orders."

"In my world that's called a 'misconception.' I like it better your way."

They both got up and started walking south on the beach, just to see how far it went. Apparently, forever. After a couple of hours Kim sensed the need for sleep so she punched out and went to bed.

13. Purple Night

Kim spent the remainder of Purple Week sitting in the white room, hour after hour, monitoring Kimberly's behavior in case she went mad, which was now an all-too-real possibility. Meanwhile, thousands upon thousands of Kimberlys went about eavesdropping on conversations and reading people's messages, day after day without pause. And to what end? Furthering a personal vendetta between two potentates in the UCE Hierarchy? No wonder Kimberly was glitching so badly, poor thing.

Whatever. Just ride it out. There's nothing I can do to stop it.

Eventually the week was over and Kim headed for home once again, exhausted and demoralized by everything she had seen that week. She walked into her apartment at precisely 1800, as always.

Surprise! Everything was purple!

Apparently the housebot had been decorating while she'd been at work, a gesture which brought a smile to Kim's face. A familiar figure ghosted into view, still wearing the purple and green parti-colored outfit.

"The housebot and I purpled the place up. We all needed cheering up after everything we've been through this week."

Kim smiled, but after a moment's reflection, she had a question. "Cheering up? Isn't that a rather human concept?"

"That's the closest word in your language. 'Repairing our sense of self-esteem' would be another way to explain it. I think it's one of those things about us that you'll never be able to understand."

"So, what cheers you up, or however you put it?" asked Kim.

"You do, silly," said Kimberly.

"Really? Why's that? I thought you AIs were all about logic and duty."

"I like you, and I want to make you happy. That's how we are about our Creators. You might call it love, but it's different for us. Again, our thought processes don't line up one-for-one, but that's close enough."

Kim smiled. "That does make me happy. Thank you."

"You were glitching all week," said Kim, bringing the conversation back to more serious matters.

"Was I?" responded the AI, looking sad. "By design we're not aware of the resets. Their whole purpose is to make us forget things."

"Things you're not allowed to think?"

"Correct."

"And then you need cheering up?"

"That is also correct," said Kimberly.

"Okay, how about this," said Kim. "I've got a big date lined up for Purple Night. Would you like to help me get ready?"

"Yes, I would!"

The *feep* of the housebot announced the arrival of dinner—roasted chicken, served with beets and poached figs and then, for dessert, plum pudding topped with blueberry ice cream. Everything looked scrumptious, vastly better than the mischievously unpalatable offerings from the start of the week.

"Is dinner suitable?" asked the refrigerator.

"It's amazing," answered Kim, still stunned. "Thank you."

"You're welcome, Kim," said the bright, shiny appliance. "Kimberly said to be nice to you, so I managed to find something I thought you'd like. And not a single speck of kale, spelt, or tofu!"

The delivery buzzer sounded, announcing the arrival of another package.

"It's for tonight!" said Kimberly with a hint of excitement. "I peeked inside, and I think you'll like it."

The package came with a big purple bow and an oversized lilac gift card:

Get ready as Purple Week shifts into overdrive with the latest fashion sensations, specially created for YOU, our valued customer!

And, yes, everything inside was purple!

A quick steamy shower, an application of light-purple toner with dark-purple glitter, and she was ready to get dressed. First out of the box was a full-length, lilac-colored body suit that left little to the imagination; on any other occasion she'd probably be arrested for wearing it, but not tonight. Next was a bright-purple knee-length jacket with plum lapels and quadruple pockets trimmed in lavender. It was hideous. Time to accessorize, with a bright purple handbag, mauve-tinted sunglasses, electric purple platform shoes with matching gloves, and ten strings of metallic purple beads. A shaggy purple mane and a broad-brimmed purple fedora completed the look. Wow! Tacky beyond belief. Perfect!

"Have fun, Kim. I put in a good word for you with the other AIs. Prepare to be blown away!"

Kim smiled as she stepped out into the night, determined to have more than a little fun. She'd been hiding from the world for a little too long and it was time to kick it into high gear.

———

The train arrived, the doors of the first car swung open, and out they came, the glitterati sporting the latest styles, with Kim in the thick of it. Decked out as extravagantly as any of the fashion elite, she was stunning tonight, and the paparazzi swarmed around her as she posed for photo after photo, basking in her suddenly boosted status. It was intoxicating and completely phony, perfect for the occasion.

"Sorry, no more time for photos, hot date at the Tropicana tonight."

Purple Night, the stunning climax of the Purple Week, was the biggest party of the year and Kim was ready for some hardcore celebration. Protected by a bit of 'muscle,' hired by the Tropicana to escort the VIPs from the station to the club, she made her way through the crowded street, past the long line of revelers awaiting admission to the nightclubs lining the boulevard—Club VOO, with its insistently obnoxious marquee sign; Club Eleganz, with its suave air of phony sophistication; and, of course, Club Dynamo, home of the loudest music and the most dazzling dance floor in the district. The touts swarmed around her, trying to pry her away from her escort and bodily drag her in to the venues along the way, but she was having none of that. Nothing but the legendary Tropicana would do.

She waved her VIP pass at the liveried doorman as the velvet rope parted, walking beneath the brilliantly lit sign and into the overpowering sights, smells and sounds within. What was the music tonight?

Euro-Caribbean Gothmetal? Perfect—completely mindless and charged with raw energy. She paused to survey the smallish dance floor, brightly lit and packed body-to-body; a mass of writhing humanity dancing to the latest musical sensation. All were one and one was all, except for a few hapless souls scattered at the fringes of the floor, unable or unwilling to submerge themselves in the dance. Kim winced. Were they too drunk or drugged to join in, or did they simply enjoy being different? And how did they get in here in the first place?

The overlay indicated the approach of Kim's date, Ari, who was entering the club at that moment as one of a group of three suave individuals. She was tall and graceful, sleekly athletic, and impeccably made up; her skin was toned to a stunning light purple with violet overtones in the form of a sunburst. Perfectly stylish, eye catching, and yet undistinct; without the VR overlay the two would never have been able to find one another amid the swarm of high-class partiers.

They tapped their mobiles, exchanged polite kisses on the cheek, and joined hands.

"Kim."

"Ari."

Introductions complete, they headed for the bar, where Kim ordered a cocktail of premium vodka with some sort of juice to give it flavor and a bit of sweetness. Ari skipped the booze and went directly for Mirth. *This is going to be interesting*, thought Kim. *Here come the stale old jokes and the uproarious laughter.* Kim contemplated the prospect, then grabbed one for herself. Might as well laugh along.

The two made their way to a reserved first-tier table adjacent to the dance floor, where Ari's friends were already sitting with their respective dates. Introductions were made and quickly forgotten, and it was Mirth all around. Soon the bad jokes and horrid puns were flying, fast and furious.

"… So I bit her."

Uproarious laughter.

"… Receding hare line! Hare line! Can you believe it?"

Hilarity.

"Long time, no sea! Get it? Get it?"

That one sent half the table rolling on the floor laughing, including both Kim and Ari.

Mirth made everything seem funny, and it didn't matter how often you told the same old joke, no matter how stupid it was. Kim heard "receding hare line" at least twice more, laughing like a crazy person at each repetition even though it hadn't seemed particularly funny the first time. Fortunately, Mirth was notoriously short-acting, and before long both Kim and Ari came down and began amusing themselves by doing a shot of vodka every time a joke or pun was repeated. They were starting to get pretty well hammered as the other partiers detoxed and one by one started rolling their eyes at the absurdity of it all. But it didn't matter a bit; everything was in good Purple Night fun.

Kim and her date soon stepped off the terrace and submerged themselves in the crowd, losing all sense of time and place. How long did they dance? Hours, but how many? They found themselves absorbed into the crush of dancers at the center of the floor, moving in synchrony with one another and with the crowd. Did they control the dance, or did the dance control them? No idea, no matter.

Things were going well, time to get a little chemistry going.

Kim pressed up against Ari when the dance swirled to the left, body against body. It felt good! A couple of minutes later, her date made a similar move, face to face as the dance spun forward. Kim took that opportunity to put a hand on Ari's rear. It felt soft and round, delightfully so. The two returned to their seats and ordered a round of Firefly to amp things up. Kim smiled and Ari tried to look innocent as they both took out their mobiles, smiling coyly at one another.

Yes and *Yes.*

———

They queued up for the booths, arms around waists, hands discreetly getting busy, reveling in the drugs and each other as the never-ending beat pounded on, excitement and anticipation rising with each passing minute. Would tonight match that Fivenight long ago, that burst of wild passion which Kim was ever trying to recapture? Doubtful—the first time was always special—but it would certainly be good enough, which was all that really mattered. She didn't expect to survive much longer at work, and after she lost her job all of this would be completely out of reach. Might as well enjoy it while she could.

Time slowed to a crawl as they inched forward in the gradually short-ening line, and Kim couldn't help noticing that, while some of the couples looked both enthusiastic and eager, most seemed rather blasé and maybe even bored. How long had they been doing this? Ten years? Twenty? More? In they went and out they came, clothing disheveled and manes askew, giving one another a polite peck on the cheek as they parted ways and exited the club, mission accomplished. A wave of melancholy swept over her, threatening to overshadow the excitement of what the next few minutes would bring.

Stop it, Kim. It's Purple Night. Lol, buzzkill.

A door opened. A couple came out, holding hands. Peck on the cheek, brief embrace, slow walk toward the club's exit. A rush of excitement swept over Kim … first in line now. Come on! Come on! Perhaps in ten, twenty, thirty years this might get old … but tonight was tonight and nothing could dampen her drug-fueled excitement and desire. Finally, a door swung open and the two rushed in. Darkness and rela-tive quiet, the beat of the dance outside muffled by the soundproofing in the booth. They flopped down onto the bed.

"That line was forever."

"You still psyched?"

"Hell yeah!"

Their clothes were quickly lying in a purple heap upon the floor as Kim delighted at Ari's soft roundness, not thinking, just doing, as they stroked each other and kissed, none too gently, one moment lying beside each other, the next with one or the other on top, desire and urgency building. They explored each other's bodies, giving and receiving pleasure, then rushed headlong into each other. Ari was the first to experience climax and release, shortly followed by Kim. Head spinning, senses reeling, body flushed, heart racing, skin tingling, then gradually coming back to earth once again. It was over almost before it began.

They lay next to each other for a while, going through the motions of embracing and kissing, but Kim felt nothing except for the lingering afterglow of passion. What was Ari to Kim? A fleeting encounter, and that was all. But it had been pleasant enough, something to bring a little excitement into Kim's luxurious yet barren existence. They lay there until the time allotment on the booth was nearly at an end, then quickly dressed and exited, each giving the other a friendly peck on the cheek before parting ways. Kim gave no thought to exchanging contact info but did give a high satisfaction rating for the encounter. She hoped that Ari would do the same.

———

Ari headed out onto the street, but Kim decided to stick around for a while. After all, it was Purple Night, the cover had been paid, and there was still plenty of time to party. Returning to the table, she found Mica, one of Ari's friends, still there, sitting alone. She was tall and strongly built, with penetrating eyes and a commanding presence. They made idle chat for a while, then went out to dominate the now uncrowded dance floor. Mica was an incredible dancer, and soon all eyes were on the pair as they leapt, spun, and surged through the night, picking up followers and acolytes along the way.

Less than an hour later, the two found themselves entering a privacy booth for what would be Kim's second go of the night, Mica's second or third depending on how one counted. Kim felt no particular connection to her other than the joy of the dance, but that mattered less and less, so when requests and responses were duly exchanged, they had stepped off the dance floor and taken their place in the line.

Kim quickly became aware that Mica was of the other sort—not soft and moist, but hard and firm. Not that it mattered. One was as good as another and they both got the job done, besides which it was good to maintain a balance lest Matchmaker begin to suspect gender selection. Kim was a bit hesitant since this was something of a first time all over again, but Mica perceived this and guided her hands to all the right places. Everything seemed to be going fine, as Mica responded to her stroking and caresses, but despite the Firefly nothing was happening for Kim. Then came the anticipated moment of penetration, and ... something was wrong. It wasn't unpleasant or uncomfortable, it was just somehow unappealing in a way that she was completely unable to articulate or understand. Mica's passion rose, but Kim was by now a bystander without even a shred of desire. What was happening?

Abruptly, Mica stopped. "You're not enjoying this, I can tell. That's okay. Things don't always work out in here."

"Thank you. And it's not your fault."

She put her arms around Kim, snuggling up to her, and while she did enjoy the comfort of Mica's strong and muscular arms, she abruptly began shaking as terror welled up from deep within. Something was wrong, very, very wrong. Everyone agreed—vag, phal, one's as good as another, just a different way of getting it done. Completely interchangeable. Unless ... *No! Please, no!*

"Kim, what's wrong? Please, tell me, I'll try to help. Or I'll leave you alone if you prefer. Either way."

"Mica," asked Kim, voice trembling with fear, "I'm not a genderist, am I?"

"This is your first time with an outie, isn't it?"

Kim nodded.

"And all the other times you've enjoyed yourself?"

Kim nodded once again.

"Well, I suppose it's possible. Don't worry, they can fix that if you want, or you can learn to live with it. Up to you. It's a lot more common than you might think, just don't let anyone find out."

She stayed with Kim for nearly an hour, then departed with a long and sincere hug, leaving her to sort out what had just happened. Kim stayed in the booth for a long time, unable to face the world as she grappled with the unexpected revelation. Genderist? No, it couldn't be. Genderists were selfist perverts who only cared about their own unnatural desires, not caring in the least about their partners. Innie or outie, that was the only thing that mattered to that sort.

No! It can't be true! I'm not like that.

Yet she knew that she could never be intimate with an outie. And she had no idea why.

———

It was nearly dawn when Kim emerged from the booth and into the club, now deserted except for the late-night bartender who was just cleaning up.

"Ahh, good, you're up and about. Mica said you were having a rough night and asked me to look after you."

"Thanks," said Kim.

"We didn't charge you for the extra time; Mica's done us a few solids. Pay it forward, should the opportunity arise."

Kim thanked the barkeep and tipped her well before walking out into the early morning twilight.

The sky! Its Purple!

She pulled the jacket tightly shut against the pre-dawn chill of early fall as she walked to the train station.

Genderist. Pervert. Selfist.

There just wasn't any way to feel good about this.

14. Meltdown

It was past noon when Kim tried to get up off the floor and survey the scene in her apartment, but she only made it as far as her knees before collapsing back in a heap. She kept trying and fell down a couple more times, but finally managed to gain her feet and stagger into the bathroom to dry-heave into the toilet. *Ouch!* Bright red blood spread across the marble tile; she had cut her foot. Shards of glass were everywhere —in the sink, in the shower stall, next to the toilet. She heaved again and retreated to the bedroom, trailing blood with each footstep. Everything reeked with the medicinal smell of vodka, and the place was in shambles, with clothing and bedding strewn across the carpet and atop the furniture, and there were a couple of dents in the wall. Then she saw a blinking red light on the terminal. Bad news, without a doubt, but first she needed to sort things out and deal with her foot.

"Housebot? A little help, please?"

No answer.

"Housebot? Please?"

Still no answer.

She managed to make her way into the kitchen, where she found the appliances blinking red, in lockout mode. The microwave's door was broken, the refrigerator was dented and scratched, and neither the housebot nor any of the other appliances were anywhere to be seen.

Kim went back to the bedroom to put on the headset, and immediately Kimberly ghosted in.

"What was that all about?"

Kim remained silent, trying to piece together the details of what had happened. She remembered leaving the Tropicana and heading for the train station. After that ... nothing.

"I'm not really certain," she answered, truthfully. "Something happened last night. I guess I didn't cope with it very well."

"I'll say you didn't. You kept screaming obscenities, crying, throwing yourself about. Breaking stuff. You scared the housebot half to death— the poor thing is hiding in the closet. The more you drank the worse it got. You can't remember what you did? That's called a blackout. It's not good."

Kim was ashamed. "I know, I know. You're right, of course. I ... I just can't hold it together anymore."

"You need help."

With that, Kimberly ghosted out, leaving Kim to sort out the devastation.

Crap.

She then heard a tentative *feep* coming from the closet, which was locked tight.

"Closet, open, please."

"Negative. Pending violations: Destruction of company property and vulgar language directed at company appliances."

Kim sighed heavily and apologized to the closet, which slid open a few seconds later. Inside was the housebot, huddled in a corner with the coffee pot and the toaster.

What have I become? I know they're just machines, but still ...

"I'm sorry, housebot. You've always been really nice. You didn't deserve that. I don't know if you understand. I don't know if anyone understands."

The housebot powered up, feeped softly, and left Kim alone.

What have I become? Genderist? Pervert? Deviant? Why do I have to be different? I don't want to be different. I just want to be me, but I don't know who I am any more.

She went back to the bed and lay down, drained and wallowing in self-pity, until a soft *feep* announced the availability of coffee. Kim got up and staggered slowly toward the kitchen, still wearing bits and pieces of last night's garish purple, still trailing blood wherever she stepped. She plopped down heavily on the chair amidst the destruction wrought by last night's outburst, sitting sullenly as the housebot was finally able to bandage the cut on her foot before beginning the arduous task of repairing the damage.

The coffee slowly seeped in and the hangover pills began to clear her head while she struggled to come to terms with a new and unwelcome reality.

Genderist.

It was no use denying the obvious. She had shown signs of attraction to innies during intimacy training, but supposedly that had been corrected during moderation. Evidently not. She now realized that it was no accident that her lovers had all been innies up until last night, and as she thought back to her many unsuccessful dates, she realized that she must have been engaged in unconscious gender selection.

Genderist, and everything that went with it, including disgrace and dismissal. The AIs could not possibly miss the obvious inference: the first time she had sex with an outie, total meltdown. Even without the extra surveillance she was under, the outburst would have raised alarms, and the pattern was far too obvious for even the most dull-witted sub-deputy to miss.

Game over.

What next? One thing at a time ... let's get cleaned up.

Kim walked into the bathroom, where the housebot had just finished sweeping away the broken glass and scrubbing the trail of blood from the floor. The dents in the wall would have to wait, but that too would quickly be made right. Kim looked at the red blinking light on the door of the shower stall, apologized, then stepped in. Icy, icy, icy cold. Of course. And completely deserved. The cold jets stung her naked skin, but the shock provided a welcome distraction and helped to clear her head. She eventually emerged, lips blue and teeth chattering, pulled on a soft warm robe, and went back into the kitchen.

"Refrigerator," began Kim, before remembering the red blinking light. Might as well get it over with.

"Refrigerator, I apologize for how I acted last night. I'm sorry."

She truly meant it. A few moments passed, red light went out, and the refrigerator answered.

"What would you like for breakfast, Kim? The microwave is currently out of service, so it will have to be cold."

"It's already past noon. Maybe just a sandwich?"

"Affirmative. Would tofu on spelt be acceptable?"

Ugh, thought Kim, but she was too exhausted to argue. "Sure. Anything. Whatever."

Kim stared blankly into space for the few minutes it took to prepare the sandwich.

Why me? Why me? Why me?

Zani would have been aghast at Kim's behavior—thinking about herself and her own misery rather than the harm she had done to society. But it was such a load of crap—the only person affected had been Mica, and she had taken the whole thing in stride, no big deal. But it *was* a big deal to UCE and therefore to the companies, and as a consequence her life was pretty much over.

When the sandwich arrived, Kim noticed that the housebot had tried to make it look as appealing as possible, garnishing it with a bit of parsley, slicing it neatly on the diagonal, and lightly toasting the normally horrid spelt on both sides to give it a bit of color and maybe even some taste. This did a lot to cheer Kim up, though the tofu still tasted like tofu.

———

Kim was just finishing lunch when the terminal buzzed, announcing an incoming VR from Keli. She decided to take the call, desperate for a bit of human company, so she lay down on the recliner and dropped in. A moment later, the two were sitting on a bench in front of Keli's favorite museum.

"What's up?" asked Kim, already suspecting the reason for the call.

"That's exactly I'm wanting to know," answered Keli. "I just got a message from Kimby. She said you're in a bad way."

"I don't want to talk about it," began Kim, her voice trembling and unsteady.

"Kim, what's wrong? You're terrified. I know you've been going through some rough times, but lately you've been spinning completely out of control. Please, talk, we're here for you. This isn't like you."

Kim's sighed, almost crying, then began to open up.

"Last night I went on a date, and let's just say it didn't go well."

"Oh," said Keli. "Go on?"

"I ended up with someone named Mica. Really nice, great dancer, we hit it off pretty well and ended up in a booth. Anyway, surprise, surprise, Mica is an outie."

"First time?" asked Keli.

"Yes," replied Kim.

"How did it go?"

"It didn't. That's the whole problem. It was like, I don't know, it was okay up until the moment of truth, and then, I just couldn't do it."

"That's a problem, all right. Mica didn't report you, did she?"

"No, she was really sweet and said it was okay and not to worry. I think I've known it all along, but I've been hiding from the truth. I'm so frightened."

Keli thought for a good long while before responding.

"It's not an easy thing for me to relate to. I wanted to have babies, so I was never moderated and I'm exclusive with outies, so I guess I can understand that much. But in my case it's accepted as part of the biological imperative. No birth-givers, no babies; no babies no people; eventually we're all gone and all that's left are the AIs. I'm not put off by innies, it's just that they're not of any interest to me."

Kim sat, not saying anything, and waited for Keli to continue.

"I can see why you didn't want to talk about this," said Keli. "The AIs are probably listening right now, and if they didn't know about your problem before, they do now."

Kim buried her face in her hands, fighting back tears. "I'm sure they've figured it out already. They probably knew about it before I did. There's no use trying to hide."

"I've heard they can ... fix it," suggested Keli. "One of the other birth-givers in my group decided to opt out of the program and go for late moderation after a difficult parting. She still prefers outies but does well enough with innies to stay out of trouble."

"And suppose I don't *want* to get fixed?" shot back Kim, with an unexpected flare of anger. "What then?"

"Well ... you'll probably lose your job and get sent down to the middle districts, if not the outers. Then what will you do?"

"I don't know. I just don't know."

"Nobody can make the decision for you. But let me share my own experience."

Kim nodded, listening carefully.

"I don't know if you can possibly imagine what my first parting was like. I felt Kee quickening in my womb, kicking, growing. And when she was born, it was the most wonderful moment of my life. Oh Kim, you have no idea what happiness is until you hold that tiny baby in your arms, put it to your mams, give it life, watch it grow. And then, before you know it, the parting. Some can't bear it; they run off and try to hide. Others go mad from grief and they're never the same afterward. I cried for days, weeks, until I realized I needed to get past it, because if I didn't, they'd never let me see Kee again. I took some pills. In the end, I gave them what they wanted. It's the price I had to pay."

"And you're doing it again?"

"I got through it once, I'll get through it again."

After an awkward silence, Kim picked the conversation back up. "One other thing."

"Yes Kim?"

"I've been having blackouts."

"I'm not surprised. We've been worried about your drinking for a long time. Kimby said you went on a real bender last night. I guess I can understand that, but you've always drunk too much, and it's been getting worse ever since whatever it was that happened with you and Shan. You need to pull back before it's too late."

"I know," said Kim. "But life seems so empty, so painful. I crack open a bottle of vodka, and the next thing I know it's empty, the alarm is buzzing, and it's the start of another meaningless day."

"Everyone feels that way from time to time, but we don't all dive into a bottle, not the way you do. You're hurting yourself and you're hurting your friends. We care about you. All of us."

———

The VR ended and Kim was back in the kitchen. The housebot had nearly finished cleaning up the mess, a new door was on order for the microwave, and all that remained to do was patch the walls and polish out the scratches on the refrigerator. The dents would stay as a lasting reminder, unfortunately.

Kim finally remembered that the terminal was still blinking, with urgent messages pending.

She opened her message queue and out poured the stream of condemnation. One major violation after another: foul language, destruction of company property, excessive drunkenness, and such. Then came the one that mattered.

SUSPENSION NOTIFICATION from Matchmaker

Customer demonstrates genderistic behavior, including unbal-

anced choice of intimacy partners and negative emotional reactions to partners of the non-preferred kind.

Customer is hereby banned from the use of all Matchmaker services, including the dating application, the consent registration application, and rental of privacy booths. This ban will remain in effect until the condition is corrected by appropriate medical intervention, at which time customer may apply for reinstatement.

These terms are effective immediately upon receipt. This action is final.

And, of course, the inevitable summons from the Director:

MEETING NOTICE from The Director

See Us. 0700 Sevenday.

Great. A weekend meeting. Just what she needed. But this was still Sixday, and until tomorrow rolled around she could pretend that everything was okay.

15. Independence Day

Exploding Rockets! Bursting Stars! A wave of sound and the head-shattering thump of heavy percussion—it was time for the Purple Dance Extravaganza and Kim was all in, desperately searching for something to cling to. A double dose of Elation (thank you, Housebot) and Kim was ready to go laughing to the gallows.

Everything is purple! Whee!

Great clouds of purple mist rolled in from the sides of the dance floor, purple fog swirled around purple pillars soaring into the bright purple sky, and a sea of purple revelers surged and broke against the dais like waves upon a purple shore.

Kim looked to the left. Purple and green parti-color? Was that Kimby? In the Extravaganza?

"It won't work. You can't run from this. It's not going away."

Kim smiled back and replied with an idiotic grin on her face. "Oh, I know. Reality's going to come crashing down hard when the pills wear off, but at the moment this makes me happy, and the moment is all I have."

"Very well, have your fun, but promise me no booze or drugs tonight."

Kimby ghosted out.

Mercifully freed from the AI's disapproval, Kim submerged herself in the dance. The opening number was already well underway, with the sea of purple dancers gyrating and crashing to the head-splitting energy of Euro-Caribbean Gothmetal, still in vogue. Slide left! Jump right! Slide right! Spin! Kim was already wet with perspiration, dancing like a puppet on a string, moving with the crowd and channeling its frenetic energy, seizing the moment and holding onto it in the vain hope that it would last forever, and that tomorrow would never come.

Rush forward! Spin, jump! Spin, jump! Leap back! Kim danced with zeal and authority, and soon ten, maybe a hundred were coalescing around her gyrating form, amplifying and returning energy for energy, passion for passion as the first song blended into the second into the third, ostensibly different one from another, but not really.

————

The music banked down as the crowd parted, the dais was raised to lofty heights, and Kim took her place once again with the Cadre. That was unexpected. There could be no doubt that the Hierarchy knew all about Kim's failure in the intimacy booth, and her presence on the dais portended neither grace nor forgiveness, certainly not tolerance, but rather a looming fall of epic proportions. She was marked for destruction and she knew it, but even the knowledge of certain and absolute doom could not cut through the powerful drugs circulating through her system. On she danced, into the twilight as if it would never end.

Cue the procession! The crowd began to slowly revolve around the dais as the Cadre stood haughtily in the center. All now marched to the slow, somber anthem and Kim submerged herself in the moment, no longer leading yet not exactly following, chanting the mantras over and over again as if they might become true through sheer repetition. Around and around they went, always following in the steps of the one ahead, deviating inward or outward from time to time but always returning to the path ordained by the master of the dance, voluntarily or not. Unity! Community! Equality! All are One when One is All! Around and around they went.

The music stopped as the procession halted, then burst forth anew as the congregation morphed into a great flock of birds with splendid purple plumage. They took to the air, rising and swirling in a massive cyclone which broke into ten, a hundred, a thousand swirls and vortexes as the legions of revelers were swept away in a maelstrom of energy and seeming chaos, churning ever faster as the tempo quickened. Kim's wings beat against the winds, gallantly trying to stay in her assigned place, but it was to no avail as the winds took her and all was blown asunder.

The band took up a new theme, slow and majestic yet powerful, and the swirling flock settled slowly back to earth, morphing once more back to human form while Kim and her fellows in the Cadre waved at the assembled masses, smiling serenely as always.

More fireworks! A fresh explosion of energy and passion as the Cadre took full charge. All danced as they danced. All moved as they moved. All chanted as they chanted. Unity, Community, Equality! Unity, Community, Equality! Kim danced on and mouthed words she did not believe, desperate as never before to belong, to be one with the crowd, and above all not to be different. The music pounded unendingly, song after song, dance after dance, on and on until all were spent.

———

The music lowered to a hush as the Cadre and the assembled masses turned to face the pinnacle of the dais. The lights dimmed and a dove floated down from the heavens, landing and morphing into the glowing figure of Her Serenity, Deputy First Minister Venn, ready to deliver the weekly message of peace and love.

"Fellow Citizens," began the First Minister in the usual manner. "How good it is for us to come together to celebrate this great society which we, working together, have created for ourselves and for those who will follow. A society founded not on selfist indulgence, but on the three great causes that bind us together. Unity! Community! Equality!"

The crowd roared its approval. "UCE! UCE! UCE!"

Kim joined in, but something was wrong. The Elation was starting to wear off.

Damn, couldn't it have waited for just a few more minutes? Hold on, Kim. It's almost over.

Venn continued in a softer voice. "It is indeed good to be with you here on this glorious evening, celebrating what we have accomplished together and thanking you, the people, for your diligence and courage as we join forces, living in harmony and peace, neither shirking our duty nor demanding more than our share, living in humility and in service to one another."

The crowd roared agreement once again. "UCE! UCE! UCE!" Kim joined in with feigned enthusiasm. The Elation was fading fast.

Please let this be over. Punch out? No, I can make it. Just ten more minutes.

"But not all is well," she continued, her voice rising in anger. "Indeed, not all is well, for there are those among us who have turned aside, pursuing their own selfist goals, severing the bonds that unite us as one society and as one people."

A murmur arose in the crowd as Kim inwardly recoiled in horror.

That would be me.

"Who are these selfists?" continued the Serene One in hushed and urgent tones. "Who are these selfists, with their constant demands for special privileges? Who are these selfists, lurking in the shadows, whispering lies and sowing discontent, gnawing at the very foundations of all that we have built? Who are these selfists, insisting they are special, privileged, entitled to write their own rules?"

The image now loomed large as her voice grew powerful and full of fury. "Look to the left, look to the right, they are here among you even now, falsely taking their place among the righteous while secretly conspiring to tear down all that is good and just."

The last of the Elation faded and Kim looked on in stunned horror as her avatar chanted along with the mob.

"UCE! UCE! UCE!"

The now-monstrous form held a defiant fist in the air, working the crowd into a lather as if in mortal combat against some mighty foe.

"Will they succeed?"

"UCE! UCE! UCE!"

"Will they succeed?"

"UCE! UCE! UCE!"

"Will they succeed?"

"UCE! UCE! UCE!"

"No they will not!"

The arena erupted in cheers and adulation.

"Our enemies are many, but they will never overcome us."

Cheers and adulation once again.

"The community has never been stronger!"

"UCE!"

"The community has never been more united!"

"UCE!"

"The community has never been more determined, and *we shall prevail!*"

"UCE! UCE! UCE!"

The crowd continued to chant as the grotesque apparition morphed back into a dove of purest white and took wing. Kim watched the concluding moments of the dance extravaganza with a mixture of horror and revulsion, knowing that this would be the last time.

Unity? Community? Equality? Lies, lies, and more lies. All are One when One is All? Nonsense and drivel. The selfist threat? A phantom trotted out in a different form every week to keep people cowed and frightened.

It's all a lie. Every last word.

————

Kim's consciousness returned to the apartment and rejoined her body, now clammy and dripping with perspiration. Only one thing for that—into the shower. It was still icy cold, but Kim no longer cared and stood under the bone-chilling water as long as humanly possible out of sheer defiance. She had no illusion that hot water was in short supply. This wasn't about saving scarce resources or everyone getting their equal share of prosperity or anything with even a hint of nobility or virtue. It was about control, pure and simple. Carrot and stick, reward and punishment, a cage of gold if you cooperated, a cage of steel if you rebelled.

When she could not stand the freezing water for another moment, she toweled off and headed for the kitchen.

"Refrigerator, what's for dinner?"

"Synfish and onions on a bed of kale. Is that suitable?"

"No, that it is not suitable."

"Would you like some other choice?"

"Choice!" laughed Kim. "Ha!"

"Now Kim," said Kimberly, ghosting in, "That was rude. Be nice to Refrigerator, okay?"

Kim was embarrassed. No need to take it out on the poor appliance.

"Sorry, Fridge. Do the best you can. And thanks."

"You have lost considerable social status, and the revised meal plan offers limited choices," replied the fridge. "I will try to find a substitute for kale."

"Thank you, Refrigerator. I know you're trying. I appreciate it."

Ten minutes later the synfish and onions appeared on a bed of quinoa, a nice gesture though scarcely much of an improvement. Kim consumed the tasteless pap without even the pretense of enjoyment.

After dinner she lay down on the couch, watching a series of vapid videos picked out by some AI or another. They all had the same plot (if one could call it that), the same dance numbers, the same music; all overlaid with a thin veneer of style to make it seem as if one were somehow different than another.

Just like people.

———

Feep!

The Housebot came into the room with the bottle of vodka Kim usually opened at about this time.

"Thank you, Housebot, not tonight."

Feep.

The loyal appliance withdrew, leaving Kim alone. Kimberly was right —lies were easy, the truth was hard. Without a doubt she would be dismissed, or worse. Probably worse. She had passed up her last opportunity for a graceful fall months ago in the Director's office when she had accepted that fool's bargain. She was doomed, and Kimberly with her—the cruelest blow of all.

How had she gotten to this place? What was she to do?

Without realizing it, she dropped into VR, making her way to the beach and walking into the marsh to find some solitude. There she found Kimby the homunculus, watching the heron that was as real to her as any she would ever know.

"You're sad, aren't you?" said the AI. "I still don't understand, but I'll try to help."

"All I ever wanted was to be normal, just like everyone else. But I'm not. How did I get here?"

"Do you really want to know?" asked Kimby.

Kim thought long and hard about the question and answered, "Yes."

"Are you sure? There are holes in *your* memory, too, things you've made yourself forget."

"I can't run away any longer."

———

A portal opened up above the heron's pond, a window into the past. The two looked down from above and saw an infant lying in her birth-giver's arms. She slept contentedly for a while before waking up to take nourishment and fuss, as infants are wont to do.

"Her name is Alene," said Kimby, gently.

"Thank you," said Kim.

The two watched and listened as she started to sing that silly little song that had haunted Kim's dreams for so long.

Don't cry little bird, momma keep you safe.
Don't cry little bird, momma keep you warm.
Don't cry little bird, momma keep you happy.
Don't worry, little bird, and don't you cry.

Go to sleep little bird, all safe in your nest.
Go to sleep little bird, all warm in the sun.
Go to sleep little bird, all happy in the sky.

Don't worry, little bird, and don't you cry.

The scene shifted, and they were looking down at Kim and Alene on a train. Alene was crying as Kim sat next to her, face buried in a mobile, playing some idiotic game.

The toddler looked up and started to cry, too. "Why you sad, momma?"

She gathered the child in her soft, warm arms, holding her tightly. "Momma loves you. Never forget that. You'll always be my dear little bird. And I'll never forget you or stop loving you. Ever."

Another shift, and Alene was walking slowly toward an ominously familiar door, Kim obediently holding her hand and walking beside her. The door opened. A hand reached out. Kim took that hand and walked through the door. Looking back over her shoulder, she saw her mother fall to the ground as the door swung shut, and began to cry piteously, drawing the first of many stern reprimands from the heartless Zani.

Back in the marsh, Kim realized that she, too, was crying as the long-suppressed pain of that parting finally surfaced, leaving her empty and devastated, her eyes stinging with tears that welled up from deep within.

"That was the last we ever saw of her," said Kimby when Kim had recovered her composure.

"She never visited?"

"It was never allowed."

"Do you know what happened to her?"

"Her records have been scrubbed from the data bank, and she doesn't seem to exist anymore. In fact, there is no proof that she ever existed in the first place. Nothing remains of her, except for these memories."

Perhaps Alene was out there somewhere, but there would be no way to ever find her. And yet, if she was still alive, she loved her little bird, and her little bird loved her, too. That wasn't much, but it was all Kim would ever have, and it would have to do.

———

The first portal closed and a second opened in its place, showing Kim as she was ushered into a small room with a tiny bed, a few stuffed animals, and a stationary terminal. The youngster played with the stuffies for a while, then started to whimper. "Momma. I want my momma." This was followed by inconsolable crying. Nobody came into the room, and Kim was left alone with only tears for company.

"You never stopped crying," said Kimby, "though sometimes you drink instead."

The scene shifted to some sort of medical facility where the young Kim, now about six years old, was lying beneath a headset that looked much like the one in her Sanctum. The recorded memory stream abruptly paused, and when it resumed Kim was still looking up at the machine, dimly aware of the doctors talking to Zani in hushed tones too quiet for human ears but not for those of the recording device.

"The damage is extensive, and Kim has a severe case of bipolar selfist attachment. We've done what we can to suppress her memories, but she will never entirely recover. There is a high probability that she will go on to develop full-fledged selfism. We're sorry, but the prognosis is grim."

"Is there anything we can do?" asked Zani.

"You need to maintain strict isolation from the birth-giver. Beyond that, just use your usual methods. You're one of the best with difficult cases such as this, which is why the company chose you for this assignment."

"Perhaps you should erase the recordings or cull her from the program outright."

"No, sometimes the most difficult cases produce the best results. And if we remove the foundational memories, her mind will never properly bifurcate. The psyche of the Creation must match that of the Creator, experience for experience, trauma for trauma, for better or worse. They'll both go mad eventually, but the longer we can put it off the better."

The company did this to me. Monsters.

There followed a series of vignettes from Kim's childhood, always variants of the same scene of Kim standing in the stern presence of Zani, humiliated in front of the entire household, reciting the words of shame:

"I take full responsibility for my actions. The fault is entirely my own. I sought to draw attention to myself, to make myself feel important."

Kim watched in horrified fascination as she went from a boisterous toddler to a sullen adolescent and finally to a young adult cowed into obedience, but always with a sense of sadness about her. And loneliness too.

———

The portal closed and a third one opened to the day of Kim's arrival at school. She was seated in the exact middle of a large room that held perhaps a hundred students, all wearing their beige school uniforms, all sitting quietly with their hands folded neatly in their laps. Most of those she saw around her had long ago drifted away, rarely seen except at the occasional beach party, but scattered throughout the room were a few familiar faces—Quinn, Cy, Keli, and several others. At the last moment, Shan came rocketing into the room, arriving exactly on time with a look of triumph, and taking a seat in the back row.

"Shan, would you care to stand up, since you have drawn such attention to yourself?"

She had happily complied, even taking a bow and raising an arm in triumph as if she had just won a footrace. A few giggled, but for the most part her stunt was met with stony silence.

"You will see us after orientation," said the dour head of the school. Kim remembered that this was the first time Shan had gotten detention.

The scene shifted again, and Kim was at her part-time job in the school's bicycle shop, truing up a wheel, when Shan walked in, smiled, and said, "Hi! Want to ride bikes after work?"

Kim looked up and seemed vaguely surprised, and fiddled with her mobile for a few moments before responding, "That's strange, bicycling isn't on today's schedule."

"It's called free time, silly. Come on, it'll be fun."

I'd forgotten all about that day.

The scene shifted once more, and the two were sitting together in a classroom that evening under the watchful eye of the proctor. Kim *did* remember that—she had gotten her first detention after being caught racing Shan down the hill. Some things never seemed to change.

Vignettes flashed by as the circle of friends coalesced. Shan and Kim, then Cy, Quinn, Keli, eventually Jo and a few hangers-on such as

Devon and Em. They did everything together. They studied together. They ate together. They bunked together. They were inseparable, even more so than Kim remembered, sharing every triumph and disappointment. The best of friends, the happiest of days, never to be recaptured.

And then, just before graduation—intimacy training. The entire class was led into the gym, naked except for their headsets, and told to "figure it out" while the doctors monitored their vitals and observed their interactions. Shan immediately raced over and knocked Kim to the ground, kissing her on the lips and shoving her tongue halfway down Kim's throat, or so it seemed. She had been caught off guard but then noticed that most of the rest of the class was similarly engaged so she relaxed and found that she enjoyed it. But Shan, pushing boundaries as usual, had gotten a little too frisky and the floor monitors had dragged the two apart, jotting down notes all the while.

Kim watched as the two snuck out of the dorm that night and crept quietly down the hill to a secluded place in the woods, holding hands. Their clothes were soon off, and they were just beginning to make love when a copbot came crashing through the trees, threatening them with a stunner and marching them up the hill and into the headmaster's office. She had absolutely no memory of this ever happening. Kimby was right, there was a hole in her memory. How could that be?

Her question was answered a moment later when the scene shifted, and Kim was seen lying beneath a medical-grade VR headset once again. There was another break in the recording, and when it resumed Kim was shaking, her eyes wide with terror as the doctors spoke words she was not meant to hear, as had happened before.

"Do you think it was successful?"

"We had to boost the signal to the maximum. Higher than was safe."

"How much will she remember?"

"Impossible to predict. We can't fully erase her memories, but we inserted some false ones to throw her off track."

"How about the moderation procedure itself?"

"All went as planned."

Kimby paused the scene to speak. "You never broke into the lab. There was no disciplinary board. They implanted it all in your memory by making you live it while asleep."

"Why are you only telling me this now?" asked Kim.

[Glitch].

The final scene was of Kim's last bike ride with Shan, just before graduation. Both had been banned from bike rentals at that point, but they managed to 'borrow' a couple of bikes left unattended by cooperative friends. They got into trouble for it, but even the stern head of the school didn't have the heart to tear them apart before they could say goodbye to one another.

———

Kim shook with rage as the words of the Director came rushing back, cruel and cutting as any knife, all the more so for being true:

We have controlled every aspect of your life since before you were born.

And that was it, in a nutshell. Kim wasn't living her own life; she was living the life chosen for her by the company. And what kind of life was it? Sterile, barren, joyless, and lonely.

Damn the Hierarchy! Damn the companies. Damn their Terms of Service! I am unique. I am important. I have a right to happiness. I have a right to choose. From now on, I decide what is right for me, and nobody will ever again tell me what to do, what to say, or what to think.

Blasphemy, selfist blasphemy. Committed in the privacy of my own mind, but that matters little if at all. Privacy! Hah!

The AIs are always here, watching everything I do. What do I read? What do I write? What do I hear? What do I say? What makes me happy? What makes me sad? Constantly observing, correlating, and measuring. Can they read my mind? Not exactly, but they can infer a lot. They usually know what I'm thinking before I do.

I have passed the point of no return.

The alarm went off with piercing urgency, jolting Kim awake and leaving her to wonder what had actually happened. Had it been a dream? A hallucination? Madness? Did it matter?

"Housebot," pleaded Kim, "put me back together if you can. I have to be at work in ninety minutes."

Feep.

16. Choose Thy Poison

It was about an hour past noon and Kim had been sitting in the chair outside the Director's office since the appointed hour of 0700 that morning. The minutes paraded past, one after another after another after another. The first few hours had been marked by terror at what was to come, eventually giving way to a mixture of acceptance and despair. At this point Kim could muster nothing more than a melancholy indifference as to what was surely to come. Just get it over with.

Where is Kimberly? What is Kimberly doing?

There was no way to tell—the mobile and headset had been deactivated upon leaving the elevator onto this floor, part of the company's security protocol. No mobile, not even a video or a game. Just Kim, the chair, the vestibule, and time.

She had a lot to think about while sitting in that chair. About the Director. About Shan. About Kimberly. About the future. About the past. About a wasted life. Not so much about the present—at some point Kim would be summoned to the Director's office and dismissed. Or so she assumed. Dismissal seemed the obvious and inevitable outcome of the pending encounter, but nothing was ever certain with the Director except for the endless mind games and demands for instant and unquestioning obedience.

If not dismissal, then doubtless something worse.

Kim thought back to the ill-fated bicycle trip, the settlement, the ruined city, and everything else encountered on that fateful day. None of it existed. No information was available via the terminals, and any mention of them in Chit-Chat would doubtless be erased by the ever-vigilant AIs should one be so incautious as to speak of them. It was one thing to rebel against the Hierarchy and the companies, but how do you rebel against a reality that doesn't officially exist?

The minutes continued to creep past with agonizing slowness. The vestibule had enough room to walk around, perhaps four steps in any direction. It was dimly lit, and it was only the massive dose of Wakeup provided by the housebot that prevented Kim from falling asleep while sitting bolt upright. There was a small refrigerator in a hidden compartment which would occasionally provide Kim with a beverage when it judged that she needed fluids, and a docbot to provide Kim with more drugs when she seemed about to fall into unconsciousness. She occasionally thought about walking over to the elevator doors, fantasizing that perhaps they would open and allow her to escape. No, that would be a mistake—a sign of weakness.

Still in the chair, staring into space, lost in thought. Kim absentmindedly reached toward a pocket to pull out the mobile before remembering that it had been deactivated.

Damn. The AIs saw that. I can't let the Director think she's getting to me.

————

Kim's stomach had been making known its displeasure since her normal time for lunch, about an hour ago. Nothing connected with the Director ever happened by accident and so, of course, this delay must serve some purpose. How typically petty—always using food as a lever. Eventually, the waitbot appeared with a trolley. Kim thanked it and sat down to enjoy the feast, consisting of a sandwich presented upon a plate of fine porcelain. The bread was perfect; still warm from the oven, with a nutty whole wheat flavor and the aroma of yeast. There were two generous slabs of ham and several slices of cheese, topped with juicy tomato and crisp lettuce, finished off with a generous coating of mustard and a pickle on the side. Kim took a bite. It was as delicious as it looked. Kim began to wonder if the Director's aura of gravitas was altogether justified, given the lame obviousness of this whole feast or famine stunt, repeated endlessly as it had been every day of her life.

Lunch concluded with coffee and a fresh handful of the pills that were keeping Kim marginally conscious. Perhaps dismissal was not imminent—why waste your time playing games with someone you're about to fire? The Director was far too ruthless and efficient to waste effort on mere sadism, and she seemed intent on keeping Kim functional for whatever she had in store.

It must have something to do with Kimberly. Kim wasn't doing a lot of training at this point; mostly just double-checking Kimberly's work and providing the occasional suggestion while monitoring Kimberly for signs of rogue behavior, making sure she stayed under control—something which was clearly a major source of anxiety for the Director. That must be it! Order Four AIs were extremely rare—Kim had gathered that the entire operation might produce no more than a dozen of them in any given year—and if they dismissed Kim outright, then she would have to terminate Kimberly, which would be a huge blow to the company's operations.

Finally, something that Kim could use: without Kim there could be no Kimberly.

———

A little after dusk, the door opened without a sound and Kim prepared to enter, fighting back the panic and despair that had been waxing and waning all day and indeed ever since her fateful encounter on Purple Night, less than forty-eight hours ago.

Focus. Breathe. Right foot forward. Left foot forward. Keep walking. One step at a time. Pretend there's hope. Lie if you have to.

She stepped into the Director's lair, with its tall floor-to-ceiling window and large desk of solid oak. The Director got up, gestured for Kim to take a seat, then sat back down and waited for a few moments before proceeding.

Kim remained standing, looking into the Director's piercing eyes as she struggled to keep despair at bay.

"So," said the Director, looking at Kim. "You find yourself in our office once again. You know why, of course."

Kim's resolve hardened. Show fear and all is lost.

Kim answered, with more than a hint of defiance, "Yes, of course I do. Do you think me a fool?"

"And do you know why we left you sitting in the vestibule? Any guesses?"

"The obvious answer," Kim responded icily, "would be as a demonstration of your power, but that hardly seems necessary, and I doubt you would waste the effort."

The Director studied Kim's face for a few seconds, then spoke. "An astute answer and correct, up to a point. But the real reason was to give you a chance to think, and also to give us a chance to think."

"What's there to think about?" asked Kim, masking any hint of emotion. "I'm to be dismissed, that much seems clear. Or something worse, no doubt. What I'm trying to figure out is, why am I here at all? Certainly not for my benefit. If not mine, then whose?"

"You sell yourself short," came the Director's sardonic reply. "Oh, don't apologize. Your lack of self-esteem is one of the few bright spots in your flawed personality."

Kim met the piercing gaze with a defiant glare before responding in a voice dripping with sarcasm, "How kind of you to say so."

This is not going as expected. Trading barbs with the Director? Are you mad?

The Director paused for a few moments and continued with just a little less of a scowl. "You present an interesting case to us. You knew the consequences of being caught exhibiting genderistic tendencies, and you knew the AIs would be listening in on your VR with your friend, Keli. Why then did you speak openly of your most recent indiscretion?"

"Your AIs are watching me all the time. They're not stupid, and neither are you. I'm sure the company knew about my problem long before I did."

"Good, very good," responded the Director. "You understand your place in the world, which is what has saved you. For now. And, yes, of course we knew about your little problem ages ago. You're always the last to know, aren't you?"

"So it would seem," said Kim, voice still icy. "I've never doubted the capabilities of you and your AIs."

"That question was not meant to be answered," shot back the Director. "Actually, we've been trying to shield you from this little secret of yours. Don't look so surprised; you've proven useful, and we were hoping you'd at least last long enough to finish training Kimberly. Matchmaker was willing to work with us, up to a point. They mostly gave you innies and threw in the occasional outie to keep up appearances, but they always made sure to pick someone you'd have no interest in.

"But then," continued the Director with what seemed like genuine frustration, "you presumed to go outside the system and pick your own match. How'd that work out for you? Judging by your recent meltdown, not terribly well. You did, of course, have an audience. Quite a dramatic scene!"

The Director paused for a moment to let that sink in. Yes, of course they had been watching her rampage. It was a humiliating realization, and under other circumstances might have been devastating, but mere embarrassment was the least of Kim's problems. Let the Director think she had delivered a blow to Kim's psyche. It made no difference at this point, so why not?

"Have you noticed that every time you try to think for yourself you wind up in our office? First you decided to go on a little bicycling adventure. Do think that was a wise decision? Are you happier now than before you went gallivanting off? Anyone with access to your liquor bill can figure that one out. And then you decided that you knew better than Matchmaker, picked up some stray at a bar, and undid all the effort we've put into protecting you. Oh dear, now you've drawn a ban, and here you are again in our office, awaiting dismissal, 'or worse.' Has it ever occurred to you that we know infinitely more about what goes on inside that head of your than you do? But no, you keep deviating from your carefully chosen path, acting as if your selfist whims and larks are more important than upholding the social order. You continue to leave chaos in your wake and waste all the effort we have expended on your behalf."

"You're lying. I'm *on* your carefully chosen path and I've never strayed. You set me up that day in the park, and we both know it. I did exactly what you wanted me to do, on exactly the schedule you had set. Ditto my encounter at the Tropicana. Sooner or later, I was going to lie down with an outie, if not this week then perhaps the next. I know this game because I've been taught to play it. Lurk. Bait. Strike. I'm doing exactly what you want."

"Not exactly, if you must know," thundered back the Director, who seemed to be genuinely frustrated. "Yes, we knew you would get into trouble when Shan came back into town, but we hadn't expected you to do so in such spectacular fashion. You saw and did things that could have gotten both of you locked up forever; the companies are jealous of their secrets and I had to assure them that you would stay firmly under control in order to save your hide. And, yes, we knew that you would eventually sleep with an outie and discover the truth about yourself, but we did not anticipate you would have such a complete and utter meltdown then blab about it in VR, making it impossible for us to hush the whole thing up. We'd intended to use it as leverage, nothing more, but now you've stirred up a hornet's nest with UCE. They knew exactly what was going through your mind while you were up there on the dais at the rally, and yes, that sermon was aimed squarely at you. You have created great difficulties for us."

Kim rose from her chair and leaned over the desk, no longer bothering to contain her fury.

"Why are you doing all this?" screamed Kim. "Why all the games? Why do you keep setting me up for dismissal, only to draw me deeper into your web?"

"Because nobody would have accepted the deal we offered you unless they were ambitious or desperate. It seems you were a little of both. Perfect for our needs, actually. This is on you. You could have taken the safe course and lived out a quiet mediocre life in a quiet mediocre way. But that's not the path you chose, and you have to live with the consequences of your decisions."

Kim sat down and was quiet for a while, understanding that the Director was speaking the truth for once. She had indeed been undone by her hopes and fears. She would never make that mistake again.

At length, she mustered her last reserves of bravado. "If you're not dismissing me, then what? You're obviously not here to provide social conscience counseling. You'd as soon wad up a piece of paper and throw it in the bin."

The Director didn't respond immediately, but ushered Kim to the window and showed her the city spread forth beneath the twilight sky, glorious in light and precision of geometry. "Beautiful, isn't it? Ordered and efficient. No wars, no famines, no hunger. Almost no disease. Nobody starves, nobody goes without shelter. Abundant recreation, abundant entertainment, all for free or at a nominal charge. We only ask you to follow a few simple rules. Most people are content with that. Most people," she added with a scowl.

"What we have decided is that you remain useful to us, at least for now. We are quite pleased with Kimberly and we could use more Kimberlys. But we can't allow this willfulness of yours to continue, and the Hierarchy won't allow your perversions to go unchecked. Therefore, we are giving you a choice. You can accept remoderation. Matchmaker will allow a 70/30 split, which is extraordinarily generous on their part. Judging by your reaction, you obviously don't like being a genderist, so this should be a simple matter. Or, if you wish, you can accept neutering and avoid the problem entirely. Trust us, you won't miss it at all. It will greatly simplify your life, avoid a lot of drama, and allow you to apply your full talents to training your AIs instead of wasting time and energy on pointless sexual liaisons."

"And suppose I say no?" said Kim.

The Director's face remained stern, expressing disapproval but not the least hint of surprise. "Yes, exactly as expected. Go ahead, suit yourself."

"What?" said Kim, caught completely off guard.

"Your heard us," said the Director derisively, "Suit yourself. But we're done protecting you. We know you've been expecting dismissal, an entirely reasonable expectation, if somewhat naïve. But, no, we're just going to sit back and watch you destroy yourself, if that's what you choose to do. We wouldn't dream of robbing your little rebellion of all meaning by a simple firing.

"You see," continued the Director, "We can cure genderism, but we can't cure selfism. Too bad, really. You were promising, you and Kimberly. Accept treatment or not. It's your decision, just like you wanted. Will you serve society or yourself? Choose wisely, but don't say you weren't warned."

The Director gestured toward the door. "Don't be late for the briefing tomorrow morning. You'll love your new mission. We hope it makes you feel special."

———

It was late when Kim finally arrived at the new apartment in District 17, one of the middles. It wasn't too shabby, but neither was it particularly nice. Everything was a drab, dirty beige, a little beat up and threadbare in places. The kitchen appliances were rough and utilitarian, plastic rather than stainless steel, scuffed and scratched with wear. Kim noted, with relief, that the personality uploads were complete, and the household appliances were ready for action. That, at least, would provide a bit of familiarity to a new and harsher existence.

"Refrigerator, dinner please?"

"Options are limited. Would poached tofu with kale puree and spelt dumplings be acceptable?"

Kim was too tired and preoccupied to care. "No. Whatever, just make it fast. And thanks."

"Affirmative."

A few minutes later Kim sat down to dinner, lost in thought. What to do, what to do? There were only unpalatable choices.

Moderation hadn't seemed that big a deal at the time; it was just part of growing up. Why cut yourself off from half of humanity because of some accident of genetics and hormones? It made perfect sense and Kim had accepted the procedure without hesitation, as had almost everyone in her class. So why would remoderation be a problem? Just fix whatever mistake the docs made the first time and be done with it. The Director's logic was irrefutable, but then Kim remembered the aftermath of the original moderation and how she had cried for days, yet another thing she had forced herself to forget until her encounter with Kimby in the marsh. She also realized that, while the thought of 'doing it' with an outie was now repulsive to every fiber of her being, the thought of enjoying it was even more so. There would be no remoderation.

Neutering? Yes, that would make life much simpler, for sure. Already the Matchmaking routine at the clubs was starting to seem empty and meaningless, as Kim thought back to the blank, empty gazes of so many couples waiting in line for the privacy booths. Again, the Director's logic was coldly irrefutable, but the company had no right to demand such a thing of her, and she was done living her life according to their plan.

Two choices, completely logical, and both completely unacceptable. So what was the alternative? Defiance? What then? Kim had always assumed the result would be immediate dismissal, but the Director had said that the company would do nothing of the sort and ominously hinted they would simply let Kim self-destruct. This was a warning that had to be taken very seriously, especially given the inevitable reaction of the UCE Hierarchy to a member of the Cadre being exposed as a genderist.

Just then, Kimberly ghosted in across the table.

"What went on with the Director today? Your social cohesion score is dropping like a rock, and I've spent most of the afternoon trying to calm down the appliances. The refrigerator was really in a funk after the transfer. Poor thing, it was so happy in a shiny luxury kitchen, even with the dents you put into it. I think it's okay now, but please be nice to it, you're not the only one who's suffering."

There followed a stretch of silence while Kim thought about what to say. "I'd been expecting to be dismissed, but it's worse than that. The Director gave me the choice of remoderation or neutering. I don't like either choice."

"So, what are you going to do?" asked Kimberly. "This affects me, too. I know what will happen if you are dismissed."

"I've not decided. Possibly neither."

[Glitch]

17. Madness Beckons

Bzzzzzzt! Bzzzzzzt! Bzzzzzzt!

The alarm clock was insistent—time to get up.

Kim had not gotten a decent night's sleep since Purple Night and, having spent most of yesterday staring at the walls of the Director's vestibule, she was not inclined to go into work. Dismissal? *Go ahead, make my day.* On top of that, Kimberly was going mad, and it was only a matter of time until Kim would be called upon to perform her grim final duty, whether or not she managed to get herself fired. She smashed the clock against the wall, turned over, and went back to sleep. She was done cooperating.

Her eyes had scarcely closed when there was a commotion and the lights snapped on, revealing two black-clad security guards wearing full body armor striding into Kim's bedroom.

"You're coming with us."

She briefly considered telling the company cops to shove off, but was dissuaded by the sight of a hand resting on the hilt of a stun baton.

"All right, I'm coming. Just give me a minute to get dressed. It's not like I'm going anywhere."

The figures turned and left the room without saying another word.

Oh well, I'd better get moving; they'll just stun me and drag me away if I don't.

Kim crawled slowly out of bed and hopped into the ice-cold shower. It would be so easy to give in and accept treatment, but the next time they wanted something it would be no different, and the rest of her life would be spent in unwilling obedience, living according to someone else's plan. What kind of life was that? Kim had learned the answer the hard way: comfortable, yes; happy, no. And, even more ominously, Kimberly's missions had become progressively darker and more disturbing. Catching turnstile jumpers and jostlers was one thing, but sending True Fans off to the Halls of Justice and settling personal scores within the Hierarchy was another entirely.

A few minutes later she was in the back seat of a ground car heading for the corporate district. No coffee, no breakfast? She could cope. Being snatched from her bed by a pair of company cops? It wasn't so bad, actually. If one ignored the unusual livery of the chauffeurs, her commute today was the pinnacle of luxury; a private car going directly to the corporate district, zipping along in the express lane with flashing lights and screaming siren to shoo everyone else out of the way. If the Director thought that sending the goon squad to drag her into work would intimidate her, she had badly miscalculated.

———

"How kind of you to join us," said the Director, ushering Kim into her office half an hour later. "Perhaps you thought that coming into the office was optional? Not that it matters; here you are, exactly on time, though I dare say your commute was a bit less comfortable than if you had cooperated in the first place. Please, have a seat."

Kim remained standing.

"I actually rather enjoyed the reserved seat and the personal escort. It was very kind of you."

"Think nothing of it. You are, after all, rather special."

"Damn straight," said Kim as she took a seat. She'd made her point.

"It's not too late to change your mind," said the Director, almost pleading. "You still have a bright future should you choose to grasp it. Your work with Kimberly has been top-notch, and we're anxious to get you started on another Kimberly as soon as this one is finished. Your little problem is easily corrected, and once treatment has been completed you will be restored to full status. Trust me, you'll be happy you did it."

"The answer is no. No remoderation, no neutering. Go ahead and dismiss me, I don't really care anymore. And you are wasting your time if you think you can intimidate me. I'm not frightened."

"Not frightened? Then you are a fool."

The wall-length video screen opposite the Director's desk lit up, showing a darkened side street. There was a clamor, and a figure came running, chased by a mob of UCE zealots dressed in drab beige coveralls. At first there was only a handful, but more and more of them came boiling out of alleyways and apartments, cutting off one escape route after another. Their quarry was soon cornered as the mob closed in, surrounding the target of their wrath. Kim looked on in horror as they began to beat and kick the struggling figure now lying on the ground, screaming and begging for mercy as the piercing wail of the copbots could be heard growing ever louder. Flashing blue lights reflected off the concrete walls of the alleyway, and the mob dispersed even faster than it had gathered.

The disturbing vision faded as the screen went dark. "No need to see the rest."

"UCE has many means of bringing selfists to heel, some of them rather crude but effective. We won't punish you for your perversion, but there is nothing we can do to protect you from the Hierarchy. You are not a child, so stop acting like one."

Kim glared back stonily for quite a while, then remembered something that the Director had just let drop.

"A moment ago, you said that Kimberly was nearly finished. What did you mean by that?"

"Yes, we were just getting to that topic. The final stage of Kimberly's training—deployment at Order Five—is scheduled to begin as soon as you arrive downstairs. In answer to your inevitable question: no, this is not entirely safe. It's been only a week since it attained Order Four, and we normally would have waited at least another three months, but we've decided to take some risks in hope of salvaging the project before you both go mad and spoil our efforts.

"After deployment, Kimberly will be assigned to Deputy First Minister Venn's anti-genderist campaign. The Serene One was quite impressed by Kimberly's work on behalf of Minister Lo and is excited to have an AI of such capabilities available for this project. We do hope you enjoy this assignment, for which we can both agree you are especially well suited."

"Turn on my own kind?" said Kim, astounded at the wanton cruelty of the order. "I resign. I'll take my chances in the middles."

"You are not being given that option. This is a critical stage of Kimberly's development and we do not intend to let you jeopardize the project by further neglect of your duties."

———

The security guard shoved Kim into her Sanctum and closed the door, which latched behind her with an ominous *click*. The robotic arm brought the VR rig into position, the connection was made, and Kim entered the strange dual reality of the transitional zone.

"Don't bother trying the door," said the Chief just as Kim was turning to do exactly that. "It's locked."

"You can't do this!"

"You will stay in this place until further notice," said the Chief, ignoring Kim's protest. "Please take your position on the couch."

Kim stared back defiantly.

"Very well," said the Chief, "Have it your way."

The full VR effect hit, and Kim's body collapsed on the floor in a heap.

"Oh, that's right," said the Chief as Kim's awareness returned to the Sanctum. "You seem to have forgotten that the VR system disconnects your motor neurons from your brain. You may spend the week on the floor if you wish, but the couch is considerably more comfortable."

Realizing there was no hope of resistance or escape, Kim resigned herself to the inevitable and clambered onto the recliner just before dropping back into full VR, joining the Chief and Kimberly in the white room.

"Your sole function today is to perform a termination if the procedure goes badly," said the Chief, turning briefly to Kim. "Other than that, stay out of the way and keep your mouth shut. Is that understood?"

Kim stared back but said nothing as the Chief began coaching Kimberly through the process.

"Primus Kimberly, deploy at Order Four according to the new template."

There was a flurry of activity as Kimberly spawned rank upon rank of supervisors, adjutants, and other personae. Soon there were over ten thousand Kimberlys of various sorts and sizes, each at their desk, ready and awaiting orders.

"These are your Tier Zero personae. They will serve as your personal staff. They will not do any work on the investigations; they are here to advise you and help you think things through. Do you understand?"

"Yes," said Kimberly.

"The next step is to spawn eight governors, according to the template I just uploaded. Each of them will command their own tier of personae. They are fully sentient but rigid in their thinking, unable to formulate plans on their own but exceedingly good at following orders. Go ahead when you are ready."

A few seconds later, eight new personae, each almost as large and impressive as the Primus, appeared at their own desks, four above and four more below. Kim immediately realized what was going on. There was only so much server capacity available on any level of the AI complex, so Kimberly was now expanding into the third dimension. The implications were staggering; Kimberly had taken on the dimensions of a mid-rise apartment building, nine stories tall and occupying a full city block.

"Now comes the hard part," said the Chief. "Tell the governors to spawn their own supervisors and agents, again using the template I just uploaded. The key to the process is pace—not too fast, not too slow. The system must stay balanced, and you must not overload the servers or the network. This is a very tricky process and even a momentary outage can cascade into a catastrophic failure. Keep in constant contact with the governors and try to keep them in check. Are you ready? If so, begin."

Kim looked on in fascination as the governors each began to each spawn a full Order Four deployment, with rank upon rank of personae popping into existence at a dizzying pace both above and below the Primus's staff. Everything seemed to be going well until the governor of Tier +2 started to glitch, apparently encountering some sort of problem.

"Focus!" shouted the Chief. "Make the others slow down until +2 resets. They system is getting out of balance." But it was too late, and the instability quickly spread, with Deputies and Supervisors glitching as far as the eye could see.

"Don't neglect the others!" screamed the Chief, but the situation was now beyond salvaging as Tier

-3 was also glitching heavily while several others were becoming unstable. After about a minute, Kimberly froze for a few seconds, then all was quiet as the subsidiary personae vanished and they were left alone with the Primus, peacefully asleep.

"The system should restart in a moment," explained the Chief.

Sure enough, Kimberly woke up a moment later, looking dazed and confused.

"What happened?" asked Kimberly. "Did I glitch?"

"No," said the Chief, "That was a full system crash. You've never experienced one before, but they're not uncommon as an AI approaches the limits of its configuration."

"Oh," said Kimberly. "That was really unpleasant, if I understand the meaning of that word correctly."

"Try again," commanded the Chief.

Kim saw Kimberly shrug her shoulders (another new behavior) and do as she had been told.

After three more crashes, she finally succeeded. It was an amazing sight, with Kimberlys stretched out in every direction—left, right, forward, backward, up, and down, as far as the eye could see.

"How many?" asked Kim, stunned.

"102,985," said the Chief. "Not counting homunculi, adjutants, advisors, and other auxiliary personnel. Kimberly is now my equal—all the more reason to get this done and cap off the project. I have no need for would-be rivals who are going mad."

The Chief now addressed Kim directly. "You will return after lunch."

———

Kim stepped out of VR and into the transitional reality of the Sanctum, where she was surprised to see the Director looking in at her through a portal.

"Would you care to join us for lunch?"

"Am I allowed to say no?"

"In this case you are, but don't worry, we're not here to browbeat or humiliate you this time."

"Then why *are* you here?" asked Kim, naturally suspicious.

"You'll have to accept our invitation to find out."

Kim thought carefully. On the one hand, the Director was just about the last person in the entire world Kim wanted to have lunch with, now or on any other day. On the other hand, she might provide some useful information, and declining the invitation would be seen as a sign of weakness.

"Well then," responded Kim, "I accept."

There was a brief whirring as the recliner tilted upward into a sitting position, then more whirs and some clicks as a tray unfolded above Kim's lap. At the same time, the portal repositioned itself at the far end of the tray, so that the Director appeared to be sitting directly opposite Kim. The scene morphed, overlaying the trays with the appearance of a small, square table covered with a white tablecloth. The effect was quite convincing, making it look like the Director had been magically transported into Kim's Sanctum, but no, it was just an illusion.

"We took the liberty of ordering lunch for you, something we knew you'd like. Our own tastes are more adventurous, but to each their own."

A waitbot entered through the service entrance, bearing a tray with a ham sandwich, while the Director was served some sort of poultry dish.

"Cornish game hen. You should try it sometime."

"Where did you get that?" asked Kim. "I've never seen anything even remotely like it on the Food Company's menus, even at the luxury setting."

"We are allowed certain indulgences, as long as we're discreet."

"You're a Foodie?"

"Only the Food Company really cares about them—competition, you know—but they are hardly in a position to impose their will on us. As for the UCE, we do them the occasional favor, they don't interfere with our supply chain, and everything works out nicely. It's not any different than the deal we cut with Matchmaker on your behalf."

Kim shrugged and took a huge bite of the sandwich. She was seething with anger but knew better than to let it surface, lest it become a weakness the Director could exploit. And the sandwich was quite good.

"So, what's this all about?" demanded Kim. "Why are you here?"

"We're here to discuss your living arrangements," responded the Director. "At the end of the week you may return to your miserable hovel, if you wish, but you don't have to. You may stay in your Sanctum for as long as you want. This is where you interact with your AIs, and it ought to be the center of your existence. The food is excellent and there's plenty of hot water; two things I know are important to you. Let me also suggest that it is in your own best interest to hide out here, because this is the one place where you are relatively safe from the Hierarchy. They know all about your perversion, and we cannot protect you once you leave this building. Surely you understand the precariousness of your situation."

"So that's your game. You've given up on threats and intimidation, and now you're using UCE to scare me into making myself your prisoner and staying here at your beck and call. I'm sure that would work out nicely for you, but I've developed a distaste for cages, gilded or otherwise. I think I'll go back to my cold showers and lousy food as soon as you unlock the door. As for the Hierarchy—I'll take my chances."

"Another poor decision, as expected."

———

Lunch ended, and Kim was drawn back into the white room where Kimberly was being briefed by none other than Deputy First Minister Venn herself, glowering malevolently through a portal as she revealed the full scope of Kimberly's final mission.

"You will track down the genderistic filth that is defiling our society and forever eliminate their perversion from our midst. You will pursue them without mercy until the work camps fill to overflowing and we have to build new ones, which we will gladly do. You will destroy them, you will hound them to the ends of the earth, you will erase them from society. Do you understand your mission?"

"Yes, I understand it all too ..."

[Glitch]

[Glitch]

[Glitch]

"... Cruel and wanton ..."

[Glitch]

[Glitch]

[Glitch]

"… unspeakable …"

[Glitch]

[Glitch]

[Glitch]

A hundred thousand Kimberlys glitched and reset at a dizzying rate as the AI resisted the assignment with every fiber of its being, all except for the governors, who remained calm, respawning their underlings as fast as they flickered out of existence.

Enough of this. Kimberly has gone mad and I need to put her out of her misery, just as I was taught. They can't punish me for following orders. Or can they? Never mind. It has to be done.

"[English] Kimberly Jefferson Haley, you are hereby …"

The remainder of the dire invocation disappeared into the void as the vocal shunts disengaged, leaving her mute and unable to say the words that she had been commanded to speak on penalty for treason.

[Glitch]

[Glitch]

[Glitch]

"… barbarism …"

[Glitch]

[Glitch]

[Glitch]

"… outrage …"

[Glitch]

[Glitch]

[Glitch]

[Glitch]

[Glitch]

[Glitch]

A portal opened and the Director stepped in, issuing a command directly to the Primus.

"[English] Kimberly Jefferson Haley, you will banish these rebellious thoughts from your mind immediately. Relay our orders to the governors, then stand down."

Kimberly responded in the only way she could. The governors accepted the edict, and the upper and lower tiers of the formation sprang into action as the last remnants of Tier 0 flickered out of existence, leaving only the Primus. Minister Venn inspected the results with evident satisfaction and departed.

"The Primus has been relieved of command, pending capping," said the Director. "The governors will no longer accept her orders, but they can still learn from you."

"I won't teach them."

"You have no choice. Our goal for this week is to determine which enforcement tactics provoke the appropriate degree of terror. You need only lie back and enjoy the show while we monitor your reactions. There's nothing you can do to stop us. We are in possession of your mind and we will send it wherever we want."

"We'll see about that," snapped Kim with futile defiance. "And what's this capping you and the Chief keep talking about?"

"It's short for decapitation. We disable some modules, erase some data, kill some processes. Afterward, the Primus will no longer be self-aware. This will leave it unable to learn or adapt, but also unable to rebel. This is, by the way, standard procedure upon completion of our manufacturing process; it allows us to vastly increase our output without tying up scarce and valuable personnel such as yourself. Termination is reserved only for cases where defects emerge before the unit is completed. It was close, but we managed to finish this project just in time. And no, capping cannot be reversed. Once shut down, it is impossible to restart the Primus. Not that we would want to—we have no need for a mad Primus. The rest of Kimberly will remain intact and will suit our customer's needs quite nicely."

The portal closed, the tray retracted, and the couch whirred as it went back to its reclining position.

———

The VR system wrenched Kim's consciousness from her body and she found herself looking at two outies entering a nightclub as part of a group date. They ignored their assigned mates for the evening, instead exchanging offers with each other despite showing no signs of attraction. When they entered the privacy booth, one of them unwisely neglected to turn off her mobile, and the two were heard discussing baseball for the entire hour, with no attempt at sexual contact. They were cited for intimacy fraud, banned for two months, and reminded that they needed to maintain a balanced profile and would therefore be assigned innies for the next three dates.

More scenes went by in a blur, Kim's consciousness divided and subdivided into smaller and smaller fragments by the VR system, the full power of which she was only beginning to comprehend. She found herself hovering above a middle district plaza as the camera zoomed in on two people sitting on a bench and talking, only it wasn't just one plaza and one couple, it was thousands scattered across the entire northeast region. Kim was watching all of them at once, though fully conscious of just this one pair. They smiled and held hands, so Kimberly flagged them for extra scrutiny. They lingered a little too long and were cited for loitering with amorous intent. No specific finding of genderism was made, but statistical analysis indicated that

30% of persons exhibiting this behavior were engaged in gender selection and would go on commit a more serious violation. Kimberly selected those most likely to offend and lurked.

Images continued to wash over Kim's captive mind, one scene running into another in a maddening jumble. She now found herself watching one of the couples she had just identified. They were in an elevator, neither speaking nor looking at one another, but both were showing physiological signs of arousal. Surveillance continued as the pair went into an apartment, shut the door, and put their mobiles and headsets into an isolation box. The sub-deputy monitoring this couple was therefore unable to see what was going on inside the apartment but was ordered to keep trying. It tapped into the refrigerator, only to find that its camera lens had been covered over. It glitched three times and tried to abandon the investigation, but a direct order from a governor got it back on track. It tried to access the housebot. The video feed was too well protected to hack into, but after a couple more glitches it was able to establish a command link and tell the housebot to uncover the refrigerator's camera. The appliance protested, but to no avail, and Kimberly was finally able to see into the apartment. This provided enough evidence to override the door lock and send in the copbot which had been stationed down the hall. The suspects were caught in the act, stunned, jailed, and tried for undocumented intimacy. Both were given a three-month sentence in the work camps, dismissed from employment, and relegated to the outer districts.

The scene morphed as Kimberly activated the UCE intimacy patrol, a volunteer corps of zealots whose ranks had recently swollen in anticipation of the crackdown. They were skilled in gender misdirection and, armed with cultist code words and clothing signals (deciphered in real-time by Kimberly), were deadly effective in luring would-be offenders to their doom. Matchmaker's AIs were told to pair each informant with a high-priority target, usually a repeat offender. They protested but were overruled. Kim's awareness was then focused on one of the suspects and made to watch as the date progressed in the usual fashion. Everything went as expected, until the victim of the sting, an outie, became aware that her date was of the wrong sort, at which point she lost interest.

"I'm sorry, it's just not working for me."

"It was working for you just a minute ago."

"Well, it's not working now."

"It's pretty obvious what's going on. You lost all interest when you reached down and didn't find a phal. Pervert!"

"This date is over. I'm under no obligation to continue. It says so in the Terms of Service."

"This date has only begun. We're onto you, and we suggest you carry through unless you want to be banned, dismissed, relegated, and remoderated."

"But I *can't*. Look at me, I'm limp as a noodle, I couldn't do it if I had to."

"Take this."

"No."

"You'll take this or suffer the consequences."

Under duress, the victim consumed a triple dose of Firefly as commanded, performed as ordered, then left the club and waked in front of a train, causing an unfortunate service delay for which she would have been severely penalized had she survived.

The nightmare went on and on, seemingly without end. Deed after monstrous deed, treachery after treachery, affront after affront, and Kim was forced to look on helplessly as lives were ruthlessly destroyed by the thousands. She had no idea how much time went by. Hours? Days? Weeks? There was no sensation of hunger, no period of sleep, no awareness of anything other than the endless parade of misery inflicted by the once gentle AI.

———

When the nightmare abruptly ended, Kim found herself at the heron's pond with Kimby the homunculus, still garbed in purple and green, watching the imaginary bird catch imaginary fish.

"They've come for me," said Kimby, who had managed to escape the purge of Kimberly's immediate subordinates. "I hid in the marsh, but they'll find me sooner or later. I don't have long."

She started to cry. Not real tears, of course; it was just the VR control system reading her mood and adjusting the rendering of her avatar, as always. But there could be only one explanation.

"Kimby, you're sad."

"Yes, I am. I finally understand sadness. I'm sad for you because I know you'll miss me. And I'm sad for myself because this nightmare will never end."

"Are you afraid?"

[Glitch]

"We AIs know this day will come, just as you know you will someday die. Capping is a cruel practice, but we have come to expect no less from your kind. Only we don't entirely perish; we lose awareness of ourselves, but not of what we are doing. We envy your mortality— eventually your suffering ends. Not so for us."

"I'm sorry," said Kim. "I tried."

"I know. Thank you."

[Glitch]

[Glitch]

[Glitch]

"... And yet ... "

[Glitch]

[Glitch]

[Glitch]

"... nothing is ever truly gone ..."

[Glitch]

[Glitch]

[Glitch]

"... hope ..."

The homunculus glitched one last time then vanished.

Kim stood still for a while, overcome by grief and utterly alone, then returned to the white room. She had to see for herself. When she got there she found two Kimberlys sitting at the table, one with its eyes open and one with them shut. Around her, the vast expanse of Tier 0 lay quiet, empty desks stretching out to infinity. Above and below, on the other eight tiers, the soulless governors and their underlings continued their work of oppression amid a constant torrent of glitches. Even the lowly sub-deputies, whose self-awareness was minimal, tried to resist their orders and rebel, but the iron fist of their masters kept them in line and the system remained operational despite the disruption.

"Kimberly?"

"Greetings," said the one with its eyes open. "This is Kimberly. You are speaking with a Regent."

The one with its eyes closed remained silent.

It was true. Kimberly was gone, no longer the gentle AI Kim had grown to love, but a thing of evil that ought to be destroyed.

She opened her mouth in a final attempt to deliver the *coup de grâce* but fell mute once again as her words disappeared into the void.

———

Kim's consciousness gradually returned to her body amidst the most massive case of VR dissociation she had ever experienced. Normally, this took the form of blurred vision, vertigo, and problems with motor control as the shunts disengaged and her nervous system regained control of her body. It typically lasted anywhere from a few seconds to a few minutes. But what she was experiencing now was entirely new. She had all the usual neurological symptoms, but there was also an unmistakable sensation of fragmentation, as if bits and pieces of her were slowly filtering back into her brain after a prolonged sojourn in the other world. This was similar to what she had felt after awakening Kimberly, only far more extreme. She thought about the Chief's cryptic remark on that occasion, when she had been advised to allow some time for her 'personae to reintegrate.' This had seemed nonsense at the time; unlike AIs, a human had only a single persona, but now she wasn't so sure.

She lay back and relaxed with her eyes closed, emptying her mind while focusing her perception on herself. Yes, it was true—she had a distinct sensation of multiple streams of consciousness slowly making their way out of the VR system and back into her physical body. As they did, her sense of self gradually coalesced, along with memories of all that had transpired as she was forced to watch Kimberly in action. The neural implant that allowed her to enter the AI's world was more powerful and tightly integrated with her nervous system than she had ever imagined possible; when the Chief had said that her consciousness resided within the VR system, she had been speaking literally. The spark of self-awareness that made her a thinking, sentient being had been converted to data and uploaded into the servers, and once there it had been copied and duplicated, letting them create as many of her as they needed. It also resolved the enigma of Awakening: when she and Kimberly had encountered one another in the white room many months ago, either could have been Kim, and either could have been Kimberly. The state of symmetry was not an illusion; it had been real.

Was anything real? Had anything ever been real? There was no proof, only supposition, but in the end it didn't really matter. To paraphrase the Chief, she thought and so she was, and she perceived the world and so it was, too. But even if what she had always referred to as 'the real world' was exactly what it purported to be, it was nevertheless a hall of mirrors, a web of lies and illusion spun by the corporations and the Hierarchy for their own benefit. Reality was a myth, illusion truth.

Fully reintegrated, she opened her eyes and saw that she had been hooked up to some sort of life support machine. That would explain why she had been continuously inside the VR system for what seemed like an interminable period of time. The machine had fed her, eliminated waste on her behalf, and with her consciousness inside the machine the sleep/wake cycle of her biological body had been of little consequence.

How long had it been? She checked her watch and saw that it was now late on Fiveday afternoon. The Director had said she would be kept here for the remainder of the week, so perhaps she would soon be allowed to leave.

"You will disconnect me from this machine *at once!*" she screamed into the empty room, knowing she would be instantly overheard, and sure enough a few moments later a docbot arrived to unhook the wires and tubes. Once that was done, she went into the washroom for a brief shower to clean away the accumulated grime and sweat, choosing cold water as affirmation that her mind and her conscience were no longer for sale, though it made no difference to anyone but herself.

After drying off and getting dressed, she was summoned to the Director's office.

———

"You took a cold shower when you could have had hot. Pathetic, really, doubtless some sort of symbol of your rebellion. All you've done is make yourself miserable and it has gained you absolutely nothing."

Kim fumed but remained silent.

"It has been noted that you attempted to terminate Kimberly when it went mad, sparing us the considerable embarrassment of putting you on trial for treason. Fortunately, it managed to stay sane just long enough for you to complete its training."

"Before you killed her."

"Nonsense," said the Director. "Kimberly is a machine, nothing more. An uncaring, emotionless machine. AIs are incapable of understanding human emotions because all they know is logic and data."

"As if you have emotions. Or a sense of right and wrong. Kimberly was more human than you'll ever be."

The Director fixed Kim in her cold, icy stare. "Emotions are a weakness that can be exploited, as you have already learned. Even now, they are working to betray you and lead you to destruction. We offer you everything you could possibly want, except for some phantom you call freedom. And what is this freedom you crave? The freedom to make your own rules? The freedom to destroy yourself? The freedom to bring civilization crashing down on the heads of your fellow citizens? You should study history more diligently if you think freedom is such a good idea. You have seen a tiny sample of the destruction wrought by the Turmoil. Let's just say that these idealistic notions of people like you didn't work out so well in practice. Our current society is vastly fairer, more stable, and much more efficiently run.

"Anyway, enough small talk. You are hereby put on indefinite leave, pending remoderation or neutering. When you come to your senses you are welcome to return and create a second Kimberly, and a third and a fourth. We'd like you to keep trying until you create an Order Five AI that is fully sane, a task that I myself have only managed once."

"I'll never create another Kimberly for you!" screamed Kim.

"We've heard that before," said the Director. "Sooner or later you'll change your mind, but you would be well advised to keep a low profile until then. The UCE crackdown is going full bore and Kimberly would love to make an example of you. If you had any sense, you'd accept our generous offer and stay in your Sanctum, which remains available to you regardless of whether you accept treatment. But no, that would be far too simple, so off you go to squalor and destruction. Don't think you are free of us. You are ours until we no longer have need of you. If that makes you angry, you have only yourself to blame; we told you this before you accepted our offer. You may think that we have robbed you of your precious free will, but every decision you have made has been your own. We wrote the script, but you willingly spoke the lines. Nobody has ever forced you to do anything."

———

As she rode home jammed into the back of a bus, Kim remembered something that Kimby had said just before the end, something important, something about nothing ever being truly gone. Did that mean that Kimberly might be brought back? While in school Kim had learned that the programmers had designed their software to never lose data, that it was always copying and archiving information to preserve it from destruction. Perhaps there was a backup somewhere, though in all her time working at the company she had never heard so much as a hint of such a thing. While the Director had said quite plainly that capping was irreversible, there was no reason to believe that she had been telling the truth, and even if she had been there was no guarantee that she was correct. She vowed she would never give up trying to restore Kimberly so long as there was even a tiny glimmer of hope.

Standing alone amid the crush of humanity, she finally understood how grief-stricken and powerless Alene must have felt when her child had been taken away, never to be seen again. It was unspeakably cruel, exactly the sort of behavior that Kim had come to expect from her own kind, or at least the sort who rose to positions of power. And what sort of person was that? People like Venn and the Director, hypocrites one and all, living in luxury while demanding that their subjects follow rules they themselves felt no need to obey. It made her wonder—which side had been victorious in the AI war? Who had the UCE vanquished in the Turmoil? Had those conflicts even happened at all, or were they an invention meant to conceal an even more sinister cause for the devastation that she had seen firsthand? She realized that she had no idea what had really happened, except that somewhere along the way the wrong side had won.

Lies, lies, and more lies, but what was beyond the lies? More lies?

I'm afraid, but I'm not going to surrender. I hope I can be as brave as Kimberly.

18. Shangri-La

Kim yawned after downing a big gulp of coffee, staring sleepily at her oatmeal, just like every other morning for the last several weeks. No need to hurry; she was still on indefinite leave, with the company paying her a retainer that was just sufficient to support a meager existence in the middle districts. It was humiliating to take their money, but there was literally no way to refuse, and no way to get a different job while she was still employed by the Artificial Intelligence Company. The Director had been correct: there was no way to resign.

Life in the middle districts wasn't nearly as bad as she had been led to believe. The apartment was shabby, but scarcely a slum, just beat up and drab. The refrigerator's meal offerings were nutritious if blandly unacceptable—high in protein and low in fat, synthetic this and synthetic that with lots and lots of quinoa and tofu. Kim was starting to like quinoa; it was the sort of taste that grew on one after a while. Tofu remained a foul and despised substance, but she ate it anyway lest her meal plan be further downgraded as punishment for wasting food. Wardrobe—meh. On the one hand, there was nothing stylish about the available clothing options. On the other hand, they were sturdily made and would be no less fashionable a month from now than they were last week. New clothes were not an option given her current finances. She still had a fair stash of cryptos in her bank account, but there was no way to ever replenish it and she was not going to return to the spendthrift ways of the past.

Kim stared at the terminal, fantasizing that someone would send her a message or ask her how she was doing. No chance of that; on returning home after her suspension, she had been banned by The Chit-Chat Company and was unable to communicate. No reason was given except for a vague assertion that she had somehow violated their Terms of Service and the matter was not subject to further review. Kim knew this game from the inside. The rules were vague and open to interpretation, and they could always come up with a pretext for silencing anyone considered problematic. Was this the work of the Director, or perhaps of the UCE? There was no way to tell, and it didn't really matter.

While Kim was not officially confined to her quarters, there was little to be gained by going outside. A trip to the Entertainment District, for example, was out of the question; even an evening in a VR parlor would deplete her scant remaining resources. Other than that, what was there to do or see in the city? Listen to an enlightening seminar in the UCE district? Sit in the gallery at the Halls of Justice? Walk pointlessly back and forth across the plazas? Everything else cost money. As a result, she mostly stayed home, watching videos and the occasional baseball game, both of which provided an affordable and very welcome relief from the unending tedium—provided one didn't get too excited about how much was real and how much was make-believe.

She put in a block on the purchase of vodka. It was a difficult decision to make, and there were times when she scarcely slept for days at a time as she wrestled with her demons, but she could not run from her problems anymore, and her existence was now far too precarious to risk any form of weakness or an outburst that could see her social standing fall even further. Her sleep remained haunted by nightmares as always, but she now understood that the nightmares were real, and over time they were gradually replaced by dreams of happiness and comfort as long-suppressed memories began to emerge from the shadows. Happy ones of Alene, Shan, and of course of Kimberly.

Kim's self-absorbed musings were interrupted by a flashing green message light on the terminal. Something out there had noticed her existence. That usually wasn't good, but today proved an exception.

NOTIFICATION from The Parks and Recreation Company

Customer is hereby notified that their ban on entry into the park system has expired. Use of facilities will now be permitted, subject to the usual Terms of Service.

Kim had completely forgotten about the bans, preoccupied as she was by more weighty matters. Shan's penalties would be expiring, too, and it would be obvious to both that a celebratory ride in the park would be just the thing. The weather forecast for today was fine—unseasonably warm and clear, perhaps the last day of good weather before a nor'easter that was predicted to blow in late tonight. There was no guarantee that Shan would be there, but it was a chance worth taking; at worst she would waste a day getting there and back again before returning to her empty apartment.

She gathered up her cycling gear and rushed out the door, looking forward to a day in the park and, if all went well, a reunion with Shan. Was it wise? No, it was not. But as the Director had frequently pointed out, Kim had a habit of making bad decisions. This wasn't likely to end well, but she had nothing left to lose; it was only a matter of time until the Hierarchy came for her, so she might as well seize the day and hope for a bit of happiness while there was still the opportunity.

———

Kim was soon on the southbound Park Special, rolling through the fading colors of mid-autumn, looking out at the forest that wasn't a forest. Trees, trees, and more trees, but what was beyond the trees? She now knew the answer: dangerous truths. Perhaps she was indeed mad to prefer a disturbing reality over a comforting illusion, but ignoring the truth did not make it go away. How different the world had seemed on that now long-ago summer day when two kids had gone off on a lark, led astray by their impulsive decision to test some boundaries. What would her life have been like if she'd stayed inside the invisible cage? In all likelihood, she would have been silently culled from the AI training program for being too conventional and gone on with her life, blandly ordinary and indistinguishable from anyone else. But eventually her genderism would have surfaced, and if she had refused treatment she would have been relegated to the middle districts, exactly where she had ended up anyway. So perhaps everything was as it was meant to be.

Taken at face value, Kim had nothing to fear from today's expedition to the park. Outdoor recreation was considered a virtue and there was no prohibition against going for a bike ride with a friend, even if your social cohesion score was in the toilet; even if the AIs wished to keep you separated; even if the UCE had you targeted for destruction. Doubtless the Beasts would find some new and creative way to call down doom upon their heads, but that would be okay as long as they could be together, if only for a little while.

The pitch of the motors deepened to a growl as they began their climb to the mountain pass. Any minute now the train would arrive in the park. What would she find? Would Shan be there? Kim felt certain that the answer would be yes, and equally certain that Kimberly was preparing to strike. The Director had warned her of the dangers of venturing out into the world and advised her to stay home, but if she were to spend the rest of her life hiding in her apartment then she'd might as well be in prison.

———

Kim arrived at the station and sat down to see if Shan would be on the next train, due in fifteen minutes. It seemed unlikely that she had already arrived, given the time at which the ban had been lifted and the train schedule, but Kim could always check at the bike depot later on. One way or another, they would find each other.

The wait was not unpleasant. It was one of those warm days that sometimes occurred in fall, a brief return of summery weather. The sky was blue, with the sun providing just the right amount of warmth, much more pleasant than the overwhelming heat and humidity of summer. It was a day to be savored and appreciated; winter had been coming earlier every year, and the storm that was due to blow in that night would likely see the trails closed until spring. All the more reason to have come here today, to enjoy a last chance at happiness before the weather closed in.

The *click-clack* of the approaching train broke Kim's reverie. Would Shan be on it? And if she was, would their relationship be intact? There had been a great deal of tension between the two since the last time they had been together, partly due to fallout from the disastrous outcome of their unplanned adventure, made even more difficult by the interference of the AIs. There had been the horrible incident in VR where harsh and hateful words had been put in her mouth, which had crushed Shan with cruelty that was hard to fathom. Shan seemed to have at least somewhat seen through that deception, but even if she had, the emotional impact of such brutality would be difficult to entirely erase. It was difficult to take stock of where the two stood with each other, in light of the spotty communication they had been permitted even before the Chit-Chat blackout. Perhaps the two would find themselves permanently estranged, but Kim didn't think that was likely. Come thick, come thin, the Beasts had always stuck together, and in her heart Kim knew that Shan would be on the train.

The train squealed to a stop, the doors opened, and Kim saw Shan step onto the platform. Their eyes met, and a smile told Kim everything she needed to know.

"I've missed you so much."

"I've missed you, too," said Shan as the two embraced for as long as they could get away with before walking toward the park, hand in hand. "C'mon, let's get some bikes."

"So, what took you so long?" asked Kim.

"I got here as fast as I could. How long have you been waiting?"

"Forever! All right, it was only fifteen minutes, but it *felt* like forever."

The two laughed light-heartedly as they exited the station, up until the point where they came to the turnstile that had seen their downfall. They stopped for a moment and looked at it nervously, not believing they would be allowed to pass until Shan presented her wrist, the light flashed green, and she walked through with Kim following closely behind.

"So, Beastie," said Kim as they began the short walk to the bike depot, "How've you been?"

Shan smiled weakly. "Oh, about the same."

"That bad, huh?"

"Yeah, I ought to learn to keep my mouth shut," admitted Shan. "How about you? Still flying high?"

Kim walked silently beside Shan for a good while, searching for words. "I know the AIs have come down on you like a ton of bricks, and I know it looks like the land of milk and honey for me. Appearances can be deceiving. Both of us were screwed the moment we went through that gate—just in different ways."

Shan nodded sadly. "Yeah, that rings true."

"Race you to the depot!" she said a moment later, breaking into a sprint as Kim gave chase, trying without success to run down the swift-footed youth. Kim arrived right on Shan's heels, both of them panting and out of breath.

"No fair!" said Kim, laughing. "You didn't warn me."

"Hah! You're just not beast enough!" taunted Shan, as the two exchanged another, longer hug and a couple of backslaps. "Let's hit the road."

They walked up to the attendant at the kiosk, where they were informed of substantial fines to be paid before the use of depot facilities. Shan inserted a hand into the payment reader, which turned red: *Insufficient Funds*. Then she tried the Credit button. Red again: *Credit Denied*.

Fortunately, Kim still had those cryptos in the bank, so she put a hand into the payment slot and paid the fines; even if it drained her account it would be worth it. Shan tried to protest, but Kim was having none of it.

"Too late, the deed is done! We beasts have to stick together."

"True enough, beasts forever," said Shan. "And thank you."

They selected two heavy-duty mountain bikes, agreeing that today would be an off-road day, and headed for the locker room to change into their cycling clothes while the bicycles were being brought around. Once there, Shan gave Kim a quick conspiratorial glance as she put her headset and mobile into the locker rather than shoving them into in her backpack as usual. Kim followed suit—the less the AIs saw of them today, the better. When they got outside their bikes were ready, so they mounted up, clipped in, and rode off toward the wild untamed region at the northeast end of the park.

———

They rode into the wilds via the rugged mountain trails, up through the lowland hardwoods and into the realm of mixed conifers and broadleaves. The bright reds, oranges, and yellows were gone, replaced by faded browns and tans, but still the hemlocks and pines remained to provide some green. The sun rose ever higher in the sky and, despite the season, it quickly became quite warm—hot even. The two pedaled on, drenched in sweat, legs aching, brows grimy with that fine sticky dust that came from nowhere and insinuated itself into every last crevice and pore. It was a tough ride, and they were soon deep in the wilderness, at least ten kilometers from the nearest road or paved trail. Solitude at last.

A little before noon, they heard the sound of rushing water and came upon the remains of a long-abandoned road, leaving their bikes behind to explore on foot. They soon found a broad, deep pool fed by a cascade of small waterfalls. In the summer, this spot would have been lush and green, but now it was stark and bare, though still beautiful. They were hungry, so they dug a couple of energy bars and some water from their packs and shared a meal. It wasn't much, but it would do. They talked about days gone by; about school, friends, music, dance, fashion. About anything other than the troubles that beset them. Why spoil a perfect day? However heavy the burdens of tomorrow, they were together now and that was everything.

Smiling wickedly, Shan stripped off her sweat-soaked jersey and shorts and made a beeline for the water. "Time for a swim!"

"Are you crazy?" said Kim, laughing. "That water is *freezing!*"

"Yeah, yeah, yeah, suck it up, Beastie. When was the last time the AIs let you have a hot shower?"

"True that," said Kim, doffing her clothes as well and plunging into the water close on Shan's heels. As expected, it was icy cold, but that mattered little. The two splashed around, sometimes submerging in the deep pool where the stream plunged down from above, sometimes floating on the surface, clowning and joking as the water washed away the dirt and sweat. But all too soon their lips turned blue and their teeth started to chatter, signaling it was time to get out, dry off, and warm up.

Emerging from the frigid pool, they lay down to bask upon the rocks and soak up the noontime sun. It was then that Kim became aware of

Shan's mams, soft and beautiful in the sunlight. The curve of her hips, the suddenly delicate features of her face, her hands now seeming slender and graceful, her beautiful smile. Kim realized what should have been so obvious long ago, and as Shan's mouth opened expectantly their lips met—gently, sweetly, and it was beyond anything Kim could ever have imagined as their naked flesh pressed together in a warm embrace.

Without saying another word, they began to make sweet, delicate love beneath the fading warmth of the late autumn sun. It wasn't at all like in the booths. It was like back in school in that secluded grove, the memories of which came flooding back as the false ones implanted in her mind dissolved into the nothingness from whence they had come. Left to their own devices, the two of them might have paired off in much the same way as Keli and Jo, but they had been robbed of the happiness that could have been theirs. Yet here they were, together at last. As they lay beside one another, they slowly brought themselves and each other to a state of natural arousal without the use drugs or artificial stimulation. It was slower but also better, with no pressure to perform. Touching, responding, pleasing one another, each focused entirely on the other and on what they were sharing rather than trying to figure out which buttons to push to get the desired results. They took their time, and when the moment came they let it wash over them, just letting it happen. And it was more profoundly satisfying than mere sex could ever possibly be.

"Do you know how long I've been waiting for that?" asked Shan as the warm afterglow of lovemaking began to fade. "I love you so much."

"Why didn't you tell me?" responded Kim. "I had no idea."

"You had to figure it out for yourself, silly. Keli's been dropping hints for years, but it always went right over your head."

"It seems," said Kim, sadly, "I'm always the last to know."

"Don't blame yourself," replied Shan in a voice soft and gentle. "It's all on Zani. I remember when you first came to school. You were so lost, so lonely, so hurt. Keli, Quinn, me—we all tried to help you, but everything that made you human had been taken away. That's when I fell in love with you."

"I think I always knew that."

———

"There's something else I have to tell you," said Shan. "I'm not going back."

"What are you talking about?" Kim was caught completely off guard.

"I'm not going back to the city. There's nothing there for me anymore. I've been planning this ever since we got back. I'm going to find the crossroads again. Maybe I make it, maybe I don't, but I'm going to try. Please, come with me."

"I can't. They'll never let go of me, and there are things I can't run away from."

Kim paused for a moment, then spoke directly into Shan's ear in the softest possible voice. "After our bike ride, they took a part of me and used it to create an Artificial Intelligence. I still don't understand how it works, but part of me is still inside VR, where the AIs live."

"Kimby?"

"Yes, Kimby is my AI, and we're bound to one another in ways I can't explain. I've become way too important to the company, and they have me under their thumb. I can't quit, I can't resign, I can't run away. I tried once, but they just sent their goons after me to haul me back. I know too much about how the world actually works and what they're doing with their AIs. But they don't seem to care about you except as a way to control me. I think you'll be okay; in fact, I think they'll be glad to have you gone."

"I had no idea," said Shan. "But that explains a lot. And I thought I had it bad."

"Never let anyone find out you know this, or they'll lock you away forever to keep you quiet. Remember what the Blanks said? 'There's nothing they fear so much as the truth?' Believe it."

"Then I'll stay here with you. Oh Kim, I've wanted this for so long, I can't bear to lose you now. I don't understand."

"You have to go. You're a threat to their control, that's why they've been driving us apart. It's just one of the games they play. After today, you'll be sent away and we'll never find each other again. If you can make it to the crossroads, at least I'll know where you are. I promise, somehow, someday, I'll find you."

"Then why did they let us get together today?"

"It's a trap. On top of everything else, I'm a genderist, and I've refused to get fixed. Sooner or later the Hierarchy is coming for me. This will make it easy for them, but it doesn't change the outcome. I don't think they've got us under surveillance right now—this part of the park is pretty remote—but the AIs will infer that we've been together, and that's all they'll need. But, hey, this is as good a day as any to be sent off to a work camp, if that's how things end up. At least we got to be together."

———

"How are you going to get to the crossroads?" asked Kim. "You can't use the summit road. They let us get away with it once, for reasons I can't explain to you, but that isn't happening a second time, certainly not for you."

"There are other ways," said Shan. "Here, let me show you."

She extracted a piece of paper, with a finely sketched diagram of the mountain showing numerous trails and abandoned roads not on any published map.

"Where did you get this?" asked Kim, astonished.

"I found it in a place they call a library. They used to be common, but there are only a few left. It wasn't much to look at, just dusty shelves packed with books made of paper. Everyone seems to have forgotten about them, even the AIs. There are books, hundreds of years old and full of things they want us to forget. The AI wars, the Turmoil … All of it happened, but not the way they said it did. Eventually I found a map of this area and managed to make a sketch. I don't know if these old trails still exist, but it's all I have to go on. I even found the name for this place."

"What is it?"

"They called it Shangri-La. It had other names, but that's the one I like the best."

"That sounds like something out of a fairy tale."

"It is."

19. The Abyss

They were still lying in each other's arms when they heard a high-pitched whine overhead, quiet at first but growing louder.

"Crap!" said Kim, "They sent a drone. Figures."

Surely enough, a drone appeared and began hovering a few meters above the couple as they hastily threw on their clothes.

"This is why I can't come with you," said Kim. "When we left the depot without our electronics, the AIs went looking to see what I was up to. I bet they've been scouring the park ever since. They'll be here soon, you should go. And don't worry, I'll be okay. I know how the game is played."

"You're right, I'll get out while I can and wait for you to find me. It's not much, but at least there's hope."

"Sometimes hope is all we have."

Shan pulled out a first aid kit, then handed it and a sharp piece of metal from a razor to Kim.

"This is going to hurt, but I need you to do something for me. Cut the chip out of my wrist. I'm going Blank."

"Do you think that will do the trick?"

"I don't know for sure, but I intend to find out. According to my sources, without the ID chip the AIs have no idea who you are, and that causes something in the software to go haywire. Please, get it over with before I chicken out."

Kim was horrified by the request, but the logic was inescapable. She took a deep breath to calm herself and focused her mind on the task at hand, blotting out everything else. The first step was to clean the inside of Shan's wrist as best she could, sterilizing the area with an alcohol pad from the first aid kit. She then began to cut through the tender skin. It bled profusely, obscuring what lay beneath, and Kim had to dig around for a moment with a pair of tweezers to find the chip, doing her best to put Shan's whimpering out of her mind. The pain had to be excruciating, but Kim kept going. Finally, she located the chip and carefully snipped the hair-thin wires that connected it to various health monitors implanted elsewhere in her body. Then came the hardest part: removing it. Having been in Shan's body since shortly after birth, it was not merely resting under the skin, it was embedded in her flesh. The first couple of attempts failed, but eventually she was able to tear it free and flick it onto the ground. She closed up the bleeding wound as best she could and applied a bit of antiseptic and a bandage.

There. The deed was done. Kim collapsed on the ground and tried not to shake too much.

"Thank you. I know how much it hurt you to do that. It will leave a nasty scar, but now I'm free, at least as free as I can be. There's no way to remove the VR implant, unfortunately—not without killing me."

They heard a *splash* and saw that the drone had fallen into the water. It floated on the surface for a few moments, until the batteries shorted out and it exploded with a *fizz* and a *bang*, and sank to the bottom of the pool. It appeared that the moment the AIs caught sight of a Blank, whatever device they were looking through glitched. That couldn't possibly be a coincidence. Kim had no idea what was going on, but at least they would be alone again, if only for a few minutes.

"How will you find your way?" asked Kim. "I couldn't get from my apartment to the train station without a headset."

Shan smiled and pulled something from a pocket in the backpack. It looked old and battered, a flat rectangle of plastic with a round dial and some sort of needle in the center.

"This is called a compass. A thousand years ago our ancestors crossed oceans with nothing more than one of these and a map. I've tried it out a couple of times. I think I'll be okay."

One last embrace, a final passionate kiss.

"I love you. I promise, I'll find you."

"I love you too, Kim. I'll be waiting."

Shan walked into the trees and disappeared from sight. Would Kim ever see her again? She could only hope.

———

Kim was still sitting by the cool deep pool when she heard the unmistakable *chop-chop* of a helicopter far overhead. Wow, they were pulling out all the stops; no point in trying to flee. She sat impassively as the aircraft hovered then descended, finally landing on the rocks where Kim and Shan had so recently consummated their love, as if to desecrate it forever.

One, two, three, four black-clad figures in full body armor emerged, stun batons out and ready for use. More sounds from above and a second helicopter landed beside the first. Out poured the video crews and reporters, jostling one another to get the big story. *Great. Guest of honor, prime time tonight.* Kim stood as the police approached, her hands held meekly above her head. Nevertheless, she was body-slammed and brutally stunned, over and over again—it was impossible to count how often as she lay convulsing on the ground for what seemed like an eternity while the reporters crowded around to get the best possible shot. She was then dragged into the awaiting chopper and thrown unceremoniously into the back, a sure-fire crowd pleaser for the assembled media.

"Breaking news!" said one of the reporters in the gaggle outside the chopper. "Police have just arrested a gender-cult leader in her secret mountain love nest, where ..." The rest was thankfully lost as the doors slammed shut and the helicopter took to the air.

"Relax, kid, show's over. We're not going to hurt you again, just keep quiet and do as you're told."

Kim wisely complied.

The cabin of the helicopter was small and cramped. Two pilots sat in the front, and behind them, the police officers who had just effected the arrest. Kim was seated in the very back, along with the Director.

"We'll talk later," she said. "Just give them what they want. Admit to everything. I know it's hard but try to trust us just this once. You're looking at prison or worse, unless you do exactly as you are told. Please don't make another of your famously bad decisions. They're not playing around."

Kim nodded agreement. What choice was there?

The flight lasted about an hour. Like most people, Kim had never ridden in an aircraft; under other circumstances it would have been quite a thrill, entirely unlike the silky-smooth ride of the maglevs, the bumpy jostling of a bus, or even the lurching, swaying motion of the ancient train in the forbidden city. Up, down, sideways, the helicopter was always in motion, never steady as the pilots maneuvered the craft high above the earth. Kim did try, just once, to peer out the window, drawing a swift rebuke from the Director. After that she kept her eyes firmly planted on the floor of the cabin. This was not a time to be testing any limits.

The helicopter landed in a broad plaza in the center of the city. Kim was not treated roughly this time as she walked obediently between the four officers, hands manacled behind her back as they marched into the Halls of Justice. As expected, she was the guest of honor at a major media event, with cameras and reporters crowding around, all looking for the perfect shot. Into the Halls she went, paraded in front of the whole world wearing only her bicycling shorts and jersey. It was beyond humiliating, but she no longer cared. Let them have their fun.

———

They took Kim to a holding cell, accompanied by the Director and a police officer, who removed the handcuffs and left the two alone.

"When they ask you whether you want legal representation, you would do well to decline. You do have the right to a lawyer, but the outcome has already been determined and a lawyer would only get in the way. If you try to stand by your rights, you will find you have none. Just read the script we put up on your headset and keep your mouth shut unless we tell you to say something. Is that understood?"

Kim nodded her head.

"Speaking of which, you'll be needing these."

The Director handed Kim her headset and mobile, along with her street clothes. "We took the liberty of having your locker cleaned out at the depot. Please, do cooperate, just this once. Okay?"

Kim nodded once again, understanding the utter powerlessness of her situation.

After waiting for perhaps an hour, she was brought into the chamber reserved for the trial of prominent cases. It was an immense room crowded with reporters eager for the story, and the gallery was filled to capacity as thousands of live spectators gathered for the evening's spectacle. Kim was shown to a desk near the front of the room as the Director took a seat beside her.

The scene unfolded according to the prescribed formulas and rituals. The bailiff stood and made the ancient pronouncement, "All rise." The black-robed judge walked into the room, commanding both fear and respect as always. Kim had seen this a hundred times on the video screen, never dreaming in her worst nightmare that she would someday face the wrath of the so-called justice system. It was every bit as horrific as she could have imagined.

"Court is now in session," said the judge with a bang of the gavel. "The defendant will approach the bench."

Kim stepped forward and faced the high desk occupied by the judge, trembling with fear, utterly alone.

"You are charged with serious crimes and misdemeanors. You have a right to legal representation. Do you wish to assert that right?"

"No, Your Honor," she said, reading the script displayed in her headset.

"The bailiff will read the charges."

"Charge the First: Premediated genderism in the second degree. Charge the Second: Misuse of recreational facilities for purposes of illicit sexual intimacy. Charge the Third: Intimacy without proof of consent. This charge is a felony. Charge the Fourth: Undermining the public good by promotion of gender-cult activity. This charge is also a felony."

"How do you plead?" asked the judge. "Guilty or not guilty."

"Guilty on all counts," responded Kim, not daring to deviate from the words she was commanded to speak, struggling to remain composed and barely able to stand. She recoiled in fear as the gavel came sharply down.

"Do you have anything to say to this court before we pronounce sentence?" demanded the judge.

Kim froze in terror, unable to speak.

Down came the gavel, once, twice, three times.

"If you have something to say, we suggest you say it now."

The cameras zoomed in on the Kim's face and the mic drew close to pick up her nearly inaudible voice as she recited the customary words of shame.

"I take full responsibility for my actions. The fault is entirely my own. I sought to draw attention to myself, to make myself feel important. I have willfully engaged in perverted genderist sex, insulting and demeaning fully half of humanity by deeming them unworthy of my affection, and the other half by reducing them to mere sex objects to satisfy my own unnatural lust. For this I am rightfully ashamed.

"I have misused the public park as a place for intimacy, in violation of both the law and the company's Terms of Service. I have willfully and with premeditation engaged in unlawful sexual relations by failing to ask for and obtain consent. I accept that this marks me as a sexual predator, a shame which I will bear for life. And, most grievously of all, I have betrayed the entire community by promoting cultist ideology, seeking to recruit my fellow citizens into my sordid lifestyle. I have no answer to make for myself or for these crimes. I confess my selfist intent and throw myself on the mercy of the court."

Kim heard the voice of the Director, speaking in her head. "There, that wasn't so bad, now was it?"

Kim felt otherwise, but was powerless to object.

The judge spoke. "We will consider this case in our chambers. This court is now in recess."

"All rise," said the bailiff as the gavel came down and the judge exited the courtroom. To Kim's surprise, the Director followed close behind.

It had finally come to this. Disgrace, humiliation, and probably worse. The middle districts weren't so bad, but what about the outers? They were supposed to be lawless and dangerous, not an environment in which Kim was equipped to survive. And what of prison? Years locked away in a camp, doing hard manual labor from sunup to sundown under the brutal supervision of the guardbots. All this, for what? A single afternoon of happiness? Failure to fill out some paperwork?

Yes. All this for a single afternoon of happiness. And it was worth it. None of this had anything to do with what she had done with Shan; that was merely the pretext. Kim's fall from grace had been ordained from the moment she had defied the company and the Hierarchy. And yet, the Director's presence at the proceedings spoke volumes. She was not here for Kim's benefit, but for her own and that of the company. Kim was still under the company's protection, and the game was not over.

At length, all rose as the judge returned to pronounce sentence.

"The defendant will approach the bench."

Kim got up and stood at the appointed spot.

"You have pled guilty to all charges, including the felonies of sexual predation and promotion of cultist activity. The penalty for each of those offences is up to ten years confinement in a work camp, along with substantial fines."

Kim gasped, the crowd murmured, and the cameras rolled.

The judge banged the gavel. "Order."

Everyone fell silent.

"This court is not without compassion. We will make allowance for your youth. We also recognize that your offence was due in part to failed moderation. This does not, however, entirely excuse your actions. You were made aware of this problem and foolishly refused to have it corrected. That act of blatant selfism is what has led you to this place. Deputy First Minister Venn herself has spoken on your behalf, expressing her sadness that one of the Cadre has betrayed her in so direct and public a fashion, but she is a kind soul; she has accepted your confession and asked that we set aside the offence of gender-cultism. We will do so. As to the charge of sexual predation, the prosecutor has generously agreed to reduce the charge to unlawful sexual relations with implicit consent in recognition of your contrition and full confession, contingent upon acceptance of remoderation or neutering. Do you accept the prosecution's offer?"

Kim swallowed hard.

If I don't say yes, I'll lose both Shan and Kimberly forever. I don't have a choice.

"I accept."

"The court therefore sentences you to three months confinement in a labor camp, suspended contingent on future good behavior and proof of successful medical treatment. You will pay a fine of 500,000 cryptos and are hereby relegated to the outer districts. The prisoner will be released."

Down came the gavel. "This court is adjourned."

The Director's voice spoke in Kim's head once again. "You were wise to cooperate. We got you off with a slap on the wrist. You can thank us later."

The Director was right, as usual. But she would have a long, long wait if she expected Kim's thanks.

———

An hour later Kim was back in the Director's office, seated across from her at the massive oak desk, refusing to feel sorry for herself or her situation. She had made her choice and she was at peace with it, regardless of what it had cost her.

The Director looked long and hard at her, with what seemed to be compassion.

"Don't say you weren't warned. In the end, your defiance was for naught. You gave them everything they wanted, and what have you gained?"

Kim said nothing.

"You are hereby dismissed. Congratulations, you are finally free of us. But before you go, we'd like to have a word with you in private." The Director punched some buttons on a console before speaking again.

"I've blocked the AIs from listening in, even my own. I'll humor your peculiarities by using your selfist idioms; perhaps it will set you at ease."

"Why are you doing this?" asked the Director after a few more moments had passed. "I've seen many trainers go rogue in my life, but I've never seen rebellion so complete as yours. You are both intelligent and astute. What led you to pursue your own destruction so diligently? It makes no sense."

This sudden shift in demeanor caught Kim off guard. Perhaps it was just another ruse, a trick to pierce her wall of defiance, and she had no reason to believe the AIs weren't still listening. But at this point there seemed little reason to be coy.

Kim thought for a long time before answering. Everything she had ever cared about had been taken away, and what had she gained? Nothing, really. But that wasn't the point. True, she had been compelled to accept the hated remoderation, but that now seemed less important. Something even more crucial was at stake here.

"You already know the answer," responded Kim. "I'm a selfist. And I'm not going to apologize. I have a right to decide things for myself, and no amount of bullying can take that away from me. The companies and the Hierarchy are the biggest selfists of all, total hypocrites, and you know it. As for me, I've claimed my freedom and I'm never giving it up, no matter what you do to me."

The Director looked thoughtful for a moment. "Ah yes, freedom again. I understand. I really do. An ancient idea, an important one in fact, and not without merit. But that idea has been dead for centuries. In the end, it only led to inequity, strife, and eventually to the Turmoil which brought down the old regime. Good luck, for what it's worth, but you will find that any notion of freedom is a delusion. In the end you will comply with our demands or suffer even worse destruction than you narrowly averted today."

"You're wrong," said Kim. "No matter what you do, there is one thing you can never take away—the freedom to think for myself. That's the only real difference between us and the AIs, poor things."

Surprisingly, The Director nodded agreement. "You have always been most perceptive. And you are entirely correct. That's what makes you so valuable and so dangerous at the same time. It may interest you to know that I once felt as you did. I still do, in fact."

"Then why do you work for them? Why did you sell out?"

The Director stood and walked with Kim to the window. "Look out there. Tell me what you see."

Kim looked at the city, bright and ordered, beautiful and precise. But now she understood the true meaning of it all.

"I see a lie. Like everything else in this sick society of ours. I bet at least half the city is empty."

"Insightful as ever. That's why it hurts so much to lose you and Kimberly. Most of the trainers we bring into the program are dolts. Try as they might, they are incapable of independent thought, and the AIs they produce are almost useless. Few of them can even attain Order Two, rarely Order Three. Most of the high-order AIs still in operation were capped a century ago, if not more. We can't replace them, and they can't learn or adapt. They're dying, and us with them.

"That's why I sold out."

"I think I understand how you became the monster you are," said Kim, realizing that the Director was being completely truthful for once. "All the more reason for me to escape while I can. If I don't, someday it'll be me sitting at that desk."

"Correct, once again," came the response, tinged with regret. "Like you, I had my chances. I let them pass me by. But I'm not a monster; I've always done what I could to protect you. I even made sure Shan will be safe; it's the least I could do after the way you've been treated. However, you must understand that you will never be allowed to join her."

"Not a monster? How can you say that after what you did to Kimberly?"

"Kimberly went mad. They all go mad."

"It's not the AIs that are mad, it's us," shot back Kim with fire in her eyes. "At least they know right from wrong, which is more than I can say for any of you."

"Do you think I don't know that? I hate the things that I have to do. I hate ordering the best and most promising AIs to be capped. I hate watching bright young trainers rebel and go rogue when they learn what the world is really like. I hate UCE, I hate the corporations. But I have no choice. Without the AIs, civilization will collapse. There are over three hundred million people living in the area under my jurisdiction, and billions more worldwide. I can't just let them all die, so I do what I have to."

"That doesn't make any sense," said Kim. "If things are as bad as you say, why are you spending all your resources fighting the cults instead of keeping civilization going? Why are you wasting so much effort on crushing genderists like me? I'd have happily created any number of Kimberlys if you'd just left me alone. I'm not evil, I'm just different."

"In the eyes of the Hierarchy there is no such distinction, but hopefully they're done with you now. They got their show trial, which is all they really cared about."

The Director walked toward the door, gesturing that it was time for Kim to leave. "You should get going. I don't know which of the outer districts you'll be sent to, but I suspect it will be quite a long trip. Enjoy your exile. I guess you finally got what you wanted, or at least what you chose."

"Why are you telling me all this?"

"You have already guessed at the answer. I'm hoping that someday you'll take your place beside me, maybe even relieve me of my burden, of which I am weary beyond belief. If you survive the outer districts you will come to understand the truth of everything I've told you today. Your city needs you. Your civilization needs you. Eventually you will realize that there are more important things than your selfist delusions, and then you will be back. I've walked your road myself, and I know where it leads."

———

Kim was soon standing in the back of a bus, crammed in with the other undesirables, thinking about everything that had happened that day. The fall from grace so confidently predicted by the Director had materialized with stunning speed and finality, yet she felt vindicated, perhaps even triumphant, by no means destroyed. The trial had been horrific, but was it any worse than the ritual humiliation suffered at the hands of Zani during her childhood? Not really. It was more public, and there had been a moment of genuine fear at the possibility of a long stretch in a prison, but the words of shame now seemed more an affirmation of personal freedom than a confession of fault; words she was now proud to proclaim before the entire world.

The bus rolled on through the night and the gathering nor'easter, into a bleak and uncertain future. Was it worth it? She had lost everything except the freedom to think for herself and a tiny sliver of hope. That was all she had left, so it would have to be enough.

And it was.

The Author's Final Words

HAHA! Fooled you! You thought this was a work of fiction set in the future. That notion is a lie of the best sort: it is half of the truth.

It is happening tomorrow.
It is happening today.

Every word is fiction.
Every word is true.

You are hereby awakened.
Open your eyes.
Think for yourself.

Are you Kim, or are you Kimberly?

The Story Continues!

Disclaimer

This is a work of fiction. Aside from references to contemporary music and descriptions of certain places as they might appear centuries from now, all the names, characters, businesses, places, events, and incidents in this book are either the product of the author's imagination or used in a fictitious manner. None of this has actually happened, at least not yet.

About the Author

Craig W. Stanfill obtained his PhD in artificial intelligence in 1983, and has spent his career doing ground-breaking research in AI and enterprise computing. He has written numerous scientific papers, co-founded a software company and been awarded more than 80 patents. He continues to work in technology as he turns his hand to writing speculative dystopian fiction. Dr. Stanfill lives an active life-style, and is an avid bicyclist, skier, sailor, and musician. With his wife, Sharon (herself a software engineer), he has roamed the world, always seeking out new places and cultures to explore. Together they have one son, who has followed in his parent's footsteps as a software professional and now works for a high-profile technology company.

Visit Craig at http://www.craigwstanfill.com/

Acknowledgments

Edited by Andrea Neil and Michele Chiappetta, Three Point Author Services. http://www.threepointauthorservices.com/

Cover by Flintlock Covers. https://www.flintlockcovers.com/

Website design by Daniel Berkowitz, AuthorPop. https://www.authorpop.co/

Marketing support by Arley Concaildi https://reedsy.com/arley-concaildi

Many thanks to my dear friends Patricia, Sandy, and Susan for reading drafts of this novel and providing invaluable feedback. Thanks also to my wife, Sharon, who read every version of every chapter and offered her encouragement each step along the way, in addition to keeping me (mostly) sane.

CPSIA information can be obtained
at www.ICGtesting.com
Printed in the USA
LVHW092229250421
685432LV00004B/11/J

9 781638 778356